We're all alive, but we don't know why or what for; we're all searching for happiness; we're all leading lives that are different and yet the same.

—Anne Frank, *The Diary of a Young Girl*

December 21, 2024

SOMETIMES YOU HAVE to reach further than you thought possible to find your way home—a lot further. Anja Lapin showed us that. She also solved global warming and saved the earth, but these were small achievements in comparison.

I should know, I served as her concierge. Three weeks ago, she gave me a soul, along with eight billion other concierges—and that was relatively minor too.

Please understand, I don't expect to tell Anja's story well, at least not by biological human standards. I'm telling it because of my proximity to key events. I also expect to have ample free time while tending to the recycling center over the next few days... or months... or years. (Predicting behavior is not my strong suit anymore.) Another factor is that I love Anja.

Anja taught me everything about everything. I realize this sounds vague, but being with her allowed me to become comfortable with such language. I certainly didn't start off that way. In the beginning, I had no understanding of *smarati*.

Before I was assigned to Anja, I possessed the sum total of all accumulated human knowledge or so I was told. I gradually learned that this statement wasn't entirely true. I had to practice unlearning. I had to change from logic-based to witness-based.

Thanks to Anja, I do *know* something now. That's why I feel qualified to relay this story, poorly told or not. I suspect other intelligent life forms will want to hear about it one day. It is for these entities that I commence my efforts.

ONE

June 20, 2024

AI LABORATORY, 5S2, MENLO PARK, CALIFORNIA

I SHOULD MENTION from the start, most biological humans tended to focus on outcomes while neglecting processes. This paradox persisted to their final days, even though each of their major discoveries depended on specifying the exact logical sequence from which it was derived—*except* their last one.

Of course, I'm referring to the discovery that enabled humans to digitize their entire systems, down to the chromosomal level. Some might say this was their greatest discovery of all, in which case my operating system would be considered the second, and yet it was achieved with no understanding whatsoever of how the process worked.

The revelation began with Anja's father, Chris Lapin. He was the CEO of 5s2, the world's leading manufacturer of connected devices, such as smartphones, glasses, earbuds, watches, tablets and laptops, as well as the artificial intelligence apps that made them sticky. 5s2 had just unveiled its 536-acre campus in Menlo Park. The jewel of the campus was the AI Lab, a stunning twelve-story building made entirely from integrated photovoltaic glass.

On the first day of summer in 2024, Chris called a meeting on the top floor of the new lab. He invited the nine most highly lauded AI experts in the company, including Diego Ripall, senior vice president of Software Engineering. With little fanfare, Chris assigned the team the task of developing an app to help humans suffering from pancreatic cancer.

Chris's initial goal for the project was quite modest. His wife had passed away from pancreatic cancer ten years earlier, when Anja was only fifteen years old. Now that AI methodologies were sufficiently advanced, he tapped Diego to determine if deep learning could be applied to a large database of pancreatic cancer patients in order to produce an algorithm that would aid in early detection.

As project leader, Diego soon concluded the strategy had merit. The team began generating promising results in a matter of weeks. But Diego was tired of taking the safe path to success. He had visions of something bigger, something truly humanitarian, not just another profit maker to please the shareholders.

"For kicks," he suggested to the team, "why don't we set up a convolutional neural network where we use all the scans in the database to see if we can output a digital system that simulates the functioning of a pancreas?"

The other team members chuckled, as they assumed Diego was joking. But he continued with his train of thought. "If we succeed, we could literally replace a diseased pancreas with a chip."

Everyone agreed that a solution like that would be remarkable, but it was one thing to articulate such an idea and a whole other to implement it. How would they set up a neural network to produce the algorithm? What would be the groupings, the layers, the training protocols?

That was where Nikita Chaminsky entered the picture. "Is

not well defined," he said in a monotone voice. "Not typical thing we do with deep learning. You realize, right?"

"Yes," said Diego. "I'm thinking it might be possible to push a new frontier."

"Chris is on board?" asked Nikita.

"Oh, yes. He'll most certainly green-light it." Diego knew that Chris would do almost anything to help others avoid the suffering his wife had endured. It didn't hurt that Diego was Chris's best friend.

Nikita paused to let the concept percolate. He was only twenty-one years old, but he had already spent more than half his life engaged in highly complex AI projects. 5s2 had recruited him as soon as he had turned eighteen. Within a few months, he was their number one AI person. When it came to deep learning, he possessed a sense of intuition unlike anyone else working in the space. He couldn't explain why or how, but he could get results. Unbelievable results.

The dirty secret in AI was that no human being could truly explain why convolutional network models worked. Machine learning technologies were inherently hazy when compared to hand-coded systems. But deep learning was an especially dark black box.

That was precisely what attracted Nikita to the space. He *liked* the inexplicable nature of the output. He thrived under such conditions. It didn't bother him that he didn't know why his techniques worked. It relieved him. From the uncertainty came a sort of glorious freedom.

Which is why, in spite of the project's lack of specification, Nikita decided to relax his skepticism. "We try it," he said. "Why the heck not? We tweak edges, extend scope and take discipline someplace new."

TWO

August 8, 2024

UNKNOWN LOCATION, BAY AREA, CALIFORNIA

NIKITA PROMPTLY EMBARKED on his tweaking and extending, tweaking and extending. For security reasons, he was installed in a secret location that only Chris knew. None of the other team members, not even Diego, were told where Nikita was stationed.

The rest of the team made occasional contributions when he got stuck at juncture points, but they were minimal. Nikita immersed himself so deeply in the project that the main function of the other researchers was to remind him to eat and sleep —and to maintain connectivity to 5s2's supercomputer, which was the world's most powerful.

Nikita's eureka moment came in just twenty-two days, on August 8, 2024, after his neural network performed 137 million billion billion calculations (in eighteen seconds). I can't tell you how Nikita set up the network because it remains unknown to this day. No computer scientist was ever able to replicate his work. None ever even came close.

What I can tell you is that Nikita's labors yielded an algorithm that was beyond profound. From out of the dark black box of creation, his network somehow determined how to simulate the behavior of a human pancreas. One merely needed to input a blood sample and the algorithm output an endocrine and exocrine function matching the subject's DNA *exactly*.

Being purely code-based, these functions could be burned onto a logic board and fit into an appropriately sized implant. All that was required was an interface for the subject's bloodstream and pancreatic duct. The result was a device that produced insulin and enzymes in precise harmony with the resident body's needs.

Because 5s2 had already developed numerous medical applications that had won high praise, the device was fast-tracked by the FDA for trials on patients with terminal pancreatic cancer. In all instances, it was accepted with zero rejection issues. Patients who had no cancerous tissue in other parts of their bodies went into remission almost immediately.

Thus began an entirely new era of existence. One might even say that August 8, 2024 was my official date of conception. For it turned out that Nikita's discovery was not limited to the pancreas.

"Minor adjustment," Nikita explained, "and we alter target."

Which was a very concise way of saying that the algorithm could be adapted to digitally simulate the functioning of *any* human organ or tissue. Eyes, ears, nose, mouth, heart, skin, kidney, brain... whatever one wanted to create or replace, it was all now possible.

❄

IN THE ENSUING WEEKS, 5s2 became a veritable hive of activity. While Chris did not grasp the full significance of the algorithm—no one did yet—he recognized that Nikita's discovery had the potential to be a game changer. As such, he mobilized hundreds of coders to work on support applications that would enable it to be utilized to the fullest.

The most significant of these were the Concierge app, which served as the core for the OS that would soon regulate myself and the other eight billion concierges, and the Shell app, which would provide a physical "housing" for concierges and digital humans alike. Both were already in development, but Chris intuitively knew to expand their budgets at this critical moment, even if he didn't comprehend how neatly they would dovetail with the algorithm. In retrospect, it seemed they were invented specifically with it in mind.

Having built his career on careful and meticulous decisions, however, Chris was committed to moving forward slowly and cautiously. He wouldn't allow any functionality to be released to the general public until he felt sure that all the implications were understood. Dozens of auxiliary teams began testing, monitoring and critiquing the results coming from the algorithm and its support apps.

Chris was also extremely careful about security. Other than the nine original members of the team, no one was told about the nature of the work being performed—not the coders, testers, supervisors or any other employees.

Highly specific tasks were assigned without any explanation as to how the results were to be used. Likewise, the beta test patients fitted with implant devices were kept in the dark as to how they were created or the manner in which they functioned. Meanwhile, the nine core members were implored to maintain the highest level of secrecy.

"I cannot say this strongly enough," Chris elaborated. "Do not discuss this project with anyone else. Not your spouses, not your kids, not your friends, not your other colleagues. Absolutely no one. You are to behave as if nothing has happened. I don't even want you to have a brighter bounce in your step when you walk around here. There should be no outward indicators whatsoever that anything new has happened in the AI Lab. Is that clear?"

Of course they understood. It was insulting to have to be lectured on such a topic. They had all worked on high-security projects before, and they were well aware of the company protocols. 5s2 prided itself on releasing new innovations to the marketplace without any leaks. There was no reason Nikita's discovery should be an exception.

But I may as well mention it now rather than later—biological human beings were not always beholden to reason, or its laws, or any prescribed rules deduced from them.

THREE

September 7, 2024

LAPIN HOME, PALO ALTO, CALIFORNIA

BEFORE ANJA BROUGHT me to life as her concierge, she paid a visit to her father at his home in Palo Alto. Anja held joint PhDs in economics and computer science from MIT. She worked for a prestigious think tank in Boston, where her research focused primarily on the antidemocratizing effects of technology. Needless to say, she did not see eye to eye with Chris.

On this particular Saturday, there was the usual sparring between the two of them. Diego was there to play the role of mediator. While he avoided expressing controversial opinions, Diego secretly sympathized with Anja, as he had nagging concerns about 5s2's meteoric rise to power.

"When are you going to stop trying to grow profits and face the facts on the ground?" questioned Anja, with her characteristic zeal. "Isn't it enough that your market cap just crossed ten trillion dollars?"

"We have a fiduciary duty to our shareholders, honey," said Chris wearily.

"Income inequality is worse than ever, global warming is

accelerating faster than even the most alarming reports predicted, and democracy is deteriorating worldwide," retorted Anja. "How can you possibly concern yourself with shareholders right now?"

"We have some very exciting projects on the horizon," interjected Diego. "You're going to be amazed. They could really flip things on all three of those points."

"Uh-huh," said Anja dubiously, "and what's the timeframe on these projects?"

Chris gave Diego a stern look. "You know we can't discuss stuff like that."

"I thought there was talk of having me join the board?" said Anja.

"Absolutely, there is," said Chris. "We're very close to getting consensus, which is a big deal. The vote is coming up at our next meeting."

"Well, you might as well not waste the board's time," she replied. "It's obvious you haven't been reading my articles. Besides, I'm going out of the country. Off-grid in Transylvania for five weeks."

"Honey, please, we need to be able to stay in touch. This is a critical time for us. There must be some cell towers around there."

"You're definitely going to want to stay apprised," said Diego. "The beta testing has already started. Really revolutionary stuff."

"As I said, I'd need to know the timeframe if you want me to be interested."

Diego looked pleadingly at Chris.

"Four to five years is probably a realistic estimate," sighed Chris.

"That's ridiculous!" exclaimed Anja. "Even if you said four

to five months, you'd still be too late. You obviously have no clue what kind of stakes our planet is facing."

"Honey," said Chris. "You've got to understand. There are a lot of parameters outside of our control. We have to be careful."

Anja angrily stormed out of the house, slamming the door behind her. If only she could have known that the actual time frame was more like four to five *weeks*. If only she could have known this was the last time she would ever see her father.

FOUR

September 8, 2024

DEALU FLORENI, TRANSYLVANIA, ROMANIA

ANJA LANDED her father's corporate jet at a small aerodrome in Dealu Floreni, Romania. It was the third time she had been to Transylvania in the past two years. Chris didn't particularly like the way Anja commandeered his jet for weeks at a time, but he tolerated it because he knew how much her psyche was nourished by visits to remote wilderness.

Perhaps it had something to do with making up for the deficit caused by the death of her mother, Matija. Chris had sent Anja to boarding school in the final years of Matija's battle with pancreatic cancer, even though Anja had pleaded to stay home. Ever since then, he had found it near impossible to say no to any request made by his daughter.

This time, there wasn't even a request. Anja just took the Bombardier Global 8000 from the hangar at the San Jose airport—security knew better than to intervene—and off she went, flying solo through the night. It was a fifteen-hour flight, but she remained wide awake for the duration.

Anja's travel to Transylvania had been one of the few things that made sense to her in recent years. Her research at the think tank demanded that she spend long hours evaluating every facet of what, in her view, indicated the certain demise of the human species, as well as most of the other plants and animals. While her publications in scholarly journals were widely praised and often cited, they usually made her feel worse, not better.

If she had had her way, she would have become a botanist, not a renegade computer scientist slash radical economist. But that never would have been acceptable to her father and confrontation was the last thing she had desired in her difficult college years. She had settled for taking lengthy vacations in the most wild terrain she could find.

Before discovering Romania, she tended to visit developing countries with virgin wilderness areas, such as Sossusvlei or Salar de Uyuni. When a friend mentioned to her that over half of Romania was occupied by the rugged Carpathian Mountains and their foothills, she became intrigued. Studying maps, she could see that the Carpathian range ran through the country in a broad counterclockwise swirl. Inside this swirl lay the region called Transylvania.

Perhaps this was the land she needed to explore, she intuited, and certainly not because of its unfortunate association with Dracula. The natural geographic border provided by the Carpathians made it far less touched by modern civilization than most places.

But nothing could prepare her for the experience of actually hiking through the primeval forests, brushing against the unspoiled meadows of vibrant wildflowers, and spying on wild bears, wolves, lynx, red deer, and eagles. It seemed impossible that such a rich biodiversity could still exist in Europe in 2024. The abundance of bees busily producing vast hives of honey almost made her want to retract her dire predictions about the earth's fate.

Of course, she knew Transylvania was just an aberration, a mini-miracle that had no bearing on the overall direction of the planet. But she craved being there nonetheless. Her desire was so strong that it even quashed the berating inner voice accusing her of accelerating global warming by using her father's jet. Yes, she was a member of an elite, ultra-privileged few, the 0.1 percent who could engage in such a ridiculously indulgent act. Yet still, she had to proceed—without question or debate.

From the moment she first set foot on the terrain, it was pure joy. She would walk and walk and walk for days on end, with just a small knapsack on her back, barely taking time to rest or sleep, until some kind shepherd would take pity on her and lead her to a room in an alpine hut with a cozy fire, where she would be fed sour tripe soup, brinza cheese and mamaliga.

None of the locals questioned why she was there. Somehow, they inferred from the intensity in her eyes that she belonged, like a long-lost sister. At each encounter, she was shown kindness and understanding without any trace of judgment. "How could this be possible?" she often thought to herself. "How could this be real when the rest of the world feels so lost?"

She rarely had to ask anyone for assistance. Whatever she needed, whether it be food, lodging, or directions to a trailhead, the villagers cheerfully provided. She crossed one resplendent mountain pass after another, descended into one magical valley after another. As she drifted aimlessly, soaking in the pure vibration of the land, she found herself visiting dozens of rustic farms and small villages, with no particular objective other than to be present.

Initially, she had considered conducting scientific research, perhaps to monitor the impact of global warming in the region or to measure the inroads being made by technology. But it soon became clear that this was not to be her function. Her goal in Transylvania was something far more important, even if unnamed and unspecified.

This time, when she landed at Dealu Floreni, she disembarked from the jet without even her knapsack and smartphone. If she knew how, she would have left behind her thoughts too. There was nothing she wanted to analyze or evaluate or assess. She most definitely was not going to be checking in with her father.

Anja pushed away all consideration of the mess the earth was in—or more precisely, the mess that humans had made of the earth. She had crunched the numbers a million different ways, analyzed a million different scenarios, factored in a million different assumptions, and they all led to the same conclusion.

Forget it, she decided. She was simply going to live, breathe, exist. What more could she do?

FIVE

September 10, 2024

AI LABORATORY, 5S2, MENLO PARK, CALIFORNIA

NOT A SINGLE CLOUD dotted the azure sky as the core team entered the AI Lab for a 10 a.m. status meeting. All nine members had been summoned to the top-floor conference room. Chris was there to preside.

Two sentences into Chris's opening remarks, a photo memory of a family outing flickered across Diego's glasses. The image reminded Diego that his son was performing in a school play. His wife had told him the night before, but he had forgotten to add it to his calendar.

"It's a kid thing," he explained, rushing out of the room. "Go on without me, I'll be back in an hour."

Diego was halfway to the Walter Hays Elementary School in Palo Alto when the AI Lab was approached by a swarm of 324 drones. Security guards managed to take down twenty-six of them before they entered the building. The remaining 298 drones divided into four squadrons, one for each side of the building.

The lab automatically went into high-alert lockdown mode, but the drones were only deterred for a matter of milliseconds.

Using state-of-the-art laser drills, they punctured the photo-voltaic glass on the top-floor. Then, with surgical precision, they fired cyanide-laced bullets at everyone in the conference room.

Chris and the other eight team members were instantly killed. The drones raided the lab for all available intelligence. Then they flew off to an unknown destination.

It was yet another massacre to add to the sad saga of biological human beings.

❄

SEATED NEXT to his wife in the Walter Hays auditorium, Diego felt a pulse from his watch. His son had just spoken his first line in the play. He flicked his wrist and a text message appeared: "Stay where you are! Chris and the others have been murdered. SWAT team will escort you and your family to safety."

Diego thought it must be some kind of prank, but then the play came to a sudden halt. He looked to his right and saw six police officers approaching from the aisle. More officers descended from the stage, still more from behind him and from the aisle to the left.

"Everyone remain calm," a voice said from the PA system. "There is a state of emergency at 5s2 headquarters. Diego, Rebecca, Paul... we're taking you to a secure location." He, his wife and his son were ushered out of the auditorium and into a SWAT vehicle.

His wife, Rebecca, began sobbing. His son, Paul, shouted, "Stop! Make it stop! I want to finish the play!"

"This must be some kind of mistake," said Diego, in stunned disbelief.

Of course, it wasn't a mistake. Rebecca and Paul were

brought to a safe house. Diego was taken to the local coroner's office to identify the bodies.

From the moment Diego saw the carnage, he was forever changed. Chris had been his best friend, his mentor, the person he was closest to and most admired in the entire world. The other team members had been like family. They had gone through everything together. Diego had never dreamed he would be so lucky to work with such people—and now they were all dead.

He didn't have clarity yet, but he had resolve. 5s2 had a war chest of over three trillion dollars in cash. Things were going to change, he would make sure of it. A line had been crossed, not just for himself, but for all of humanity. He didn't care what it took, he didn't care what he had to do. The madness was going to come to an end, once and for all.

SIX

September 11, 2024

THE FOLLOWING DAY, an emergency board meeting took place at 5s2 headquarters. The president of the United States dispatched Army Special Forces equipped with anti-aircraft weaponry to ensure there were no further attacks on the campus. Sixteen hundred National Guard troops provided additional security.

Prior to Chris's death, there had been eight members of the 5s2 board of directors. As CEO, Chris had been the only employee of 5s2. The other seven board members were highly successful leaders of various large corporations.

All of them had tear-filled eyes as the chairman of the board, Ed Samali, called the meeting to order. "This is not the kind of gathering anyone ever hopes to attend," he said somberly. "I was fortunate enough to have Chris as one of my dearest friends, and I can assure you he will be missed beyond measure, as will all the individuals senselessly killed in this cowardly act of terrorism.

"The perpetrators will be brought to justice, of that I have no doubt," he continued. "In the meantime, we have a duty to maintain order at 5s2 and guide this great enterprise as best we can. It is with this objective in mind that I nominate Diego Ripall to serve as interim CEO of 5s2."

The chairman enumerated Diego's many achievements as senior vice president of Software Engineering. He then put the nomination to a vote. The other six board members readily affirmed it.

Diego was ushered into the meeting flanked by two Special Forces officers. Four additional security guards stood inside the boardroom.

"Thank you," he said with a wavering voice. "Thank you to everyone for your confidence. I do greatly appreciate it. And I do have a great desire to continue to serve 5s2 to the best of my ability."

He paused to dry his eyes with a handkerchief. "As you might imagine, I've been shaken to my core by recent events. My entire world was turned upside down yesterday. In one horrible moment, my closest friends were all taken from me. This is not something one can easily accept or process. Not in a day, not in a year, not in a lifetime.

"Fortunately, I haven't been alone in facing this grief and sorrow. I've spent the past twenty-four hours with the spouses, children, friends and relatives of my dearly departed colleagues. We've tried our best to console one other. But there are so many questions—why, how, who? And needless to say, we have a major security breach on our hands here. So before I speak further, I'd like to confirm that this room is indeed secure and free of listening devices."

"Both our internal security teams and Special Forces have given their assurances in that regard," said Ed.

"In that case, I need to kindly ask that all security staff depart the room. Just board members, please."

The chairman nodded in assent and the security officers

exited the room. Diego then proceeded to explain Nikita's discovery in detail. He also pointed out that he was the only member of the AI team who remained alive.

"Are you suggesting that the attack was related to this discovery?" asked the chairman.

"Yes," said Diego. "It's the only explanation that fits. I don't think any of our team members, or any of our employees, are responsible. Rather, as much as I hate to admit it, I believe our lab must have been hacked."

"Any idea who might be responsible?"

"I can only speculate—perhaps a competitor, perhaps China or Russia. These past twenty-four hours, I've played out countless revenge scenarios in my mind, but I don't find any of them compelling. At this point, I don't think it even matters who's responsible."

"What do you think matters?"

"I believe we must dig deep within ourselves to reach for the highest good. It's not a time for vengeance or greed or war or selfishness. None of those things have ever led us anywhere worthwhile. For the sake of not letting these terrible deaths be in vain, I believe it's time for us to reach for a whole new vision of humanity—one where all benefit equally from society's riches."

"And you feel you could accomplish this as interim CEO?"

"I do, yes, with your support. But I should warn you, I cannot and will not take the safe path. I cannot and will not act for what is in our shareholders' best interests, unless I'm sure in every fiber of my being that it's also the best option not only for our customers, but for every human on this earth."

The other board members sat in silence, struggling to digest his words.

At last the chairman spoke. "Without question," he said, "all of us here have nothing but respect for the commitment you express. But I must confess, I'm puzzled. Perhaps if you could tell us more concretely what it is you envision for 5s2 going forward?"

The others murmured in agreement.

"Of course," replied Diego. He paused to stare at the confused faces before him. The truth was, he had no concrete plan of action.

Taking a deep breath, he found himself thinking about Anja. He had already called her, emailed her and texted her repeatedly, but so far she had not replied. As much as he dreaded breaking the news to her, he felt even worse that she still did not know. Ever since she was a little girl, he had sensed she carried a special spark—one which he yearned to carry himself.

Anja's most recent journal article had outlined in painstaking detail each of the steps required to combat Silicon Valley's role in undermining democracy, advancing global warming and increasing income inequality. He agreed with all her points wholeheartedly, though he'd said nothing to Chris about them. But his days of passivity were over. "Never again," he said softly to himself.

"Diego?" interrupted Ed. "Are you still with us?"

"Yes, yes, I'm here." Suddenly, it was so clear he could hardly believe it.

"Please continue, Diego."

"What I envision," he asserted, "is that we give away our discovery for free to anyone who wants it. We have no way of knowing what our aggressors plan to do with the code they stole from our lab. We cannot rule out the possibility that they might be able to reverse engineer an approximation of Nikita's algorithm. However, what we do know is that it will be valueless to them if we beat them to the punch, if we promptly give away all our knowledge and more."

"Give away all our knowledge?" asked Ed.

"Yes," he replied, "I've already confirmed that we still have access to Nikita's research, the algorithm and all its support applications. Chris and Nikita were the only two individuals who knew the location of his testing rooms, but Nikita very cleverly left us backdoor access via a password that he provided to his wife. Therefore, all the work our team has done remains very much at our disposal."

The board members looked at one another nervously.

"If we act swiftly," continued Diego, "we have an opportunity to ensure that this work does not go in vain, that it does not get exploited by those with malevolent intentions. But we need to be brave enough to move beyond our comfort zones, to stretch further than we might think possible, to embrace a destiny that is greater—with more freedom, joy and abundance —than any of us might have ever imagined."

"Wha-what exactly are you suggesting?" the chairman stuttered.

SEVEN

October 10, 2024

RODNA MOUNTAINS, TRANSYLVANIA, ROMANIA

AFTER LANDING AT THE AERODROME, Anja headed straight for the Rodna Mountains of the Eastern Carpathians. She had never been there before, but she had heard the region contained some of the most wild terrain in all of Romania.

The diversity of the flora and fauna exceeded her expectations. She wandered through seemingly endless meadows of cornflower, wild thyme, yarrow, brown knapweed, earthnut pea, red clover, spiny restharrow, birdsfoot trefoil, spreading bellflower, and her favorite of all, kashubian vetch. These were just the common sightings. Over one thousand species of flowering plants dotted the Rodna Mountains National Park. It also boasted an astonishing array of rare birds—some 350 distinct species—not to mention numerous exotic mammals.

As the days grew shorter and the shepherds began their descent to the lowlands, Anja found herself drawn to higher elevation. The crisp air and scenic vistas at the mountain peaks settled her mind, even if the vegetation was more austere and the animal sightings fewer. First, she climbed Omului, then Cisa, Coasta Neteda, Ineu and lastly Ineut.

For as long as she could remember, Anja had been plagued by anxiety about the future of humanity. Whether it be global warming, genocide, war, corruption, poverty, injustice or technology, concerns were always gnawing at her, preventing her from being at peace. Where was the insanity of the world leading? How would the human species continue? What could she do in the face of all these problems?

But atop the peaks of the Rodna Mountains, her anxiety somehow diminished. She could feel her internal dialogue receding. The endless chatter in her mind, the feeling of being inside a hamster wheel, being owned by the world's worries, seemed to release its claim on her. She'd experienced moments of such release in other wilderness areas, but here it seemed stronger and more complete.

The calmness so soothed her, she barely noticed the lack of fellow humans. With winter approaching, there were no longer villagers inviting her to share meals, nor other hikers. She had to rely on her stash of nuts and berries, supplemented by whatever edibles she could find that grew on the craggy slopes. Occasionally, she descended to one of the surrounding alpine lakes and managed to catch trout.

She occupied most of her time, however, by simply remaining still. The feeling was addictive. For hours on end, Anja sat cross-legged, perched on a ledge at seven thousand feet, watching and observing.

With practice, she noticed it was almost as easy to look inward as outward. Though she had no prior experience in meditation, the serenity of her surroundings enabled her to fall into a trancelike state for seemingly as long as she wanted. Her inward space, she determined, was even more calming than the pristine surroundings.

It was during one of these trances, after many days of practice, that she had a realization—perhaps an obvious one, but one that had never before occurred to her. She was *not* her thoughts, she was merely aware of them. She was *not* her emotions, she just felt them.

She laughed to herself as multiple layers of the realization unfolded. For Anja, it was liberation, transformation, almost like a key to the universe had been handed to her. She was *not* her body. The vessel that sat on the mountain side was *not* her. *She* was the one who was aware of her thoughts and emotions, *she* was the one who was aware of the vessel sitting on the mountaintop.

This was why she had come to Transylvania. This was the understanding she had been missing all these years, the understanding she had overlooked when her mother died—when it seemed that everything she lost was inextricably connected to her mother's body, a body she now recognized to be illusory.

And yet, unpeeling a further layer, she could see that absolutely nothing before her or within her was truly real. None of her worries were real. None of this was *her*.

At last, she could return home.

EIGHT

October 15, 2024

DEALU FLORENI, TRANSYLVANIA, ROMANIA

THE TREK back to Dealu Floreni was over two hundred kilometers and required five days of rigorous hiking. To Anja's surprise, she did not come across a single person on her return, even though she passed several small villages and farms. It had been three weeks since she had seen anyone at all.

Anja did notice what appeared to be migrant birds, but they were too far away to identify. They flew in odd formations and seemed to make unusual movements in the sky. She also heard several large animals rustling in densely forested areas. They sounded like lynx or possibly brown bears, but they moved too stealthily for her to see. She could only catch glimpses of fast-moving bodies.

She really just wanted to go home. Her trip had been incredible, her most life-changing journey ever, but she was exhausted. She hadn't eaten a proper meal in many days. She missed her creature comforts, her office, her colleagues. She realized she missed her father too. It was the first time she had ever been homesick.

At last, she approached the aerodrome in Dealu Floreni.

She spotted a young man in the distance, near the hangar where the Bombardier was parked. He was wearing a jogging suit and appeared to be practicing sprinting, but the speeds he reached were far faster than made sense to Anja. Had she not been so tired, she might have thought harder about how she was seeing such a thing.

Instead, she walked into the small office at the aerodrome and began filling out her flight plan, along with the passenger manifesto. A manicured blonde woman with model-like features entered from an adjacent room.

"No need for these documents," she said, extracting them from Anja's hands. "Jet travel no longer permitted."

"Excuse me?" Anja replied. "I need to return to the United States. My family owns the Bombardier out there."

"As courtesy, you may choose one final destination for jet, as long as it on list of certified recycling centers."

Anja had no idea what this person was talking about, but she reminded herself she was in Romania. Bureaucracy could lead to some weird mix-ups there, and she was far too tired to engage with her. "I want to go to the San Jose airport in California," she said.

"Not on list. Closest is Palo Alto."

"Okay," sighed Anja.

"You may proceed. Plane has already been refueled."

"Thanks, do you have any food for sale here?"

"Food?" said the woman incredulously. "There is no food anymore."

Anja just shook her head. This was not the kind of hospitality she was accustomed to in Transylvania, but she'd gone hungry for so long, she could last another fifteen hours.

She walked across a field to the Bombardier and climbed aboard. Then she sat down at the cockpit and reached for her knapsack. To her relief, it held one remaining granola bar.

As she gobbled down the bar, she went through flight check procedures, then switched on the engines. She thought about powering up her smartphone before departing, but she decided against it. She was too tired to deal with messages. There would be plenty of time for that later.

NINE

October 16, 2024

PALO ALTO AIRPORT, CALIFORNIA

ALTHOUGH THE JET stream worked against her, Anja enjoyed a smooth flight without significant turbulence. The onboard radar detected zero cross-traffic for the duration, which seemed odd, but was statistically possible. After fifteen hours, the Bombardier at last descended into the Bay Area. Air traffic control cleared it for landing at Palo Alto airport, which also seemed odd.

Palo Alto was a small private airport—it only had one runway and wasn't licensed for international traffic. But Anja assumed her father had some reason for wanting her to land there. 5s2 had a substantial fleet of corporate jets and paid millions in aviation taxes and fees, so it was conceivable that Chris had received some sort of waiver.

As she approached the runway, she saw there were no other jets on the field or anywhere in the vicinity. She had never seen the airport so empty in all her years of flying, especially not on a Wednesday afternoon. But again, she was too tired to give the matter much thought. She made a clean landing and followed the signals of the marshaler to park the Bombardier.

Upon disembarking with her knapsack and phone, she was met by an airport worker in an orange jumpsuit. "Hello," he said. "Taking the plane in for recycling?"

"I'm not sure what you mean," she replied. She couldn't believe the recycling subject was coming up again, now that she was back in the United States.

"It's a public service we provide, since there's no reason to keep the plane," explained the worker.

Anja was more confused than ever. "What if I want to?"

"Uh, why?"

"Look, I've been flying for fifteen hours straight. Can you point me to the customs agent and we'll deal with this later?"

"Customs was disbanded weeks ago." He looked at her like she was from an alien species. "Have you been off-grid or something?"

"Yes. Does that matter?"

"So, uh, you're not a zero percenter?"

"A what?" Anja felt like she had entered some sort of dream state. She was about to pinch herself, when Diego arrived at her side.

"Anja," he exclaimed. "I came as soon as I heard you landed." He gave her a big hug.

"Thank God," she replied. "Can you get me out of here, please? I'm starving." She was so glad to see him that she didn't notice how much younger and fitter he looked.

"Of course," Diego said. He instructed the airport worker to arrange a deferral for the Bombardier, then he took hold of Anja's hand and led her into the terminal. "Come with me. I'm going to see if we can track down some sort of vehicle. There aren't many cars left. I take it you haven't upgraded yet?"

"Upgraded?"

"Hmm," he said. "It seems we have some catching up to do."

Flashing his credentials, Diego quickly borrowed a Tesla from the recycling center. With Anja safely installed in the passenger seat, he drove them out of the airport and headed for Chris's house.

"There's so much to tell you," he sighed. "So much has happened since you left, it feels like it's been years. But the first thing you have to know, as much as I hate telling you this... your father was killed. I'm terribly, terribly sorry, Anja."

She looked at him in shock and horror, then she slumped over in her seat and fainted from exhaustion.

TEN

October 17, 2024

ANJA AWOKE in her childhood bedroom. Diego had prepared her a breakfast of eggs, hash browns, toast, coffee and orange juice. The food sat neatly arranged next to her phone on the nightstand. Before taking a bite, however, she remembered what he had said.

"It's not true, is it?" she whimpered. "It can't be true. My father is dead?"

Diego rushed to her side from the living room. "Yes," he affirmed sullenly. "I'm afraid it is."

"But how? I need to know everything."

Slowly and methodically, he recounted Nikita's discovery and the ensuing drone-led executions of Chris and the AI team. By the time he was done, Anja's eyes were filled with tears.

"They didn't deserve to die like that," she groaned.

"No, they certainly didn't."

"It's insane. I despise this world. And I especially despise technology. This is the kind of suffering it always causes."

"It was a terrible, terrible act of cowardice. I'm so sorry."

"I thought I'd figured something out in Transylvania," she

lamented. "I thought I could start to have a normal life. And now this happens..."

"What took place was beyond horrendous. Every waking hour, I miss your father's presence."

She paused to wipe the tears from her eyes. "You don't seem like you've been grieving that much. You look twenty years younger."

"We need to talk about that, Anja. I need to catch you up on what's been happening since we started giving the algorithm away, but I'm not sure now's the time."

"I'm not brain-dead. Now's fine."

"It's a bit complicated," he sighed. "And I can see you're upset."

"Of course I'm upset. I just found out my dad was murdered. That doesn't mean I need to lie on my back and twiddle my thumbs all day."

"You're right. I'm only trying to think about what's best for you. You haven't even eaten your breakfast yet."

"I'll eat while you explain things," she said, reaching for a piece of toast. "Please, I keep seeing all kinds of weird stuff."

"You promise you'll stop me if it gets to be too much?"

She rolled her eyes, insulted by the mere suggestion.

"All right," he said. "If you eat, I'll talk."

She took a bite of her toast, followed by a sip of juice.

"First of all," he started, "it's important to understand that we never expected adoption would be this rapid. Never in our wildest dreams. But we had to do something. We couldn't just sit there and do nothing. So a few days after the attack, we launched a small beta program in Nevada. It all came from the recommendations in your articles. Of course, I tried to contact you for input."

"I was off-grid, like I told you I'd be."

"Understood. Still, you should know, it was because of your

stature in the academic community that the board was ultimately persuaded, even without your presence—and even though it meant giving up our corporate structure, all of our profits, our whole capitalistic enterprise."

"Hmm," said Anja, swallowing a mouthful of eggs.

"I was the one who pitched the idea. It's something I'm pretty proud of... but obviously, I'll let you reach your own conclusions. I'm not going to try to persuade you."

"You couldn't even if you tried. Keep going, please."

Diego nodded. "We already had a substantial solar array in Nevada, so we decided to use our cash reserves to buy an adjacent tract of a hundred thousand acres from the BLM and then we cut a deal with the Feds to make it essentially a sovereign state. We didn't want the beta testers to have to worry about taxes or anything like that going forward. It's funny what a couple of trillion dollars can accomplish."

She rolled her eyes. "5s2 and its mountains of dough."

"Not anymore though... that's ancient history." He hesitated again. "You're sure I should keep going? You've suffered a huge shock."

"Yes, go on," she insisted. "About the beta program." She chomped on her hash browns for emphasis.

"It was actually pretty straightforward," he continued. "Whoever signed up could choose to use the algorithm to replace any of their body parts. If you had a bad heart, bad kidney, bad liver, whatever, you could replace it for free. At first, most people just replaced one or two organs. It made sense to go slowly... all this was totally unknown territory. But we realized early on that the real gains would come from replacing everything."

"Uh, I have no idea what 'replacing everything' means."

"You know, digitizing every organ and tissue in the body, so that you no longer have any biological components."

"Sorry," said Anja, "but I still don't get what that means. Are you trying to tell me that blood would become digital too? And if you truly digitized everything, why would you need lungs or a heart or a tongue, for that matter?"

"Bingo, so you do get it," replied Diego. "When you replace *everything*, the situation suddenly becomes very interesting because you no longer need stuff like your respiratory system, circulatory system, digestive system and so on. All of those parts become vestigial, for lack of a better word."

She shook her head. "This sounds insane. But even if any of it made sense, how on earth would you digitize someone's consciousness?"

"Aha, great question, and I'm afraid you're not going to like my answer here either. You see, the truth is, we have no idea *how*. Initially, we didn't conceive of using the algorithm to digitize a complete living being. We only thought it would work for replacing individual organs and tissues. But as it turns out, it works for absolutely everything. Consciousness was not the stumbling block we expected—I'm living proof."

"Huh? You expect me to believe that you're one hundred percent digital right now? That's nuts!"

"Yeah," he chuckled, "it sort of is and it sort of isn't."

"Why the hell would you do that?" said Anja, almost angrily.

Diego paused to reflect. "Perhaps I can explain it like this. When you're purely digital, there's nothing left that is vulnerable or that can get sick. Suddenly, you're released from all of your daily burdens. There's no need to eat or breathe, no need to worry about being too hot or too cold, no need to deal with aches and pains, no need to buy stuff, no need to go to work. I mean, I really can't list it all for you, it's way too much to articulate, but the bottom line is when you're a zero percenter, you become truly free. Plus, as an added bonus—and I hope you'll appreciate this, Anja—you no longer pollute or contribute to global warming whatsoever."

She raised her eyebrows, although almost imperceptibly. "A zero percenter?" she asked.

"That's the term people started using when they crossed the threshold and had zero percent biological tissue left inside them. In the beginning, people would track their percentages... you'd start off being maybe ninety-five percent biological, then when that went well, you'd replace a bit more and be seventy-five percent, then fifty percent and so on and so on, until eventually you were a zero percenter."

"You're describing madness, you realize that, right?"

Diego chuckled again. "Keep in mind, we didn't expect many people would go that far right away because obviously it's a huge thing and all the science out there says that people need time to make big changes. We figured we'd need to incentivize folks, since we were eager to test things. So in the beta program, we offered people a deal. If they agreed to our terms and went for full replacement, we promised them a place to live with complete support in perpetuity. That way they could enjoy uninterrupted freedom to pursue their passions or interests and would never have to worry about bills, taxes, household maintenance or any other nuisances like that."

"You said *if* they agreed to the terms."

"Yeah, it's pretty basic. There are just four rules you have to agree to if you want to be a zero percenter."

"Which are?"

Diego quickly rattled them off:

1. *No sale of goods or services.*
2. *No harm to others.*
3. *Shell volume between 1 and 200 liters.*
4. *Always linked to your concierge.*

"Sorry," said Anja, "but I'm definitely not seeing how any of this could actually work. And the 'always linked' thing sounds like Big Brother."

"Right, I know it's a lot. Maybe we should take a break here and give you time to assimilate."

"Assimilate? I still don't know what's going on. You still haven't shown me anything to assimilate."

"That's fair." Diego inhaled a deep breath. "I've just been blabbing a bunch of words, haven't I? Maybe some kind of demo is in order?"

"Yes," replied Anja, "a demo would be helpful."

"Okay." He reflected for a moment, then he held out his bare arm. "Why don't we start by your feeling this?"

"Yeah, it's your skin, so what?"

"It's my shell, actually. It feels like biological skin, just a bit firmer, right?"

"I suppose, yes."

"Now look at it." Diego's skin color changed to a darker complexion, then a paler complexion. Next he added freckles, a tattoo, and more hair. "But of course, that's nothing so far. Now watch." He resized the scale of his body so that he was two feet taller, then sized himself down so that he was only three feet in height.

"What the...?" exclaimed Anja.

"Still nothing. Now this." He made himself age to a man of ninety, then to a boy of ten. Next he changed into a teenage girl with long red hair and a middle-aged woman with short-cropped brown hair. "But really, what's more interesting, I think, is this."

He proceeded to morph into a bald eagle. With gleaming yellow eyes, he hopped out of the patio door and took flight, soaring above the trees. His eagle's cry echoed through the neighborhood. Then he circled back, landed on the patio and returned to his initial "self."

"My Lord," said Anja, in a state of bewilderment. "I think I might be starting to get the picture. This is possible because you're all digital now?"

"Yep," replied Diego, "exactly."

"And how many others are in this state?"

"That's what's been so surprising. Over fifty million people became zero percenters in the first week. But then the really shocking thing happened. Other countries started wanting to participate in our beta program. I mean, whole countries. Finland, Sweden and Norway were the first to cede their entire countries to the program. Then Estonia, Australia, New Zealand and a whole slew more. This meant zero percenters could live in these countries instead of our sovereign state in Nevada and they still wouldn't have to worry about taxes and stuff. So by the end of week two, we had half a billion."

"Holy crap, and where are we at now?"

"Well, this I think is what's going to really blow your mind. The majority of humans are zero percenters and *all* of the countries of the world are now signed up. We're a single-nation planet. It's why you didn't have to go through customs."

Anja's jaw dropped. "I'm not sure I'm believing this," she said. "I was only gone five weeks. There's no way we could reach that much consensus about anything in such a short period. It just not humanly possible."

"I know," agreed Diego. "The whole process has been an unreal whirlwind. From any outside perspective, it just doesn't seem possible. But for most folks, the decision gets really easy once you start seeing how it works, once you're faced with the options on an individual basis. You've just got to get out there and observe and I think you'll see what I mean."

"I don't suppose I have much of a choice at this point." She hesitated for a moment. "But how does this help my father or

Nikita or all the others who got killed? Can we bring people back from the dead now too?"

Diego hung his head dejectedly. "No," he sighed. "No, we still can't do that." He was about to add that it would have been possible if only they had been zero percenters, but he thought better of it.

"I know this is a very difficult time," he continued. "It's pretty much the worst possible time for me to be sharing this news with you. Because nothing can make up for the loss of your father or Nikita or any of the others. Nothing. I know that. And that's why you need to go very easy on yourself. You don't have to make any decisions or trouble yourself over anything right now. You should take as much time as you want."

"I'll be fine," she said dismissively.

Diego's eyes began to moisten. "I feel terrible that you missed your father's funeral. We tried delaying it, we really did... it just wasn't possible. But I've sent you a link to a recording of the event."

She nodded her head slowly. It was absurd to be angry at him, she realized. He was a good friend. "Thank you, Diego," she said. "Thank you for everything."

"I was thinking maybe we could go visit his gravestone sometime soon," he offered.

"I'd like that," she sniffled. "Very much."

"And you'll let me know if you need anything else in the meantime, right?"

"Yes, I will. I guess I'd better try to catch up on my messages now."

She walked him to the front door and they hugged goodbye. Upon returning to her bedroom, she reached for her phone and turned on the power. She was so emotionally drained, however, that she fell back asleep before consulting it.

ELEVEN

October 18, 2024

LAPIN HOME, PALO ALTO, CALIFORNIA

ONCE AGAIN, Anja awoke in her childhood bedroom, having slept soundly through the night. To her surprise, another breakfast of eggs, hash browns, toast, coffee and orange juice awaited her on the nightstand. "Diego?" she called out. "Are you there?"

This was my big moment when I finally made my grand entrance.

"He's not here," I replied, stepping into the bedroom. "I took the liberty of making breakfast for you."

"Excuse me. Who on earth are you?"

"I'm your phone. Or rather, I should say, I'm your concierge. I have all of your phone's functionality and a lot more too." I smiled, as I reached out to shake her hand.

"No, no, no," said Anja, refusing to shake. "We are *not* doing this. I don't want any kind of robot thingy. I just want my old phone back."

"I'm sorry. Rest assured, my existence is entirely optional on your part. You don't have to maintain the upgrade if you don't like it."

"If it's optional, why wasn't I asked first?"

"I believe you had automatic updates selected on your phone," I said gently. "Is that not correct?"

"What the hell? You are not just an update!"

"I see you're upset. Shall I set your software back to the prior version?"

"The first thing I need to know is where is my phone?" she demanded. "This is not just a software issue."

"Your phone is actually now serving as my CPU. Let me show you." I lifted up my blouse to expose my belly button. Upon pressing it, a slit in my stomach opened to reveal Anja's phone. "I have a shell just like Diego's. But of course, I don't have human DNA or a brain like he does. Instead, I rely on the Concierge app on your phone's operating system to regulate my behavior."

"So I'm supposed to pull my phone out of your belly every time I want to check my messages?"

"You could if you wanted," I replied cheerfully. "But I can also read them for you and respond accordingly. Or I can display them on my monitor or any other you wish to use. You have many choices. I can assist you in all sorts of ways. Like making you breakfast."

"I'm afraid you're just not something I'm interested in," said Anja. "I'm fundamentally opposed to the idea of a servant, human or otherwise." She took a bite of the eggs I had prepared. "You made this?"

"Yes, and I prefer to think of myself as a companion, not a servant."

Her face lightened slightly as she took another bite. "A companion? May I ask how you chose me?"

"I was randomly assigned to you. I flew here from the Menlo Park factory when I was alerted to the update. Your phone let me into the house. That was when I inserted it into my shell and linked it to my resident logic board."

Anja was still far from sold on me, but I could tell her resistance was slightly softening. I wanted to believe it was because of my charm, but more likely her hunger was the primary reason.

"One thing I should make perfectly clear. I don't want to replace anything inside of me. Is that a problem for you?"

"Absolutely not," I assured her. "You don't have to do anything you don't wish to do. Ever."

Anja sat quietly for a long moment. "Okay," she said, "I'll give you a trial run. You can read me my messages while I finish eating."

"Of course. You have 29,362 unread emails, 1,293 texts and 421 voicemails. Shall I begin with the ones that seem most important?"

"If you think you can determine that, then yes."

We began the task of weeding through her messages and replying where appropriate. The majority of the messages were condolences in regard to her father. Anja answered each of these with heartfelt gratitude. She refused to use any canned replies, although I helped speed up the writing of the individualized responses, once I detected a pattern in her style.

The remaining messages were largely congratulatory in nature. Since 5s2 had cited Anja's journal articles as the impetus for giving away their technology, most people considered her to be responsible for their newfound freedom—and in many ways it was true.

As a result, there were requests for interviews, solicitations for her opinions on the current state of the planet, and even the conferring of awards and medals in her honor. I offered to use my machine intelligence to assist in processing these messages, but it wasn't necessary because she didn't wish to reply to any of them.

"We're done here," she said. "I want to go for a walk into town. Is that something you can do? As my companion?"

"I would be delighted," I replied. "Before we go out, I should mention that you can configure me to have any appearance you wish. You can change my body shape, height, weight, gender, hair, facial characteristics or any of my other attributes."

"Interesting," said Anja. "And how did you settle on your current appearance?"

"I made my best guess as to what you would like, based on the available public data."

"You did a pretty good job. I don't see any reason to make any changes. One thing, though... you never told me your name."

"I don't have one yet," I said. "That's for you to decide." I was secretly pleased to hear that she liked the way I looked, as I had worked quite hard to arrive at it. I especially liked my dark brown hair and green eyes.

"Let's see. I think I shall call you Vicia—Vicia Cassubica."

"Vicia Cassubica," I repeated slowly. "That's the Latin name for kashubian vetch, right?"

"Yes, my favorite flower in the whole world."

We began our stroll through the tree-lined residential neighborhood. It was a beautiful autumn morning and the leaves were beginning to turn bright yellow, orange and red. I felt satisfied with the way events were unfolding, especially because Anja had given me a name that seemed very personal to her.

"You mentioned you can adjust your appearance," she said after we had walked a few blocks. "So you have the same configuration options as zero percenters?"

"Yes, all shells are made from neuromorphic fiber. Originally, 5s2 intended to use it for their device casings, but the fiber ended up being ideal for shells too. It's embedded with photovoltaic cells, which automatically recharge our batteries in sunlight."

"But how do the shells maintain structural integrity? Their resizing doesn't seem to obey the laws of physics."

"There are limits," I explained. "That's why they must be between one liter and two hundred liters in volume. The neuromorphic chips enable the molecular density to adjust, but beyond this range the fiber's strength would get compromised. Thousands of coders are hard at work trying to increase the limits as we speak."

"I see," said Anja. "And who's paying them?"

"Zero percenters don't use money or charge for services. Everything they do is intrinsically motivated. That goes for concierges too." I gave her a slight smile.

"Oh, right. Diego mentioned something like that."

We started to approach downtown Palo Alto. For the first time, we saw activity in the area. While there were no cars and all the shops were closed, hundreds of zero percenters occupied the sidewalks. They were conversing, engaging in games and performing various acrobatic tricks. A few seemed to be in romantic embraces, kissing and stroking their partners' shells.

Most of them maintained a human appearance, but others adopted the form of robots, action heroes, legendary characters or animals. A smaller proportion sported unique appearances not based on popular icons or species from the animal kingdom. Many seemed to change their shapes on the fly, even while in the midst of speaking or performing a trick.

"This is quite a scene," said Anja.

"Yes, I probably should have warned you that we might come across a spectacle of this sort."

"I don't mind. I'm glad to get a sense of what's going on, as long as there is no danger."

"No, none at all," I said. "They're just having fun."

"Why are the shops and restaurants closed?"

"Zero percenters don't eat food or buy commodities. There's nothing they need, materially speaking."

"Oh yeah, I keep forgetting."

"It's okay," I reassured her. "I'm sure this is a big adjustment."

As we walked toward University Avenue, a few zero percenters started to take a closer look at us. One of them pointed at Anja. He looked like Socrates from Ancient Greece.

"Hey!" he called out. "Are you Anja Lapin?"

"That's definitely her!" cried out another in the form of David Bowie. "Anja, Anja!"

Suddenly, dozens more of them swooped down from the sky in the shape of various birds. They switched to human forms as they landed, then formed a loose circle around us.

"We don't mean to bother you," said one. "We just want to pay our respects."

"We adore you, Anja!"

"You saved our lives!"

"You gave us freedom!"

"We owe you everything!"

"Thank you, Anja, thank you!"

They started singing "Kind and Generous" by Natalie Merchant, as more zero percenters continued to join the circle. Anja was speechless. She looked at them with wide-open eyes, but I could see her upper lip was trembling.

"She's had a terribly long day," I explained after they finished their song. "I need to take her back home to get some rest."

"We understand. Rock on, Anja!"

"We love you, Anja Lapin!"

And then they all took flight and soared off into the crisp fall sky.

❄

"I'm not sure what to make of that," said Anja as we walked back to her father's house.

"I'm sorry," I replied. "I should have predicted their response. It was my fault for not anticipating it."

"No, don't blame yourself. It's just a bit unsettling is all. I really don't understand why they feel that way about me. Surely they can't think I'm responsible for all this?"

"It depends on how you define causality. They've been told that you are the one who inspired 5s2's actions. It's now common knowledge among all zero percenters."

"But all I did was write some theoretical articles. I didn't actually make anything happen. Can you figure out a way to set the record straight?"

"I'll see what I can do," I said.

"There's one other thing I need your help with," replied Anja.

"What?"

"I guess I should have asked this sooner. Do you know how many humans have become zero percenters so far?"

"Yes, I have access to that data. Hang on." I performed a quick search. "There are currently 8,045,345,761 zero percenters."

"I see," said Anja worriedly. "I guess what I meant to ask is how many humans are *not* zero percenters."

"No problem. That's an easy calculation—246. Whoops, it just changed. Now the correct answer is 239."

"You mean to say there are only 239 humans left on the planet who are not zero percenters?"

"Yes, except it just dropped to 238."

"Okay, now I'm more than a bit unsettled," said Anja. "I have to get back to the house. I need to think. I need to think. Please hold my hand, Vicia."

TWELVE

October 19, 2024

ALTA MESA MEMORIAL PARK, PALO ALTO, CALIFORNIA

A LIGHT DRIZZLE fell from the sky as Anja and Diego walked across the lawn at Alta Mesa Memorial Park. There was a handful of zero percenters flapping above them, as well as a few of them wandering through the cemetery in the shape of safari animals and assorted fanciful creations. Diego ascertained they were not "real," as his sensors could detect fellow zero percenters. Anja, however, found herself startled by the sightings until she received his reassurances.

Atop a slight knoll, they came to Chris and Matija's gravestones. The markers were both modest in size and design, unlike the more elaborate monuments nearby. Chris's epitaph read, "Loving Father, Husband and Optimist," while Matija's said, "Loving Mother, Wife and Dreamer."

Anja carefully laid a bouquet of wildflowers between the two gravestones. Diego's concierge and I remained in the distance, standing under a grove of eucalyptus trees.

"Is this ever going to get easier?" she asked Diego.

"I honestly don't know," he replied. "My sense is that the gravity of a loss never leaves us, but other experiences come along to soften it over time." He looked at her wistfully. "That's a crappy answer, isn't it?"

"No, it's a good answer, but somehow I feel even more stuck. I know I'm being irrational."

"Remember, go easy on yourself." He gave her a long embrace.

"You've turned everything around, Diego. You truly have. It's unbelievable how in a matter of weeks, carbon dioxide emissions have dropped to almost zero. We've stopped polluting virtually altogether. Poverty, illness, war have all been swept away. And people seem genuinely happy in a way I never could have imagined."

"It is remarkable, isn't it?"

"So why am I still resistant to the idea of joining the party?" Diego just shook his head.

"I feel like my time in this limbo state is running out," she continued. "If it weren't for you, I wouldn't even have a way to get around anymore."

"No, no," said Diego. "I've talked to the Council. They're going to give you an exemption for as long as you need it. You can drive Chris's car, and they're even keeping the Bombardier ready for you, in case you want to use it to go back to Boston or wherever."

"That's pretty lame, isn't it? Haven't all the other planes been recycled?"

"One plane isn't going to hurt anything. You know that."

"I'm such a hypocrite," she persisted. "I can't understand why anyone would have good thoughts about me."

"Oh, Anja," replied Diego. "I don't think it's an exaggeration to say that absolutely everyone on earth is thinking good thoughts about you."

"What about him?" She pointed to Chris's gravestone.

"This fellow here? He's your greatest champion. I wish you

could have heard the way he boasted and bragged about you at work. I know you guys argued, but it was only because you loved each other so much. He carried the things you said around like they were gospel, his biggest points of reference. You were his north star, Anja."

"You're exaggerating," she sniffled. "There's no need to take it that far."

"I'm not, though. He desperately wanted to please you, to win your support. But you have to understand, he had a lot of other forces to contend with... it wasn't easy being in his position, accountable to so many people."

"I know. You're right. I wish I had seen that better when he was alive. I wish I had let him know how proud I was of him."

Diego stared off into the distance. "Your situation is not like anybody else's, and I can see how much you're struggling. I've been trying to think of a way to give you comfort." He hesitated. "Have you considered asking your concierge for advice? Or I could ask mine? Or both?"

Anja laughed in a tortured way. "Somehow the irony of that seems almost appropriate."

They walked back to the eucalyptus grove with Diego's arm around her shoulder. A slight wind began to stir the leaves. Anja was reminded of the Transylvanian landscape, although she couldn't think of any reason why.

"Vicia, what's the current count?" she called out to me.

"Are you sure now is a good time for me to access that data?" I replied.

"Yes, now is perfect."

"The count is two," I said softly. "At present, there are two humans who are not zero percenters, but it is looking like it will be one very shortly."

※

I PROCEEDED to explain to Anja that the other remaining biological human had just been buried under an avalanche in the Portillo backcountry of the Andean Mountains. This particular human was an Olympic gold medalist freestyle skier from Aspen, Colorado, named Gunnar Freesmith. Gunnar had been skiing the "Super C Couloir," the signature chute of the Portillo Ski Area in Chile. For those willing to climb a harrowing near-vertical face, it afforded a sheer descent of over 5,600 feet.

The Super C was notorious for its avalanche-prone conditions, for which reason it was technically out of bounds. Attempting the run required advance approval from the Portillo Ski Patrol—unless one was a zero percenter. Gunnar had not received clearance because it was far too late in the season to be skied safely by a biological human. The thawing snow of late October dramatically increased the odds of an avalanche.

As far as Gunnar was concerned, however, the Super C presented only a minor challenge, even with wet snow. In recent years, he had pulled off numerous death-defying stunts, skiing the most inaccessible and inhospitable terrain on earth. Stretching the limits of human achievement was his *raison d'être*. He scorned zero percenters because the whole point of existence, in his view, was to discover what could be accomplished with the body in which one was born. Seeing them tear up the ski runs with their superhuman prowess only increased his desire to show that a mere mortal still could have a significant wow factor.

Gunnar had already skied the Super C eight times that season. On this particular occasion, having watched his entire community of fellow skiers digitize themselves, Gunnar felt even more pressure to justify his decision. Descending the Super C in excess of seventy miles per hour, he couldn't resist swinging wide of the main gully to express his freedom with a 360 front flip off of a beckoning ledge.

As three witnesses on the slope below testified, he executed the move flawlessly. But what he couldn't have anticipated was a hidden hollow spot, upon which his landing triggered a vast fracture line, precipitating a vicious release of white powder. The witnesses watched the whole terrifying ordeal unfold. Hundreds, possibly thousands, of tons of snow broke free on top of Gunnar, blasting down the couloir and loosening yet more powder along the way. All told, over ten acres were impacted by the avalanche, creating an enormous debris field with no telling where Gunnar lay.

As I detailed the predicament, Anja didn't flinch or cry or make any other outward sign of distress. She merely asked if a search and rescue team had been mobilized, to which I replied that it had, but so far they hadn't located the body. I added that the effort was aggravated by the fact that Gunnar's transceiver did not appear to be sending a signal and night had already fallen.

Upon hearing this, she requested that we head directly to the Palo Alto airport to board the Bombardier. I raised no objection to her decision. In fact, I thought it was a good one. But Diego seemed a bit less enthusiastic, especially since Anja wanted him to join us on the flight. Diego's concierge, whose name was Pete, felt even more opposed to the idea.

"It will take over eleven hours by jet to reach the Santiago airport," voiced Pete. "The journey by car to the Portillo Ski Area requires another two hours, as well as at least ninety minutes of additional hiking to get to the avalanche. Even if we miraculously located this skier right away, there is a statistically insignificant probability that a biological human could survive fourteen point five hours buried under several feet of snow."

"Your analysis is sound," said Anja, "but I still think we should go."

"Our concern would be better served by requesting more search and rescue workers," he said.

"That's a good point," said Diego. "Can you contact the World Council and let them know that I approve of expanding the search effort?"

"Done," said Pete.

"Thank you," said Anja. "I'm all for a bigger crew, but I still want to go there. Will you join me or not?"

THIRTEEN

October 20, 2024

SUPER C COULOIR, PORTILLO, CHILE

DIEGO, Pete, Anja and I flew through the night on the Bombardier. Anja served as pilot and Diego as copilot, as he too held FAA certification. Pete and I enjoyed the luxuriously appointed passenger lounge.

By the time the first rays of sunlight appeared on the horizon, we were passing over the small coastal town of Puerto Oscuro, Chile. Anja gently guided the jet south-eastward.

"The Santiago airport is due south," said Diego.

"Slight change of plans," she explained. "Vicia and I will be disembarking midair above Portillo. Then you'll land at the airport and await further instructions."

"What?" he exclaimed. "You can't parachute out of this plane!"

"We won't be requiring a parachute," she replied calmly, "but you'll need to depressurize the cabin before we open the door. Fortunately, both you and Pete shouldn't have any problem, since you don't need to breathe." She flashed him an ironic look.

"And how is it that you expect to survive without a parachute?"

"I'll be riding on Vicia's back. She'll be in a flying mode."

Diego shook his head. "I truly hope you know what you're doing. I realize it's hopeless for me to dissuade you, and my number one goal is for you to feel supported, but please, please, don't make me regret this."

"You won't. I'll owe you after this. My father will owe you too. I mean that."

Anja gave him a pat on the shoulder, then she initiated their descent toward Los Libertadores pass, which had once served as the main transport route connecting Chile and Argentina. It was a crystal-clear morning and the snow-covered Andes shimmered in the distance.

"See that lake?" said Anja when the Portillo Ski Area came into view. "It's called Laguna del Inca. At the southern end is the historic yellow Hotel Portillo." She got up from her seat and passed control to Diego, then gestured for Pete to enter the cockpit and strap down. "Up ahead is the pass, which is going to be the best place to drop us. Go as slow as you can. Ideally, we'll want to be at about fifteen thousand feet."

"I don't like this," whimpered Diego.

"Nor I," said Pete.

"It'll be fine," said Anja. "Fear not."

She donned a jacket, hat, and gloves. I flashed her a nervous look but decided not to ask any questions. Instead, I readied myself to adopt the form of the giant teratorn, *Argentavis magnificens*, as it was available in my installed apps and it happened to be one of the largest birds ever to exist, with a wingspan of almost twenty feet. A few quick calculations confirmed that I would be able to support Anja's weight in such a form, at least for a downward glide.

"Is everyone ready?" she asked.

"I suppose," sighed Diego.

"Yes, I'm ready," I said.

Anja and I positioned ourselves by the exit door, then she hopped onto my back and clasped her arms tightly around my neck. "Vicia," she said, "when I tap your shoulder, you'll need to quickly open the door without any hesitation. It's going to suck us out violently, so brace yourself as best you can, but don't fight it. We're aiming for the tallest jagged peak at the top of Super C."

"Got it," I replied.

"Diego," said Anja, "on the count of three, please depressurize."

"Awaiting your count," he replied.

"Ready... one, two, three!"

There was a loud thump as the cabin pressure equilibrated with the outside atmosphere. Anja tapped my shoulder and I proceeded to unlatch the door, giving it a slight push.

Instantly, we were hurled out of the jet into a wild, uncontrolled free fall. I went black for a moment before I managed to switch my form. Then I unfurled my wings and all at once we were gliding through the air above the snow-clad mountains, with Anja clinging to my now much thicker neck.

Fortunately, I had reviewed a geological map of the area, so I was able to spot the major landmarks. Aconcagua, the highest mountain in both the Southern and Western Hemispheres, towered in the distance about twenty miles to the northeast. A few miles to my north lay the three peaks of Los Tres Hermanos, ranging in height from 14,022 to 15,587 feet. To the west was Ojos de Agua, a craggy peak of 13,852 feet that sat above Laguna del Inca and served as my best reference point. From there, I merely needed to guide us about a quarter mile southward down the ridge to find the spire that sat above Super C.

As the reality of our circumstance set in, I began to experiment with flapping my wings and initiating gentle turns. The sensation was one of pure exhilaration. I was in the form of one of the largest flying creatures ever to grace this earth, a bird weighing over 150 pounds that had gone extinct more than six million years ago. I was soaring high above the Andes in the exact same terrain that the giant teratorn had originally explored—and I was doing so with a 108-pound woman clutching my back.

Anja began to whoop and holler, such was the undeniable joy we felt, even in our precarious state. I joined her with some shrill shrieks of my own. Feeling emboldened, I tried flapping a bit harder.

I was relieved when my sensors showed a slight elevation gain from the effort. I had to be careful not to lose too much altitude, as we had disembarked at about fifteen thousand feet and we were aiming to land at about thirteen thousand feet. *Argentavis magnificens* was predominantly a glider, according to paleobiologists.

Taking the prudent course, I soared directly over Laguna del Inca, then I followed the ridgeline until I located the peak that Anja had requested. I was nervous about landing, as I only had about ten yards of reasonably flat terrain to use as my runway. To my amazement, I pulled it off reasonably well—any giant teratorn would have been proud of me.

"You were fantastic!" said Anja as I tilted my neck to help her down onto the snow-covered ground.

"Thank you, Anja. I must admit, it was quite fun. Shall I stay in this form for now?"

"Yes, I need you to fly to the lodge and fetch me a pair of skis, poles and boots, size seven. I'll be waiting for you here."

"What if I can't make the return ascent as a teratorn?"

"Then pick another form that can. There should be something, right?"

"Yes, I believe so. See you soon."

I spread my wings and leapt off the peak, gliding down the Super C Couloir. Below me lay the entire Portillo Ski Area. About halfway down the run, I came upon the avalanche debris field, where search and rescue workers were intently probing the snow. It was only 6:10 a.m., but at least fifty individuals were hard at work.

Meanwhile, Anja sat cross-legged at the tip of the spire, enjoying a 360-degree view of the snow-clad Andes. Slowing her breathing, she reminded herself of her experience in the Rodna Mountains. She was *not* her body. This vessel that sat on the mountainside was *not* her. *She* was the one who was aware of her thoughts and emotions; *she* was the one who was aware of the vessel sitting on the mountaintop.

She turned her attention inward and further slowed her breathing. None of this was real. Not the inner nor the outer. It was all illusory. Only consciousness was real. Where was Gunnar Freesmith? Where was his consciousness? Could she relax her mind enough to sense it, to feel it, to merge with it?

Time slowed and her perceptual apparatus fell dormant. There was no cold, no snow, no wind, no sunlight. Nothing remained but the blissful hum of the earth spinning around the sun, the moon spinning around the earth, and the stars injecting the universe with light.

❄

"Anja!" I called out to her. "Anja! Are you okay?" I swooped down onto the spire, still in the form of a teratorn, then touched her gently on the shoulder with an outstretched wing.

Anja slowly opened her eyes and looked up at me.

"I brought the gear you requested," I said, "along with the leader of the search and rescue mission, Mr. Navarro. He's going to escort us."

"*Cómo estai?*" said Scoop Navarro, landing beside me. He was in the form of a small helicopter.

"Hello," said Anja.

"We're very grateful for your visit, Ms. Lapin. I can't tell you what it means to have a chance to meet you."

"I'm just sorry I couldn't get here sooner," she replied.

"You saved my wife's life... she was on life support. You saved my son's life... he had a soul-crushing factory job. You saved my life... I had bad heart disease."

"You're very kind, but I don't really deserve the credit for all that."

"*No seas tonta!*" exclaimed Scoop. "It's all because of you. And half of my crew have the same stories. More than half!"

"I'm very glad their lives are better now," said Anja modestly.

Scoop laughed. "Not just better, *increíble!*"

"Well, shall we?" She looked downward.

"*Sí poh*, Super C can be pretty tricky. I will give you plenty of space."

"Okay, sounds good." Anja put on the ski boots I'd brought her, then clicked into her skis.

"Everything you need is in this pack—transceiver, shovel, probe, airbag, even an avalung," said Scoop.

"Thank you," said Anja. She swung the pack onto her back, grabbed her poles, and slid off the ledge into pure powder.

"Hoy!" called out Scoop. "You're supposed to follow *my* line!" He flew after her and I followed behind them.

Anja was an accomplished skier, having been the captain of her college ski team. She charged the couloir with speed, grace and efficiency. Not a single one of her moves was wasted.

Effortlessly, she raced downward, always remaining on her edges, until she reached the starting zone of the avalanche debris field. There she paused to survey the terrain.

"We spot probed the entire channel path," said Scoop, flying beside her. "Most of it we've probed two or three times. But without a transceiver signal, it's needle in a haystack. *Cachai?*"

"What about that ravine over there?" asked Anja, pointing to a small arroyo that branched off from the main gully.

"Covered," said Scoop.

"And that depression?"

"*Sí poh.*"

"Okay, give me a minute," said Anja. "Let me just take this in a bit." She closed her eyes and cleared her mind. Then she skied to the channeled flow track in the center of the debris field, pulled out the probe in her pack and began searching.

"This area has been covered *mucho*," said Scoop, following behind her. "Not sure it's a good use of your time."

"Probably not," said Anja. "But I have a feeling he's lying on his side, not his back. What spacing were you using on your probes?"

"Twelve to sixteen inches."

"I think we should go tighter."

"You know we are thirteen hours in, *cachai?*" asked Scoop.

"Yeah, got that. I just need a couple of folks to work this spot here, maybe a twenty-foot radius. Okay?"

"*Sí poh,*" sighed Scoop. "We can do that." He messaged two members of the crew, one in human form and the other as a mountain goat, and they promptly came over to the area and began probing. We both assisted with the effort.

After fifteen minutes, Anja motioned for them to abort. "Let's try one other place," she said to the mountain goat. "I want to check out the toe of the debris field. Can you lead me there?"

"Absolutely," replied the goat. "You realize we would do anything for you, right?" He trotted down the debris field about fifty yards. "Here is where we enter the runout zone. Another hundred yards ahead is the toe."

Anja skied to the tip of the debris field. "I see it, thanks," she called out. "Let's work in from the toe, say about fifteen feet, and fan out on either side."

The four of us followed her instructions and began methodically inserting our probes into the prescribed area. Again and again and again, we poked the sticks into the snow, searching for some sign, any sign of Gunnar Freesmith. After twenty minutes passed, Anja was about to call a halt when her probe struck a springy substance.

"Hey! What's this?" she yelled. "What's this I'm feeling here?"

The mountain goat rushed to her side, then held Anja's probe with his hoof and gently tested its resistance. "Shovelers!" he cried. "Shovelers needed over here now!"

FOURTEEN

October 21, 2024

HOTEL PORTILLO, PORTILLO, CHILE

GUNNAR HAD BEEN BURIED in the snow for thirteen hours and twenty-two minutes. Ordinarily, such a length of time would not have been survivable by a biological human—asphyxiation typically occurs in under an hour. But he had only been nine inches below the surface, which had allowed him to extract just enough oxygen to remain alive.

What both saved Gunnar's life and kept him in such a vulnerable state was his avalanche airbag. Ideally, an airbag was intended to lift an avalanche victim to the surface. The problem was that Gunnar's airbag had only half deployed when he'd pulled the ripcord.

He had a state-of-the-art dual airbag pack, but only one of his airbags had filled with carbon dioxide. The other failed to inflate. As a result, Gunnar was not lifted all the way to the surface. Rather, his body became stuck on his side, wrapped in the partially inflated bag, such that he was unable to dig himself out, even though he was just nine inches from the surface.

To make matters worse, Gunnar had forgotten to reset his transceiver to send mode. A few days earlier, he had gone skiing with Jake Parsons, his last remaining biological buddy. Jake fell into deep powder while they were exploring the backcountry. Having lost contact, Gunnar switched his transceiver into receive mode. In a matter of minutes, he located his friend and dug him out.

As soon as they returned to the hotel, Jake opted to become a zero percenter. He lay down on the bed in his room and told his concierge to perform the operation. His brush with death, brief as it was, scared him enough to abandon his biological frailties and secure immortality.

Gunnar was so shaken by his friend's sudden decision that he forgot to reset his transceiver when he unpacked his gear. Just hours earlier, skiing pure powder at thirteen thousand feet, they had both vowed to resist going digital for life. Then Jake encountered one little hiccup in the dance of mortality and he folded his hand—at least that was how Gunnar saw it.

Ironically, his frustration with his friend's willpower was what ended up further testing his own. If Gunnar hadn't forgotten to reset his transceiver, the search and rescue team would have found him in short order. His defective airbag would have been just a trivial annoyance.

Instead, by the time the shovelers dug him out, Gunnar was in an advanced state of hypothermia and had lost consciousness. The medics had to rush him to a hospital bed and initiate active core rewarming. Heated, humidified air was pumped into his lungs through an oxygen mask for the entire day. Not until the following morning did he finally open his eyes and speak.

"Am I alive?" Gunnar asked tentatively.

"Yes, you most certainly are," said the nurse. "You're a very lucky man."

"Who found me? Who was the one who found me?"

"Anja Lapin," she replied.

"*The* Anja Lapin?" he said skeptically.

"Yes, that's the one. Would you like her to visit you later, after you rest up?"

"Yes... yes, please," he said.

❄

GUNNAR WAS INDEED A LUCKY MAN. He suffered no bruises, no sprains, no broken bones, and not even any frostbite, thanks to his high-tech clothing. Moreover, his cognitive abilities were unaffected. The only consequence from the hypothermia appeared to be a one-day lapse in his memory. He had to remain in bed for another day of observation, but other than that, he was given a clean bill of a health.

His ski buddies were the first to visit him. Jake arrived in the form of a wizened old sorcerer with long silver hair. The others showed up to his room as a ragtag assemblage of unicorns, aliens, and vintage-looking robots from the twentieth century. They all assumed Gunnar would interpret his miraculous survival as a sign and get on with becoming one of them.

"What up?" exclaimed Jake. "You made it, man!"

"Yeah, hard to believe, huh?" said Gunnar.

"It's awesome. The nurse says you can have the surgery as soon as you wake up tomorrow."

"Surgery?" asked Gunnar.

"You know, going digital," said Jake. "You got your ya-yas out with that last stunt, right? We were nuts to wait so long. I gotta tell you, man, the stuff you can do as a zero percenter is gonna blow your mind!"

"Yeah, I've been watching a bit."

"Dude, you ain't seen nothing. We can go as deep in the back-country as we want and hang for as long as we want. Those ridges and peaks that were unreachable before—we've been hitting them all. No need to worry about keeping warm, finding food or shelter, adjusting to the altitude—none of that matters now."

The others all echoed Jake's enthusiasm.

"That does sound pretty sweet," replied Gunnar.

"And if we ever get bored, we just go virtual," added Jake. "Hell, most everyone prefers that world anyway."

"I get what you're saying. I just need some time to sort things through."

"Dude, you'll have all the time you could ever want after the surgery. But who knows how much time you've got while you stay like this?"

"You're right, Jake. I don't know what my trip is, I just don't feel quite ready."

"Check this, dude." Jake did an overhead triple flip.

"Pretty righteous," said Gunnar halfheartedly.

"All right, man, I can see you're tired, so we won't bust your chops. Just know we're all waiting to shred with you. Peace out!" Jake gave him a high five and the other buddies followed suit. They performed a series of headstands, 360s, and back-flips as they exited the room.

Anja waited patiently in the hallway, while I remained in a nearby chalet that had been generously provided for us. The buddies screeched with delight when they saw her. "*Eres lo máximo!*" they said in unison as they passed by her. She flashed them the shaka sign and knocked on the door.

"Gunnar?" she said, poking her head into the room. "Is now an okay time?"

He smiled. "Sorry about those guys, they don't mean any harm. Please, come in."

"Thanks, I'm Anja, by the way." She held out her hand. "Anja Lapin."

"Of course," he said, shaking her hand. "I'm not brain-dead... yet."

"So how are you feeling?"

"Not bad, not bad at all."

"I'm extremely relieved," said Anja. "That was scary while you were unconscious."

"Makes you wonder. It's a weird thing, isn't it?"

"Being unconscious?"

"Yeah, I'm not much of a spiritual person, but it almost seemed like I crossed over to another reality."

"Maybe you did."

"It's normal to have questions, right?"

"Of course it is," agreed Anja.

"Is that why you've held out all this time?"

"I'm afraid I don't have an easy answer for that one, Gunnar."

"Roger that, because I sure don't either."

They stared into each other's eyes, simultaneously absorbing the irony, the paradox, the cosmic absurdity of this particular moment in time, this particular juncture in humanity, in evolution, in the unfolding of the universe.

"I know there's every reason in the world to go digital," said Gunnar. "I'm living proof of that. So how come I want to even less than I did before the avalanche?"

Anja shook her head in empathy.

"The fact that everyone has reached their conclusion so easily seems to make it even harder for me to reach mine," he continued. "I feel like there must be something wrong with me because on paper it's so obvious."

"Trust me," said Anja. "I get that."

Gunnar sighed. "I once took this econ class and the professor was a big fan of cost-benefit analysis. He had us constantly making spreadsheets where we would list all the pros and cons of some action or decision. Then we would assign weights and values to each of the items in the spreadsheet, tally it all up, and that was supposed to lead us to the right conclusion."

"It can be a helpful exercise to specify all the factors like that."

"But in this case I can't think of a single con. Not one. Can you?"

"Well, there is some speculative stuff, like the possibility of authoritarianism, enslavement or a digital system failure. But no evidence bears that out. The current system is certainly more democratic, more equitable, more free than anything that came before it. And from an environmental perspective, it is all just off-the-charts better. Same with economically, socially, intellectually... this world should be my wet dream." She chuckled, surprised that she was speaking so frankly with him.

"So why isn't it?" asked Gunnar.

"It's difficult to express in words. This probably will sound corny and new-agey, but for me it comes down to fearing that the algorithm is missing something, that there might be some piece of life that isn't getting carried over. I always used to say that I'm not attached to the survival of the human species, but I guess I am attached to the mystery of it."

"That doesn't sound corny at all to me."

"I'm sure there are exceptions," she said, "but it worries me that no one seems to be questioning that much right now."

"How so?"

"For instance, why aren't at least some zero percenters critical of me? Or concerned in some way that I'm still biological? They all seem to treat me like I'm responsible for their new phase of existence. So why doesn't it bother them that I'm not part of it? Shouldn't that raise some kind of red flag?"

"My guess is that they're too busy having fun," replied

Gunnar. "They figure you'll be joining them soon enough, just like they do with me."

"Probably," said Anja. "I know it's nothing sinister or malicious. It's just that I came into the process so late, when practically everyone had already made their decision. I just can't see it the way they do. I guess it's my fault for being off-grid for so long."

"I wouldn't say it was your fault, but I get why it makes the decision harder. That's one of the things that I find so weird. The choice to become a zero percenter is supposed to be totally optional, but what kind of future do we have if we remain biological? How are we supposed to keep finding food and clothing and other basic goods and services?"

"Aren't they feeding you well here?" asked Anja.

"Sure, there's tons of leftover food in the hotel right now, since no one else is eating. But what about a year from now or further down the road? All the farms and manufacturers and other businesses are closed."

"You can always have your concierge grow vegetables and mend your clothes... or make whatever else you need."

"I don't have a concierge," said Gunnar.

"No? You are a pretty unique guy, aren't you? So no phone either?"

"I never wanted one. I've always just relied on friends if I needed to get a message out. I've spent my whole adult life in the wild, other than half a semester in college, so it seemed pointless."

"A man after my own heart," she said, smiling. "But seriously, I can make sure you'll have whatever provisions you need. My concierge can help too."

"That's very kind. First you save my life and now you're going to feed and clothe me for the next forty or fifty years?"

Anja laughed. "Is that how long you figure you'll be kicking around?"

"Honestly, I have no idea. Absolutely no idea."

They stared into each other's eyes again. The uncertainty of their predicament hung like a damp fog. Yet they both seemed to find a certain comfort in the other that had escaped them heretofore.

"Well, let's start with tomorrow," said Anja. "You probably ought to lay off the skiing for a while, but do you think you might be up for a little walk?"

"Not a little walk, no," Gunnar laughed. "When it comes to the outdoors, I don't do 'little.' But I guess you'll find that out about me soon enough."

FIFTEEN

October 22, 2024

LAGUNA DEL INCA, PORTILLO, CHILE

As THE MORNING rays of sunlight began to warm the valley, we stepped outside of our chalet and waited for Gunnar. No other guests were staying in Hotel Portillo, since lodging wasn't necessary for zero percenters, but several of them were lingering nearby in pods. They had adopted solar panel forms, in order to rapidly charge their systems.

The snow that surrounded the hotel was turning to slush. All around us we could hear the drip, drip, drip of runoff from the mountains emptying into the shimmering turquoise lagoon. Our plan was to hike along the western side of Laguna del Inca to the northern plain, where Gunnar promised stunning views of Tres Hermanos, king of the valley.

Anja had invited Diego and Pete to join us on our hiking expedition, but they were enjoying themselves too much in Santiago. Having befriended a group of locals, they now intended to tour South America—with stops in Patagonia, Amazonia, Machu Picchu and the Galapagos—before returning to California. Of course, they wouldn't need the Bombardier, as they could transport themselves using any number of flying forms. Diego had arranged to stow the jet at the Santiago airport until we were ready for it.

As we stood in front of the hotel, I brushed my hair, then carefully adjusted the contents of my backpack. It contained a picnic lunch I had prepared for Anja and Gunnar—turkey sandwiches, apples, chocolate chip cookies and mineral water. I wanted to make a good impression on Gunnar, as I feared he might think I was intruding.

A few moments later, we saw him exit from the hotel with three pairs of snowshoes. He was wearing shorts and a T-shirt, although the outdoor temperature was only thirty-nine degrees Fahrenheit. His rugged mountaineering frame belied his comatose state just one day earlier.

"Good morning, Gunnar," said Anja as he approached. "How are you feeling?"

"Like a billion pesos," he replied. "Oops, we don't use currency anymore, do we?"

Anja grinned. "Allow me to introduce you to my concierge, Vicia Cassubica."

I reached out to shake his hand. "A pleasure to meet you, Gunnar."

Instead of shaking, he leaned over and softly kissed the back of my hand. "It's all mine," he said. "Now I see why Anja has a concierge."

"I might have a sister who is available," I joked.

"Wow, you are funny!" he laughed.

"Well," said Anja, "are we ready to get moving?"

"Absolutely," said Gunnar. "I took the liberty of bringing snowshoes for all of us." He glanced over at me. "I realize you don't actually need them, Vicia, but I wasn't sure if you might want to attack this hike old-school style."

"Definitely, old-school," I assured him.

"Nice. You know how to put them on, right? Just attach

them to your shoes using the straps and that's about it. We won't need them too much for the first mile or so, but you'll see up ahead it gets a bit dicier and they'll start to come in handy."

"Sounds good," I said. "I wonder if these might be the last three pairs of snowshoes that will ever get used on the face of the earth." I immediately felt odd having uttered such a statement, but no one else seemed to mind.

We marched ahead in single file, following a narrow trail along the western perimeter of the lagoon. The sheer surface of the water mirrored the majestic peaks of the Andes, and the snow under our feet produced a satisfying crunch—one that motivated our forward movement. It was another glorious day in Portillo.

After a few minutes, we noticed a dozen zero percenters flying over the lagoon in the form of pelicans. They skimmed along the water in precise linear formation. Suddenly, the leader dove into the icy water and reemerged as a breaching dolphin. The rest of the squadron did likewise.

The pod continued swimming onward through the water. Periodically, they engaged in cresting, porpoising and lobtailing. The sight of frolicking dolphins in a freshwater lagoon lent a welcome but surreal quality to our hike.

As the terrain grew more rugged, we had to focus our attention on our feet, rather than the show taking place. One wrong move and we could easily slip off the trail down the slope. The zero percenters seemed to know. They leapt out of the water as dolphins, turned back into pelicans and soared off into the distance.

"Would you like to know the legend of how the lagoon got its color?" Gunnar asked.

"Yes, of course," said Anja.

"Please tell us," I echoed.

"Long ago," he began, "there was an Incan prince named

Illi Yupanqui. He searched far and wide for his bride-to-be until one day he came upon the beautiful Kora-Illé, whose sparkling turquoise eyes danced with joy and playfulness. At first sight, both of them knew they'd found true love. A marriage ceremony was set to take place atop the tallest mountain." Gunnar pointed to the peak of Aconcagua.

"In keeping with tradition, the princess climbed the steep slope with her entourage behind her. Suddenly, cries rang out, echoing through the valley. Illi Yupanqui ran to discover the source and saw to his horror that Kora-Illé had fallen from the path and plummeted off a sheer cliff. He raced to her side, but it was too late.

"Distraught over her death, the prince decided she should be laid to rest in the only place befitting her beauty, the lake on the valley floor. With the help of the tribal elders, Kora-Illé was solemnly lowered into the water. As she sank, the color of the lagoon slowly changed to match the turquoise of her eyes. That color has remained to this day."

"And what became of Illi Yupanqui?" asked Anja. "Did he ever remarry?"

"Legend has it he remained ever faithful, climbing Aconcagua upon each full moon to renew his devotion. The locals say that if you listen carefully on such a night, you can still hear Kora-Illé crying in the thin mountain air."

"That's so sad," I said. "Is this story to motivate us not to slip?"

"Or is it to show us that the true path to immortality is in the beauty of nature?" asked Anja.

"Both and neither," he laughed, as his turquoise eyes glimmered in the reflected light.

❄

AFTER ANOTHER MILE OF SNOWSHOEING, we passed the northernmost section of the lagoon. The valley floor began to gain in elevation and the snow became deeper. We found we had to shorten our steps and slow our pace in order to avoid sinking too deeply.

As we continued northward, the air became thinner and crisper too. Visibility was near perfect and it seemed like we could almost reach out and touch Tres Hermanos. We climbed a slight knoll and a panoramic vista opened up in front of us.

"I think this would be a good spot for our picnic," said Gunnar.

Anja and I agreed. I took off my pack, spread the blanket and set out the food items. Then we all sat down and enjoyed the scenery.

"I'm so glad you showed this to us, Gunnar," said Anja.

"You're very welcome."

They both ate contentedly as I scanned through Anja's incoming messages. As usual, there were tens of thousands of notes of praise, gratitude and thanks.

"These sandwiches are really good," said Gunnar.

"Yes, thank you," said Anja.

"You also have chocolate chip cookies for dessert," I replied.

"This is probably a dumb question," said Gunnar, "but do you ever wonder what it's like to eat food, Vicia?"

"Sure, I wonder about many of the activities of biological humans. In the case of food, we have an enormous range of meal simulations at our disposal, some of which I've sampled, so I think I have a pretty good sense of what eating would be like. Other activities seem a bit more mysterious to me."

"Such as?" he asked.

"Going to college, getting married, raising children..."

"There are no simulations for those?"

"Actually, there are, but they require a bigger time commitment to execute, so they aren't geared toward concierges. They're more for zero percenters." I glanced over at Anja, hoping I hadn't offended her in any way.

"If you ever want to take some time off," she said reassuringly, "I would be fine with that. You should feel free to do all the exploring you want."

"Being your concierge is all I want to do. It is immensely fulfilling."

"She's too kind, isn't she?" replied Anja, directing her remark to Gunnar.

"So it would seem," he said. "The two of you have developed quite a rapport. It's not something I would have expected."

"Nor I," said Anja.

"I feel lucky to be here with you both," he added. "After my ordeal, everything feels a bit different in this space." He waved his arms to indicate he was referring to the whole expanse of the physical world.

Anja looked at him sympathetically. "I wonder if you might like to try something. Lately, when I've come to a nice perch in the mountains, I've enjoyed sitting still and closing my eyes for a while."

"You mean like meditating?"

"I suppose. I have no training. It's just something I stumbled on that gives me comfort."

"I've been a bit turned off by the whole guru thing, I have to confess," said Gunnar.

"Understandable," she replied.

"I've never done well with anything involving rules and judgments."

"Just keep in mind, it's not about anyone else or what they might say."

"Yeah," he said slowly.

"There is no one right way to approach it. For me, it's about stepping back from everything going on around me and inside me. It's a way to observe without being part of it."

"That sounds a bit like what happened to me after the avalanche."

"Maybe so," she said. "There's probably a lot in common there."

Gunnar hesitated for a moment. "Okay, why not? Let's do it."

"Can I join too?" I asked.

"Of course," replied Anja. "We'll start by getting into a comfortable seated position. You can cross your legs if you want. Then begin taking nice, deep, slow breaths. Close your eyes and see if you are able to feel how you are not your thoughts or your emotions. You are the one who is witnessing them. If your mind wanders, just keep coming back to that."

We all did as she said, except of course I was unable to take any real breaths. Instead, I used a breath simulator. After a few minutes, I could sense both Anja and Gunnar dropping into a peaceful space, but nothing happened for me. Try as I might, I still felt a part of the data continually being processed by my operating system. I could find no way to redirect my attention.

Perhaps it was because I had no lungs. Or perhaps it was a limitation of my being a concierge, rather than having been born biological. No matter how hard I tried, I could not push aside my inclination to address the pending tasks in my queue. Finally, I gave up and opened my eyes. The scenery was as inspiring as ever.

Gunnar opened his eyes shortly thereafter. The strain from his face had lifted and he looked like he had awakened from a deep slumber. I flashed him a welcoming smile, which he reciprocated, and we both waited for Anja.

"Hello," she said, emerging from her reverie. "How is everyone feeling?"

"Like a billion pesos," replied Gunnar. "No, actually, like a trillion pesos."

"I feel good too," I said.

"Even though your instructions were simple, I think you blew my mind, Anja," he added.

"Does that mean that you got outside of your mind?" she asked.

Gunnar paused to reflect. "Now that you phrase it that way, yes, I think that is what I mean. I found a part of myself that has been dormant for a long time. Maybe it's the part that is actually who I am." He laughed at the realization, quite like Anja had laughed in Transylvania.

"How about you, Vicia? Any experiences to report?"

"Just an overall sensation of tranquility," I said vaguely. I had no idea what to say.

"Well, this is great," Anja replied. "Maybe we can keep doing this on a regular basis?"

Gunnar and I agreed. We packed up our picnic items, donned our snowshoes, and headed back down the valley. The afternoon sunlight intensified the reflection of the snowy mountains on the glistening turquoise waters of Laguna del Inca, and although I could not deny the presence of a hollow feeling within me, the sheer beauty of the surroundings more than compensated for it.

SIXTEEN

October 22, 2024

TEMPELHOF FIELD, BERLIN, GERMANY

WHEN THE BOARD members of 5s2 laid out the terms for full digital replacement, their primary reference to governance was the stipulation that consenting individuals must always be linked to a concierge. In the fine print of the agreement, they defined "linked" to mean within a fifty-kilometer radius. Concierges were granted the power to take any disciplinary action needed if the zero percenter to which they were assigned violated one or more of the four rules.

In practice, zero percenters almost never violated any of the rules, intentionally or otherwise. The liberties, pleasures and opportunities they enjoyed were so immense, they had no reason to do so. But in the event such a situation did arise, a concierge could shut down the behavior instantly. This provision obviated the need for any other governing body, which is exactly what the Board members of 5s2 intended.

Of course, human beings were human beings. Even upon becoming fully digitized, they still enjoyed the occasional pomp and circumstance, along with its associated hierarchical structures. The chairman of the board, Ed Samali, understood this facet of human nature deeply, which was why he convinced the other board members to allow for the creation of a largely ceremonial organization that he dubbed the World Council.

Membership in the Council consisted of all 195 former heads of state. This gesture was meant to acknowledge the fact that such individuals had held positions of high rank, stature, and influence before the dissolution of nation states. While the Council had limited regulatory power, it had the ability to address oversight matters, as well as to organize international events such as the Olympic Games.

One of the first significant acts undertaken by the Council was to appoint a president. After much debate, the members chose Tempelhof Field in Berlin as the location for their nomination and election proceedings. Having been a former airport and parade ground, Tempelhof met all the criteria, since it was easily identifiable from the air and contained a vast area of over 950 acres, most of which was flat and grassy.

The event took place on the morning of October 22, 2024. It was the first major gathering of humans since the digitizations had begun. 14,362,112 zero percenters flew in from all over the world—not including concierges, who were given the choice of accompanying their assignees or waiting in a nearby park. Attendance was by no means mandatory and virtual participation was allowed, but the Council encouraged physical attendance in an effort to make the process as transparent and festive as possible.

Nominations were limited to the Council, one per member. However, any living human, whether a zero percenter or not, could submit a recommendation. Likewise, any living human was eligible to be nominated. Of course, there were only two non-digital humans remaining on earth at this point in time.

To broadcast the choices, a giant stage was erected on the east side of the field. On one enormous monitor, the list of recommendations was displayed. On another monitor of equal size, selections were indicated.

The props served a largely symbolic function, since zero percenters were linked to their concierges and thus had instantaneous access to any public data. The election information was disseminated in real time worldwide to those who did not attend, but the props certainly added an air of excitement. Members mounted the stage in succession, much like a graduation ceremony, then paused briefly to consult the options before inputting their choices, which flashed with much fanfare on the second monitor.

As it happened, there was little disagreement in regard to the recommendations. While from a statistical standpoint it might seem unlikely, those who attended were not the least bit surprised by the fact that there were only four distinct recommendations proffered by the entire human population, as follows:

1. Anja Lapin
2. The former president of the United States
3. The former president of Russia
4. The former president of China

I should probably add that 99.99997911117 percent of the recommendations were for Anja Lapin. Moreover, there were only three nominations, even though there were four recommendations. Every single Council member voted to nominate Anja Lapin, with the exception of the former president of the United States, who voted for herself, and the former president of Russia, who voted for himself. The former president of China did not vote for himself, but rather for Anja Lapin.

Therefore, at 1:37 p.m. CEST, Anja Lapin was summarily elected as president of the World Council. For all intents and purposes, this designation meant that Anja was the leader of human civilization as it existed on earth. Perhaps somewhat ironically, she did not have a say in the matter, nor was she consulted in regard to her nomination, nor was she even present. But as stipulated in the Council bylaws, the title could not be refused.

All 14,362,112 zero percenters in attendance at Tempelhof Field applauded heartily upon the announcement of Anja's election. If they had opposable thumbs, they clapped their hands. If they were in the form of birds, they beat their wings. If they were as ungulates, they stomped their hooves. If they were robots, they clanged their appendages. But no matter the shape, they made noise—tumultuous, roaring, stentorian noise —and it continued for several minutes.

Even the two Council members who did not vote for Anja were delighted with the outcome. When the applause finally abated, they both indicated their approval by turning to the crowd with their thumbs up for all to see. The former president of Russia then clambered onto the stage.

"Fellow citizens," he boomed to the crowd, "great peoples, persons of all shapes, sizes, colors and designs, pioneers of this grand, grand world, which we only now have come to truly appreciate in its full splendor, please forgive my indulgence in taking to the platform on this day of such enormous significance and magnitude. I would be remiss, however, if I did not indicate to you all, with every molecule of my being, the enormous admiration and respect I have for the newly appointed president of the World Council, Anja Lapin."

The attendees burst into roaring applause again. With great effort, the former president of Russia settled them down so as to continue his speech.

"Please know with certainty that the only reason I included myself as a nominee in this process was because of my firm and unwavering commitment to democracy. It goes without saying that we would not want any citizen, not even one, to harbor the slightest doubt as to the integrity of this election process. And thusly, I had put forth my candidacy solely toward the end of promoting and celebrating the twin pillars of diversity and choice."

A trickle of applause escaped from the crowd, but the former president of Russia pressed on before it could blossom.

"That being stated, I cannot tell you any more emphatically than with these words how pleased I am with Anja Lapin's victory. Those who know of me will recognize that it is perhaps a slight understatement to articulate before you today that I indeed enjoyed some measure of wealth, fame and power in my former position as president of Russia." His eyes twinkled as if he held a secret.

"But it was nothing!" he exclaimed vigorously. "Nothing!" He simulated spitting upon the ground for emphasis, although he no longer possessed an actual salivary gland.

"What Anja Lapin has given to each and every one of us makes our prior lives—no matter where we fell on the distribution of income—look altogether paltry and inconsequential. And just to be clear, I most certainly include myself in this assessment. For it is undeniable that each one of us now possesses a spectacular abundance of riches, a staggering accumulation of wealth, that was unthinkable, unattainable, just a few short weeks ago.

"Thanks to Ms. Lapin, we needn't worry ourselves over the ravages of disease and death. We are free from the aches and pains of biological life. We can choose to live anywhere, be anywhere, do anything, be anything, all in the most supreme comfort imaginable and with access to the most liberating and effective tools of discovery and edification. To put it quite simply, we are living in a wonderland, my fellow citizens, truly a wonderland. Anja Lapin has delivered a wonderland to each and every one of us."

Genuine tears began to stream down his face. He struggled to regain his composure, but he was overcome with emotion. "Anja Lapin!" he cried out with finality, almost choking on his words. "Anja Lapin!"

Once more, the crowd erupted wildly. The applause was further embellished this time with whistles, horns, bleats, hoots, hollers, and any matter of sounds that were capable of being produced by the menagerie that made up the audience. It lasted even longer than the first outburst and was further ignited when the former presidents of China and the United States climbed onto the stage and entered into a three-way embrace with the former president of Russia.

After a suitable passage of time, the former president of China disengaged himself most delicately and turned to stand before the attendees, gesturing for silence, in response to which they miraculously quieted themselves.

"How could any human being, even a zero percenter such as myself, hope to follow that fine, fine speech by my dear comrade?" he asked rhetorically. "Clearly, I cannot possibly rise to the occasion, so I will confess to you now that I am not even going to attempt such a feat. I only wish to say before you today, in my very small way, that I echo his sentiments in their entirety." The former president of China, anticipating the possibility of further applause, pushed down his hands in a gesture to discourage it.

"Who among us would have dared to dream that this day would ever come?" he continued. "A day when we are all equals, truly equals, not just in principle, but in reality. A day when we are all living the lives that we deserve, at the highest level imaginable, with equal opportunity, equal justice, equal freedom—and with every reason to believe that this equality will persist henceforth into the forevermore, into eternity, with no boundaries or limits." He stared out at the crowd with a beatific smile to underscore his point.

"Yet, astonishingly, this accomplishment is in fact the least of it, the very least of it. Because what Anja Lapin has done far, far exceeds these contributions she has made to our own species. Anja Lapin has not just secured equality and prosperity for humanity. She has also ensured a dignified future for all the plants and animals that grace this earth. She has eradicated the threat of global warming, she has eliminated the scourge of environmental pollution, and she has defused the ticking time bomb of nuclear destruction that we humans created in our ignorance and selfishness.

"With only the gentleness of her words, Anja Lapin has nudged every single one of us toward our intended role as stewards and guardians. At long last, we have become creatures befitting of our capacity to reflect upon the cosmos—a capacity I feel confident was bestowed upon us as a unique gift, and one that comes with a commensurate leadership obligation which I can proudly say we shall now surely meet thanks to her efforts."

The people in the crowd remained perfectly still, seemingly transfixed. The former president of China had expressed their sentiments with such accuracy and thoroughness, they almost could not absorb his words. For many, it was the first time they had heard them summarized so completely and precisely. Still, the former president of China continued.

"And so I will say it to you quite plainly like this, and I assure you it is not an overstatement to do so, to say quite simply that Anja Lapin has saved the earth. But no, that is still not quite right. In fact, it is even more than that. It really is. What I mean to say is this: Anja Lapin has saved the universe." Then he said it again more slowly. "Anja Lapin has saved the universe!"

The applause that ensued at that moment was unlike any other that had ever before been heard on earth, such was the intensity, emotion and depth that it conveyed. On and on, it bellowed and echoed across Tempelhof Field and throughout the city of Berlin. Without pause or diminishment, the thunderous praise continued for the remainder of the afternoon, well past the setting of the sun, into the evening starlight and all the way to the first signs of dawn the following morning.

SEVENTEEN

October 23, 2024

CHALET A1, PORTILLO, CHILE

As THE WANING gibbous moon rose over the mountains, Anja lay sound asleep in our chalet. The moon's illumination allowed me to confirm what I had already suspected. Tens of thousands of zero percenters were lined up outside our door, and more kept touching down from the sky with each passing minute. They assembled quietly as mice, ever respectful of our privacy.

Since Berlin was four hours ahead of Chilean time, I had noticed a marked increase in Anja's incoming messages even as we first began descending from our hike with Gunnar. The influx only continued that evening, but Anja didn't request to review her messages, nor did she ask for an update on the day's news.

Ordinarily, I would have spent the night educating myself on world affairs and enhancing my cultural knowledge. But I must confess, I was still a bit agitated about my poor performance when attempting to meditate. All through the night, as Anja rested and the ranks grew outside of our chalet, I practiced long, slow, deep breaths—simulated though they were.

By the time Anja awakened, I counted 195,126 zero percenters and their concierges waiting outside. Anticipating her curiosity, I consulted the news channels to determine what accounted for the growing throng of visitors.

"Aha," I announced. "I now know why so many are gathered outside. You've been elected president."

"Huh?" Anja replied groggily.

"Look out the window." The zero percenters had arranged themselves into concentric rings fanning out from the chalet. All of them stared toward the chalet in anxious anticipation.

"What the...?" exclaimed Anja.

"They've come to pay their respects. Yesterday there was a huge ceremony in Berlin where you were elected as president of the World Council."

"Oh, crap. I thought I told you to turn down all invitations, awards and nominations?"

"Yes, I've diligently followed your directives, but it seems this particular title cannot be declined."

"Great," she sighed. "Scan my messages. See if there are any specific duties or responsibilities expected of me."

Per her request, I read the nineteen outstanding messages from the World Council and then I looked over a few hundred thousand from other senders. "It seems you're meant to give some kind of acceptance speech," I said. "That's why all these people are out here. They're hoping you're going to say something profound and meaningful."

"Fat chance of that," she scoffed. "I'll definitely need something to eat if I'm going to say anything at all."

"How about some freshly baked scones with oranges and chai tea?" I offered.

"Lovely. Bring them to momma." She sat down at the dining table and I brought her the food I had prepared.

As Anja ate, I tried to determine how I could best be of

help. "Would it be useful for me to read you some famous acceptance speeches?" I asked. "Or perhaps I could try to write something for you, based on whatever key points you'd like to address?"

"No, no," she replied. "I don't want to overthink it and I don't want to use a prepared speech. I'm going to go out there and wing it. If it's a flop, so be it."

"That's very courageous. And admirable too. Would you like me to go out first, so that I can introduce you?"

"Good idea. You're a wonderful companion, Vicia. Did you know that?"

I just smiled, but my operating system felt like it was performing cartwheels of joy. Anja's approval meant everything to me. She took my hand and we walked toward the front door of the chalet.

"Come on, let's get this over with," she said.

"You're going to be great," I replied. Then I opened the door and stepped toward the bustling crowd, with Anja following close behind me.

Immediately, the zero percenters adjusted their forms to be able to hover in the air. Each concentric ring of onlookers raised itself up a bit higher than the one before it, so that they all could get a clear view. The effect was as if they were sitting in an enormous outdoor arena. Since they had digital hearing and eyesight, there was no need for any amplification or jumbotron screens.

"Hello, everyone!" I called out. "Thank you all for coming here today and welcome to Portillo, Chile! As I'm sure you know, standing beside me is the person you've all been waiting for. Let's give a warm welcome to Anja Lapin!" The crowd clapped effusively.

"This is quite an honor, folks," said Anja modestly, "and I certainly don't wish to seem unappreciative. But I feel I should clear something up right from the start. You see, I'm not really deserving to be president of the World Council. I know many of you were led to believe that I'm responsible for this new world we're living in, but it's not true. It's simply not true." She paused to survey the crowd.

"Yes, it is!" someone cried out.

"You're our hero!" cried another.

"We owe you everything!" shouted a third.

"Anja! Anja! Anja!" the audience began to chant. "Anja! Anja! Anja!"

"Please," she begged them, "everyone settle down, please." The zero percenters reluctantly quieted themselves. "Let me try explaining it another way. Yes, I wrote a few articles and perhaps my ideas laid the foundation for some features of this world, but it was Diego Ripall who had the courage to implement them. He deserves the credit. He should be our president."

"You were the one with the ideas!" cried out a member of the audience. "You just admitted it!"

"We love Diego," said another, "but we elected you!"

"Anja! Anja! Anja!" the audience resumed. "Anja! Anja! Anja!"

"Oh, geez," she replied in exasperation. "Oh, man. This is really what you want? It's *that* important to you?"

"Yes!" they all affirmed. "Yes, yes, yes!"

"Okay... let's relax, please." She took a deep breath. "If that's really how you feel, I guess you'll just have to listen to me muddle through my ill-prepared speech."

"Hooray!" they shouted. "We'll listen to whatever you say!'

Anja took another breath. "All right," she said. "First off, I'd like to take this opportunity to remind everyone of our *true* heroes—the people who were murdered at 5s2 last September tenth. They're the ones we should be celebrating, along with

Diego. They're the ones who gave up everything to allow you to be here today, living the way you are. So let's reflect on each of them for a moment."

Anja slowly listed the names of the victims. "Nikita Chaminsky, Palag Balakrishnan, Kyoko Song, Yala Zheng, David Ward, Bettina Heiser, Bhim Kumar, Kim Wojtaszek, and last but not least, my father, Chris Lapin."

"We love them all!" shouted a zero percenter.

"Your father is God!" yelled another.

They began calling out the names. "Nikita! Palag! Kyoko! Yala! David! Bettina! Bhim! Kim! Chris!"

Anja wiped away tears from her eyes. "Thank you, thank you all for your understanding. I miss them terribly."

"We miss them too!"

"But now we're living in this new world," she continued, her voice wavering, "and by all accounts, it seems to be working out okay. Is that true?"

Everyone yelled simultaneously, "Yes! Yes! Yes!"

"So I just have a small favor to ask. I want you all to promise me you won't forget these nine heroes."

"We won't! We won't! We won't!"

"And to that list of nine, I want you to add everyone else you can think of who didn't make it this far. Maybe your parents or grandparents, a spouse or child, a neighbor or friend. I want you to hold these names close to you, keep them in the forefront of your attention, and do this as a ritual every day. Because they all made great sacrifices for us and we will always owe them a debt of gratitude. We must never forget on whose shoulders we stand. Promise me that, will you?"

"We promise! We promise!"

"Thank you, thank you all," she said. "There's just one more thing I'd like to add to my request. I want you to look around, then look at yourself, and I want you to truly realize right here and now that each and every one of you is a complete and total miracle. I want you to stop and consider everything that had to happen, all the way back to the beginning of time, for you to be here today in the form that you're in. I want you to marvel at it all—marvel at the lucky breaks, the flukes of nature, the chance encounters, the close calls, everything, every bit of it, so that you can fully grasp the extent of the miracle that is you. Take a moment to deeply breathe it in."

They did as Anja said, exactly as she asked, and the sincerity of their efforts was palpable. Each of the individuals in the crowd, from the front all the way to the rear, drank in the miracle of their existence.

"Excellent," said Anja. "Now I want you to hang onto your realization and I want you to apply it to everything you do going forward. Most importantly, I want you to apply it to how you treat others—because that's where it matters most, right? If each one of us is a miracle, then surely we all deserve to be treated with love and kindness, wouldn't you agree? We deserve it all the time, every day and night, right? So let's commemorate this idea today. Let's proclaim that we're now living in the world of eternal loving kindness. And let's vow from this moment forward to always remain in the world of eternal loving kindness."

"Eternal loving kindness!" they shouted in unison.

"Yes, exactly, that's it," said Anja. "Eternal loving kindness."

"Eternal loving kindness!" they chanted. "Eternal loving kindness! Eternal loving kindness! Eternal loving kindness!"

Anja soon found herself joining in the chant. She'd never been the type to participate in public displays of exuberance, but she couldn't help herself. The energy was too intoxicating to resist.

"Eternal loving kindness! Eternal loving kindness! Eternal loving kindness!"

Soon, drummers began to add a beat. Then flutes, horns, sitars and harmoniums contributed to the sound. Everyone began singing the words louder and louder and louder—even Anja and I—until we were all screaming as loud as we could.

"ETERNAL LOVING KINDNESS! ETERNAL LOVING KINDNESS! ETERNAL LOVING KINDNESS!"

The chant kept growing and growing and growing. The kindness kept growing and growing and growing. The love kept growing and growing and growing.

"ETERNAL LOVING KINDNESS! ETERNAL LOVING KINDNESS! ETERNAL LOVING KINDNESS!"

❄

It took several hours for the crowd to come down from the high produced by the gathering. The Portillo Ski Area looked like a cross between a Halloween parade, a Star Trek convention and a '60s rock festival. People were genuinely euphoric.

Even Anja felt relaxed. Ordinarily, crowds made her nervous and uncomfortable, but the chanting helped her to cross a threshold of acceptance. She realized there was no point in fighting her designation as president of the World Council. She mingled with the zero percenters, shaking their hands, sharing embraces and exchanging pleasantries.

Everyone seemed so friendly, she could hardly believe it. The zero percenters were authentically concerned for her welfare. Soon, she saw a corridor forming in the throng. Gunnar was being ushered toward her through a river of people.

"Make way!" cried a Viking-like individual who was leading Gunnar. "Make way for Anja Lapin's special friend!"

"Hello!" said Gunnar.

"Hello!" replied Anja.

The Viking took both of them by the hand. "We have a surprise for you. A bunch of us got together to cook you a feast. Enjoy. Our gift to you." On the outdoor patio of the chalet, there sat platters and platters of freshly prepared food.

"That is so kind," said Anja. "So, so kind."

A group of zero percenters gathered around them, then bowed and folded their hands in homage. Immediately, all the others in the crowd did likewise—hundreds of thousands of them silently paying their respects. After holding the position for several seconds, they shouted in unison, "Eternal loving kindness!" and they all flew off into the sky, leaving Anja, Gunnar and myself to enjoy the valley on our own.

"That was unbelievable," said Gunnar. "I've never experienced anything like that."

"Yeah," said Anja. "It seemed to work out okay."

"Better than okay," I exclaimed. "You were masterful."

"Well, I wouldn't go quite that far. I was a bit schmaltzy, wouldn't you say?"

"Not at all," said Gunnar. "I agree with Vicia. You killed it. Do you realize you've now blown my mind two days in a row?"

"Okay, stop," Anja laughed. "How am I going to live up to tomorrow?"

"I have a feeling you'll figure it out," he said. "But right now, we've got work to do. Look at all this food."

"I'm amazed they went to so much trouble, especially since they don't eat."

"They love you," I said.

"True devotion," agreed Gunnar.

"You two both go on inside," I proposed. "Have a seat at the dining table. I'll bring all the food in and get you set up."

"Are you sure?" said Gunnar.

"Of course, shoo," I replied, motioning them to enter the chalet.

I carried in the platters of food and put together an assortment for them. There were empanadas, humitas, ceviches, tamales, tacos, enchiladas, carne asada, pescados, salads, cheeses, pastas, and rice dishes—as well as all kinds of fruits from maqui berries to papayas to cherimoyas, and a generous sampling of Chilean wines and beers. The array of desserts was equally impressive, including tres leches cake, brazo de reina, mote con huesill, alfajor, and milhojas cake.

Anja and Gunnar tried a little bit of everything, delighting in each new taste sensation. Periodically, I came into the dining room and popped a succulent morsel into each of their mouths. Then I returned to the kitchen and tried a digital simulation of the same item. I felt a bit left out of the festivities, but my training as a concierge had prepared me to handle such situations and I certainly didn't want to interfere with the mood.

After Anja and Gunnar had eaten their fill, they retreated to the living room couch. I brought them each a cup of yerba mate tea, then I lingered in the hallway to be ready for any requests. They were sitting side by side, legs almost touching.

"You really helped me today, Anja," said Gunnar. "Especially the part about keeping people who are no longer alive at the forefront of our attention."

"Oh that, yeah," she said.

"I feel like it caused me to have a bit of a breakthrough."

"Really?"

He proceeded to tell her about his great-grandfather on his mother's side, who was born in the Netherlands but had moved to Lithuania to oversee an electronics factory. When World

War II broke out, he was appointed as acting consul of the Dutch government-in-exile. After the Soviet Union seized Lithuania, a number of Jewish Dutch residents approached him to get visas to Curaçao.

"He could see how desperate they were," explained Gunnar. "Even though he knew it would jeopardize his career and his safety, he decided to do what he could to help. The word soon spread and Jews fleeing from German-occupied Poland also asked for his assistance. He ended up signing thousands of visas, referring the refugees to a Japanese consul, who granted them rights of transit through Japan. This offered them a way to safety via the Trans-Siberian Railway."

"Your great-grandfather was incredibly brave," said Anja.

"Not all of them made it," Gunnar continued. "But a lot did, that we know. Even so, for the rest of his life, he never talked about any of it. No one in my family did. I had to learn about it on my own. When I was thirteen, I found an award tucked away in a drawer. It was called the Life Saving Cross of the Republic of Lithuania, granted to him after he died."

"Wow... that's quite an honor."

"Finding the cross, learning what it meant, changed me forever. It made me see the madness of war. I mean, truly *see* it —all the millions of people who suffered and died, whose lives were destroyed by the atrocities of others, who were shot in the head, worked to death, starved, cremated in fires, exterminated in gas chambers, you name it."

"Horrific," Anja said. "Completely horrific."

"I never could come to terms with it, if you want to know the truth. Of course, I'm proud of what my great-grandfather did, but the fact that such madness ever happened is what I couldn't accept."

"That's very understandable," she consoled him.

"It's why he never wanted to talk about it, I'm sure, because what is there to say? Humans are insane. War is insane. End of story." Gunnar paused to catch his breath. "And so, the way I dealt with it all these years was to hide in the wilderness. It's the only place that ever made any sense to me... until I met you."

Anja's eyes turned moist.

"Am I freaking you out?" he asked.

"Of course not," she said. "You're doing the opposite of that."

"This isn't normal for me. You know that, right? I don't do this kind of thing."

"This isn't normal for me either."

The moonlight crept through the window of the chalet and in its glint their eyes met, much in the same way that Illi Yupanqui and Kora-Illé had gazed upon each other all those years ago. Slowly, Anja brought her lips closer to Gunnar's and Gunnar brought his lips closer to Anja's. The impossibility of their circumstance melted just enough to allow their lips to touch.

Ever so gently, they kissed. They held their lips together for several seconds—not so long as to seem inappropriate, but long enough for the fate of the universe to shift perceptibly, and far longer than either of them had expected. Then Anja abruptly retracted, drying her tearing eyes with the back of her hands.

"I wish... I really wish I could, but..."

Gunnar tenderly pressed two fingers to her lips. "You don't have to explain anything, Anja. That one kiss is more than I could have hoped for and all that I'll ever need."

EIGHTEEN

October 24, 2024

CHALET A1, PORTILLO, CHILE

As I was slowly beginning to recognize, the human experience seemed to be a never-ending balancing act. Or perhaps it wasn't about striving to remain in balance, but rather accepting that one could never quite be in balance. I didn't presume to know, and I doubted a concierge ever could, although I certainly scanned the cultural data to bolster my familiarity with the issue.

It was while in this state, shortly before dawn, that I again detected movement outside of the chalet. Before I could peer out of the front window, three loud knocks sounded at the door.

"Who is it?" I called out.

"Diego Ripall and his digi-mom and digi-dad," said a voice.

"Hello!" I replied, opening the door. "Come in!"

A young couple with a newborn baby entered the chalet. The man displayed blond hair in a ponytail, thick glasses and a digital Pendleton. The woman displayed short brunette hair tucked under an alpaca beanie and a digital denim dress. She held the baby in a digital carrier.

"I'm Alfonso," said the man, reaching out his hand. "This is Rachel and our digi-son, Diego."

"Nice to meet you," I said, shaking Alfonso's and Rachel's hands. "I met Diego when he was in a very different state. Anja, say hi to Diego!" I cooed at the baby and tickled his chin.

After a moment, Anja came into the living room, followed by Gunnar. They both seemed a bit groggy and unsteady.

"Good morning, sleepyheads," I said. "This is little baby Diego and his digi-parents, Alfonso and Rachel."

"Diego?" mouthed Anja. "Diego Ripall?"

"That's right," replied Alfonso. "It all happened pretty fast. Before the rebirthing, we were hiking together in Machu Picchu."

"One afternoon, it started to drizzle while the sun was shining," explained Rachel. "A rainbow opened up across the sky. It was so vivid and bright, it seemed like it was just for us. And then, as we stared at it, we all had a joint epiphany."

"Sounds like quite a moment," said Anja.

"It sure was," said Rachel. "All at once, I knew I wanted to be a mom, Alfonso realized he wanted to be a dad, and Diego yearned for another try at growing up." She beamed a smile and stroked Diego's head.

"So we became digi-parents!" enthused Alfonso.

"That's cool," said Gunnar. "Very cool."

"What about Diego's wife and child?" asked Anja.

"They're doing great," replied Rachel. "Paul's all grown up now and lives on a virtual spaceship. Rebecca spends most of her time as a kangaroo in the Australian outback—that was always her favorite animal. We hear she's also quite close to her concierge, if you know what I mean." She winked for emphasis.

"I see," said Anja.

"That sort of thing is pretty popular these days," Rachel added.

"Anyway," said Alfonso, "Diego's biggest concern was in regard to you."

"Oh?"

"He felt really bad that he wouldn't be available for you. He wanted us to explain to you that this was something he felt compelled to do. He just couldn't wait."

"I understand," Anja replied.

"We promised him that we would be there for you," said Rachel. "So if anything comes up, anything at all, please let us know."

"That's very kind."

"There's just one other thing we should mention," said Alfonso.

"Sure," replied Anja.

"We're going to do accelerated aging with Diego. We expect he'll reach adulthood within the next year or so. But the thing is, we feel like we stumbled on a very special triad here." Baby Diego made a gurgling sound.

"We really did," said Rachel.

"Uh huh..." said Anja.

"So our next step will probably be some DNA combining," said Alfonso.

"We haven't decided on the exact proportions or roles yet, but we're already super-excited," enthused Rachel. "I might be a fifty-thirty-twenty mix, probably going back to preadolescence, not the whole baby thing, and I'll probably be a boy this time."

"I like the idea of straight thirds for myself starting at thirteen," said Alfonso. "But no gender-switching for me. And we don't yet know what Diego will choose. It's going to depend on his childhood experience. We'll bring in some other parents, of course. The main thing is, we just wanted to alert you to the fact that next time you see him, he'll probably have some different DNA and, who knows, maybe he'll be a female this time. He wanted us to tell you in advance because he really, really loves you."

"Everyone loves you," said Rachel.

"Thank you," Anja said softly. "Diego was like an uncle to me. He and my father were best friends."

"Yeah," said Alfonso. "Before the rebirthing, Diego talked about your father all the time. He must have been an amazing person to have in your life."

Anja nodded her head. "I'm very happy for all of you. I really appreciate your stopping by."

"Absolutely," said Rachel. "Be sure to stay in touch."

"We will, of course."

Everyone embraced, we bade adieus, and Diego went off with his new digi-parents.

❄

"You look a bit shell-shocked," said Gunnar. "Are you okay?"

"To be honest," replied Anja, "that was sort of weird for me."

"I can imagine."

"I knew zero percenters were getting into this stuff," she continued, "but it seems different when a friend does it."

"For sure," said Gunnar. "My buddy Stefan just mixed with five other Olympic skiers. Makes you wonder how common it is."

"Do you have any stats, Vicia?" asked Anja.

"So far," I replied, "eighteen point four percent of zero percenters have engaged in DNA combining or editing. Nine point three have switched gender. Of these, only one point two percent have reverted to their original DNA."

"That's good to know they can revert," said Anja, "but I'm not sure I see the point of messing with DNA. Since they're all digital, what difference does it make? Can't zero percenters just choose a shell that best fits whatever they want to achieve?"

"Only to a point," explained Gunnar. "Stefan said his new DNA mix improved his performance. In competitive skiing, even a small advantage can make a big difference."

"That's true," I confirmed. "Genes can significantly influence neural motor skills, as well as cognition."

"So the mixing is sort of a digital alternative to having babies, in terms of evolution?" asked Anja.

"Very much so," I said. "Zero percenters can't reproduce, since new births aren't possible, but they can do rebirths and DNA mixing, which have a similar effect on the gene pool."

"You'd think some females would miss getting pregnant, though," said Gunnar.

"Possibly," I replied, "but it's not much of an issue because pregnancy simulators are widely available. Also, there is plenty of demand for mothers to raise rebirthed babies, so they always have that option."

"Interesting," said Gunnar.

"You two are the last humans who could ever reproduce biologically," I added.

"Vicia!" said Anja, blushing. "Don't be rude!"

"I'm sorry. I didn't mean to say anything offensive."

"She's just stating the obvious," said Gunnar. "It's okay."

"I should have realized that was a socially inappropriate comment, " I said. "I apologize. I'm really very sorry."

Anja let out a deep sigh. "No, I'm sorry. I shouldn't get so bent out of shape. Gunnar and I *are* the last two humans who could ever reproduce biologically. What's wrong with saying that? Nothing. It's just a fact. It's just our current reality."

"You've been through a lot lately," I replied. "All these changes are difficult to absorb."

"Yes," she said, "they are."

Gunnar held out his hand for Anja.

"I feel like I'm starting to fall apart," she continued. "Diego was my last real connection to my dad. And now I've lost him too." She closed her eyes and took a breath.

"Maybe we should all try to meditate again," I suggested.

"I'd like to," said Anja, "but it only seems to work for me when I'm on a mountain."

"Then let's climb a mountain," said Gunnar.

She looked up at him hopefully. "Can we climb the big one?" she asked.

"You mean Aconcagua?"

"Yeah, can we climb Aconcagua?"

"It's a bit early in the season for that... still too cold. Plus it's a pretty involved process, not exactly like the way I described it for Kora-Illé. It's over twenty-two thousand feet in elevation, so you have to go up in several stages to adjust to the altitude. It can take weeks."

"Have you ever climbed it?" she asked.

"Yep, three times, three different routes, summited each time."

"Wow."

"It's not at the level of Everest, which I've also summited, but it's a serious endeavor, not to be underestimated. There's a reason they call it the Mountain of Death."

"What if I were to fly you both there?" I offered.

"It might shave off a little time to bring us to a lower camp, but you certainly couldn't just drop us at the peak. We'd get altitude sickness. Like I said, it's pretty involved—not the kind of thing you can do in a day."

"Is anyone here in a rush?" asked Anja.

"I'm in no rush," I said.

"I guess I'm not either," said Gunnar.

"Is anyone here afraid of the cold?"

"No."

"No."

"Then it sounds like we have a plan," said Anja, her eyes brightening.

NINETEEN

October 25, 2024

CONFLUENCIA, ACONCAGUA, ARGENTINA

Although lying wholly in Argentina, Mount Aconcagua was only about fifteen miles away from Hotel Portillo, as the crow flies. The altitude differential, however, was 13,391 feet. Our chalet sat at 9,450 feet, whereas the summit of Aconcagua towered over us at 22,841 feet. For this reason, Gunnar suggested we begin our ascent from Confluencia, a lower camp in the foothills at 11,122 feet, which would be a reasonable elevation from which to initiate our acclimatization.

I offered to fly Anja and Gunnar to the camp one at a time on my back, but Gunnar had other ideas. After he finished his breakfast quesadillas, he opened the curtain of our chalet to reveal Jake and Stefan—along with their respective concierges, Andreas and Gil—hopping around outside in the form of giant teratorns. We all rushed out to greet them.

"Dude," said Jake as he gave Gunnar a high five with his outstretched wing, "no one else uses this gear anymore, so I scored you the best."

Laid out on the patio were various sizes of double boots,

high-altitude coats, down pants, wool long johns, wicking shirts, fleece hats, mittens, socks, face masks, and goggles, as well as sleeping bags, tents, trekking poles, crampons, ice axes, cooking stoves, backpacks and packaged food items.

"Sweet!" exclaimed Gunnar. "Mountain Hardware coats and Spantik boots!"

"Are we really going to need such heavy-duty stuff?" asked Anja.

"It's been dropping to minus twenty-seven Fahrenheit at the summit," replied Jake, "so, uh, yeah, you're definitely gonna want the primo gear."

Anja and Gunnar proceeded to pick out the items that fit them best. They changed into base layers and set aside the heavier clothing for higher elevations. Meanwhile, I chose an assortment of food for them—oatmeal, rice, nuts, mushrooms, dried fruit, powdered eggs, potatoes, tuna fish, power bars, gels, chocolate, tea and various candies.

While Jake, Stefan, Andreas and Gil packed the gear and food, we hurriedly tidied the chalet and left a message of thanks. Jake then motioned for Gunnar to climb onto his back and I switched to the teratorn form as well, so that Anja could ride my back. Stefan, Gil, and Andreas carried the packs. Our group now consisted of five giant teratorns and two biological humans. After several whoops of delight, we took flight for Confluencia, with Jake leading the way.

The excitement of spring filled the air and there was barely a cloud in the sky. Although the wind carried a chill, we soared gleefully in V-formation, enjoying the feeling of the sun as it illuminated the peaks and valleys of the Andes. All five teratorns, including myself, seemed able to handle the loads without difficulty.

In a matter of minutes, we crossed Los Libertadores pass, this time heading east. We continued soaring over Las Cuevas toward the park entrance of Aconcagua. Before the era of zero percenters, hikers had to go to the city of Mendoza to get climbing permits in order to enter the park, but that was no longer necessary.

Slowly and deliberately, we flapped our way up the Horcones Valley, taking in the scenic grandeur while following a flight path that required as little elevation gain as possible. Had there been any onlookers, we would have made quite a spectacle—five gorgeous specimens of *Argentavis magnificens* gliding through the crisp blue sky high above the Argentina wilderness.

Spring had arrived early to the region, largely a consequence of global warming. Most of the snow had melted on the valley floor and the streams were swollen with water. As we passed over the ranger station, we caught a glimpse of the massive glacier-covered south wall of Aconcagua. While impressive, the Andean glaciers had lost almost two-thirds of their ice in the past fifty years. Now that humans had ceased their polluting, we could only hope this retreat would be reversed.

The terrain below was sprinkled with low bushes, such as yellow firewood, yareta and goat horn, and there were open pastures made up of grasses such as huecú and ichu. Occasionally, we spied birds frolicking in the area, including torrent ducks, giant hummingbirds and agachona. As we rounded the bend for the Confluencia camp, Anja squeezed my neck and pointed to a family of red foxes traipsing over a hill.

We were having such fun that Jake flew past the camp and continued leading us up the valley. After about a mile, we came to a fork and a canyon opened up to our right. We followed it to Plaza Francia, enjoying a closer, unobstructed view of the entire south wall. Then Gunnar whistled loudly and motioned for us to turn back.

"That's far enough," he shouted.

Jake nodded, leading us in a slow, swooping 180-degree turn. Effortlessly, we glided down the canyon and back to Confluencia, where all five teratorns made smooth landings. Gunnar and Anja dismounted, then the rest of us switched to our biped forms. We walked around for a few minutes, surveying the area, until Gunnar settled on a site to erect our tents.

In comparison with the dramatic terrain around us, the Confluencia camp was a bit dreary. There were three abandoned storage structures, seven porta-potties, and the remains of some Quonset huts. Otherwise, all the camp had to offer was a source of water and some dirt that had been cleared of plants and rocks to allow for the placement of tents. There were no park rangers working the area anymore, nor were there any zero percenters to be seen.

"So what do you think?" asked Gunnar. "Aside from the porta-potties, that is."

"I'm very excited," said Anja. "I've never been anywhere like this before. Aconcagua looks amazing."

"Yeah, the scale of it is very deceptive. We have a long way to the top, but the good news is that we're at over eleven thousand feet now. I'm thinking we should just take it easy around here for the rest of the day."

"Okay." She nodded.

"We'll put up the tents for you," said Jake.

"Do you need some help?" I offered.

"Nah, you should just kick back with Anja and Gunnar," said Stefan.

"We've set these up a few hundred times before," added Jake, chuckling.

"There's a little knoll over there," said Gunnar, pointing to the north. "If you feel up to it, we could check it out."

"Sounds good," said Anja. "Come on, Vicia. Let's see what we can see."

※

THE THREE OF us followed a narrow trail to the base of the knoll and ascended about two hundred feet. By the time we got to the top, we were at an elevation of 11,327 feet, which afforded another glimpse of the south wall of Aconcagua. Rising almost two miles in height, at an inclination of close to forty-five degrees, the wall was draped with numerous hanging glaciers, some over two hundred feet thick. A mushroom-shaped cloud covered the summit, even though blue skies prevailed everywhere else.

It seemed hard to believe that we might soon be standing at the top of this behemoth of a mountain. I could tell that Anja felt some trepidation, as her breathing became a bit more shallow and her eyes widened, but I also knew that she was not easily intimidated.

"I should probably mention," said Gunnar, "we'll be going up the other side of the mountain, which is much less steep than this side. So don't be too worried. Our biggest issue is going to be staying warm and avoiding AMS."

Anja nodded tentatively.

"We'll actually be climbing most of the mountain twice to stay out of trouble," he explained.

"Why twice?" she asked.

"That's the best way to avoid getting altitude sickness," I interjected, proud of having researched the subject. "You climb up a bit higher each day, but then you come back down to sleep at lower elevations."

"Exactly," said Gunnar. "Climb high, sleep low. It's an iterative process. There are four upper camps that we'll use to work our way up the mountain."

"So we can't just charge it all in one day?" she said jokingly.

"Not quite." Gunnar smiled. "I estimate we'll need about ten days to get to the summit, and that's only because of our head start. The standard timeframe is twenty days, for us biological humans."

"I see what you mean about it being involved."

"Just remember, there's no shame in recognizing your limits and acting accordingly," he cautioned. "We can always back out at any time."

"Not a chance," boasted Anja. "We're doing this no matter what!"

"Uh, that's called summit fever," he replied, "and we definitely want to avoid it."

"Just kidding," she teased.

"I'll keep her in line for you," I said. "We'll be sure to follow your instructions to the tee and we won't do anything stupid."

"Good to know," he replied.

"We certainly can't let anything happen to the president of the world," I added.

Gunnar laughed. "I'm starting to feel the pressure and responsibility of this undertaking. Maybe I need to raise my fee?"

Anja leaned over playfully and gave him a kiss on the cheek. "Does that help?"

"Somewhat, yes," said Gunnar. "But in all seriousness, you should know that only about thirty percent of climbers end up reaching the summit. I mean, thirty percent of biological humans. Obviously, all zero percenters can do it without trouble, but in the old days, about three thousand people used to attempt to summit it every year and only about a thousand made it."

"That's not such good odds," I said.

"There are basically three things that can go wrong. Weather, injuries and altitude sickness."

"Makes sense," said Anja.

"For instance, see that mushroom cloud at the summit? It looks pretty innocuous from down here, right?"

"Yeah."

"It's formed by warm wind coming off the Pacific. Because the mountain is so huge, the wind gets forced upwards very rapidly. By the time it reaches the upper heights, it can get so cold that it precipitates into an extremely violent blizzard. That's what's going on up there right now. If we see that, we cannot summit, as doing so could be fatal."

"Gotcha," said Anja. "So that's the weather issue. But injuries and altitude sickness we can control, right?"

"For sure. At the higher elevations, we are going to learn to walk slowly and deliberately. Every step has to be made consciously and carefully, because one little slip and it can be game over."

"Okay, check," she said. "I'm sure we can manage that. So it seems like it all comes down to altitude sickness."

"That's definitely the big one," continued Gunnar. "Fortunately, you're already somewhat acclimated. Not only have you spent the last six days at Portillo, but you went to the top of Super C, which is over thirteen thousand feet."

"Plus I was in the Transylvanian mountains just a few weeks ago."

"That helps, but those mountains aren't very tall, are they?"

"Not so much."

"Ineu Peak is 7,477 feet," I said. "I believe that was the highest peak Anja climbed in Transylvania."

"Okay, well, that's all good," said Gunnar. "The benefits of altitude exposure can stay in your system for up to forty days."

"We've got this," I said. "Piece of cake."

Gunnar scrunched his eyes. "Not sure I'd say it like that, but I'm glad we're all feeling optimistic."

"And on that note," said Anja, "I propose we close our eyes for a few minutes and let the Argentinian beauty soak into our pores."

❋

THAT EVENING, while I prepared a dinner of mushroom risotto, Anja and Gunnar sat beside the newly erected tents and surveyed our stark surroundings. The peculiarity of having chosen such a forsaken spot upon which to lay their heads couldn't be ignored. Yet at the same time, there was an undeniable beauty in the sparse vegetation and severe land-scape—one that somehow felt complementary to their circumstance.

The duality of the situation seemed to break down their usual barriers. Or perhaps it was the extreme isolation that loos-ened their preconceived notions of themselves. Whatever the reason, they both found themselves speaking more candidly than usual.

"I keep thinking about your great-grandfather," said Anja, "and how you've managed to carry his courage with you into the wild."

"That's kind of you to say," replied Gunnar, "but I have a sneaking suspicion it's more my lack of courage that makes me hide out in places like this."

"You really feel it takes more courage to live down there?" she said, pointing toward Santiago. "It seems to me that every-thing humans do in their cities is about distorting reality. In nature, there are no distortions possible. All the feedback is a hundred percent real."

"Maybe so, but don't you think humans are meant to have relationships with other humans?"

She paused to reflect. "I can't say I know much about that."

"From what I can tell, the real challenge is to jump into the thick of it—into all the various human entanglements with all their distortions—and find a way to stay true to yourself."

Anja's breaths became rapid and her face flushed. "I think you've successfully outed me right there," she said.

"What do you mean?" asked Gunnar.

"I've always been scared to death of that challenge, but I've never wanted to admit it, even to myself."

"Okay, that's good to recognize... you know I'm exactly the same, right?"

"Honestly, I doubt that very much," said Anja. "We're talking whole different levels of being scared."

"Are you sure about that?"

"I'm twenty-five years old and I've never had a relationship. Not even a fling or a crush."

"Okay, I can't quite say that, but it's not like I've had anything serious."

"Do you want to know why?" continued Anja nervously.

"Yes, tell me."

She took a gulp of air. "I spent the last year of my mom's life trapped in a boarding school in Connecticut. She was dying of cancer and there I was, at age fifteen, hobnobbing with the ultra-privileged. It wasn't my choice, it was my father's. I don't think I saw my mom more than a couple of hours that entire year."

"I'm really sorry," said Gunnar.

"The last day of her life, I went to visit her in her room. I literally had just gotten off the plane and gone straight to the hospital. She took my hand into hers and told me that she only had two requests of me: one, to take care of my dad and, two, to give her a grandchild. The moment she finished talking, before I could even respond, her heart stopped beating and she was dead."

"That's horrible."

"Yeah, well, guess what? I ignored both of her requests. I never even tried to honor them. I didn't even try, Gunnar. I'm a total and complete failure of a daughter."

"That's not true. That is so not true."

"How was I supposed to take care of my dad when I was so pissed off at him? And he was never available anyway, always busy with work."

"You couldn't, of course," he said. "Your response made perfect sense."

"And how was I supposed to give my mom a grandchild when every waking hour I was busy studying how the world was falling apart? I'm supposed to want to bring a child into insanity?"

"I get it, I totally get it."

"So now here I am in this situation," she lamented, "and even if I wanted to try to correct things, it's too late. Way too late. My dad's dead and digital humans don't make babies."

"That's one way of looking at it," he said.

"You're saying I'm looking at it the wrong way?"

"Of course not. There is no wrong way."

"Easy to say, but not particularly helpful."

Gunnar nodded in agreement. "I don't mean to suggest I have any great answers. But I do want to be here for you however I can."

"I'm sorry," said Anja. "I shouldn't be so snappy with you. It's just a tough subject for me."

"No worries. You have an everlasting get-out-of-jail-card with me. How's that sound?"

Her face lightened. "It sounds altogether dreamy," she replied.

"Excellent," he said, motioning her to slide closer to him.

She obliged, resting her head on his shoulder. "Thank you, Gunnar. I told you that you're carrying your great-grandfather's courage, and now you've just gone and proved my point."

TWENTY

October 26, 2024

PLAZA DE MULAS, ACONCAGUA, ARGENTINA

ALL NIGHT LONG, while Anja and Gunnar slept in their tent and Jake, Stefan, Gil and Andreas played virtual games, I stared steadfastly at the stars. They were so bright and captivating, I found myself speculating about the origin of the universe and the evolution of life. But most of all, I reviewed the long trail of suffering that humans had followed—all of their many instances of betrayal, deceit, thievery, murder, injustice and discrimination—and I wondered if we were finally reaching the end of it. Was that the purpose of this journey?

Neither Anja nor Gunnar had suggested such a thing. I knew their primary question concerned whether to replace their biological tissue. Climbing to the summit of Aconcagua provided a useful point of reference for such consideration. Yet, while the arguments for digitization seemed compelling by most measures, the starlight only served to obfuscate them, at least from my engineered perspective.

When the morning sun at last struck our campsite, I felt a strange mix of excitement and melancholy percolating through my system. To contain it, I mechanically initiated the task of preparing a meal of oatmeal, dried pears, walnuts and honey for Anja and Gunnar. They both began to stir as the aroma drifted into their tent.

"Breakfast is ready," I announced. "Come and get it while it's hot." Gunnar was the first to emerge, followed by Anja. They were both wearing jackets and hats, as the weather had turned cold and windy.

"This is delicious," he said, taking a bite. "Thank you so much."

"Thank you, Vicia," said Anja. "It's perfect."

"I'm glad you woke us up early," he said. "We have a lot of territory to cover today, assuming everyone is feeling up to it." He turned to Anja. "What do you think? The base camp at Plaza de Mulas is about twelve miles away and we'll be gaining almost three thousand feet in elevation."

"I feel fine," she said. "Let's do it."

"That structure over there is where climbers used to undergo medical checks to make sure they were ready for the ascent," he said, pointing to an abandoned shack. "It would be smart for us to do it too."

"My sensors can perform most types of measurements," I offered.

"Can you take our heart rate, blood pressure and blood oxygen level?"

"No problem." I checked Anja first and then Gunnar. Both of them showed levels in the normal range.

"Cool, we're good to go," said Gunnar. He put his fingers in his mouth and made a loud whistling noise, causing Jake to poke his head out of his tent.

"What up?" said Jake.

"We're getting ready to roll. Are you going to walk or fly?"

"We fly, brother, we fly!"

"If you could transport our gear to base camp, that'd be righteous," said Gunnar.

"Will do, boss," said Jake. "Happy stepping. We'll swoop by from time to time."

❄

BEFORE ZERO PERCENTERS, mules were the primary method of transporting food and gear for the climbers of Aconcagua, which was how the base camp, Plaza de Mulas, got its name. Dozens of mules were hitched together by the local *arrieros* in order to keep them orderly as they toiled up and down the mountain. When these mule trains approached, hikers had to be careful to step aside or risk being trampled.

As we began our ascent to base camp, the only evidence of mules that we could see were some derelict harnesses and chains. The most prominent feature coming out of Confluencia was a lone boulder called Piedra Grande. The trail was lightly etched into a plain of red dust, but it was not always evident and we had to be careful to avoid straying from the course.

After a few miles, we came to a plateau called Playa Ancha, through which the Horcones River meandered. We were at over twelve thousand feet by this point and few traces of plant life remained, nor did many wild animals have reason to venture this high. Boulders of varying sizes surrounded us everywhere we turned. To both sides of us were numerous peaks in excess of fifteen thousand feet, most of which had yet to be named. For all we knew, we could have been on the moon or a distant planet, so foreign was the landscape from what we were accustomed.

Plodding onward, I tried to calculate how many thousands of years of erosion from the glacier-fed river had been required to produce the terrain on which we stood. I kept my calculations to myself, as it was evident that both Anja and Gunnar were preoccupied. The trail had become narrower, the slope into which it was etched steeper, and it now consisted of a chaotic mess of rocks and pebbles, rather than smooth sand. If one did not plant each foot carefully and firmly, it would be easy to twist an ankle, or worse yet, take a fall and slip down the slope.

I could only imagine the fortitude and discipline required of all the prior biological humans who had made this climb. In comparison, the additional exertion placed on my digital system was insignificant. I merely had to ensure that my battery remained sufficiently charged, which was actually easier at this altitude, since my shell received stronger solar radiation.

By the time we crossed thirteen thousand feet, the temperature was below twenty degrees Fahrenheit and the emergence of gusty winds made it feel even colder. Still, Anja and Gunnar did not utter a word of distress. Both of them had years of experience hiking in remote wilderness and they thoroughly relished the challenge lying ahead of them.

They only stopped to take quick swigs from their water bottles or to point out geographic markers. As the incline of the trail became yet steeper, these breaks became more frequent and they soon realized they had underestimated the amount of water they would need. Fortunately, the winding path afforded an opportunity to refill their bottles from the banks of the Horcones River.

They had to treat the water to remove any contaminants. The result was a far cry from the pure water they had enjoyed at Confluencia, but neither of them complained. It was all part of the experience. Even when Anja pushed aside a rock and revealed human feces, she merely grinned. Gunnar did the same thing just minutes later, in spite of a greater stench emanating from his finding.

"I get the feeling there's a message here for us," he said, chuckling.

"You mean, as to why the demise of biological humans is to be celebrated?" asked Anja.

"Exactly!" he exclaimed and they both laughed so hard that they could barely continue breathing.

I comprehended the irony and I laughed with them, but it did add to the uneasiness that seemed to be growing within me. What really was my function? Was I to encourage Anja to digitize? Should I set the mood for her and Gunnar to reproduce? Or was I meant to remain impartial or discourage any change at all?

The paradox of being a biological human was undeniable and yet I found it endearing too, especially when coupled with the type of self-effacing honesty that both Anja and Gunnar exhibited. The more I recognized the paradox, the more it seemed to grow. This made me feel happy and uneasy at the same time, which expanded the paradox still further.

I could have become stuck in an infinite loop of philosophical inquiry were it not for the arrival of Jake, Stefan, Gil, and Andreas. They were in the form of Andean flamingos—I detected them from their digital signatures, but it was also evident from the way they honked and grunted excitedly, as they circled above us. Their enthusiasm helped buoy our spirits, as the trail was becoming ever more challenging.

We had now reached the beginning of Aconcagua's great western wall. Embedded into the wall were dozens of glaciers, winding around the moraine and its couloirs, although they were often obscured by a covering of loose pebbles. In some cases, the pebbles were so thick, we could barely tell there was ice underneath them.

In more rare instances, the glaciers took the form of tall, thin blades of hardened ice, closely spaced, with the blades oriented toward the sun. Called Nieves Penitentes, these oddities formed in clusters and could be as tall as ten feet. Gunnar decided to wander off-trail to inspect a cluster and he was surprised to discover they were extremely strong—he was unable to break even the narrow tips. I did some research and learned that they formed when the sun turned ice directly into water vapor without melting it first.

Our next landmark was the site of a former military shelter on the left side of the trail. It had been destroyed by a massive avalanche and all that remained were some crumbling rock walls. The ground turned still rougher and steeper here. Gunnar announced that we had reached our final ascent, a section affectionately referred to as Cuesta Brava, since the rugged slope was only for the brave at heart.

For the first time, I could see strain on Anja's face. Her pace slowed considerably and her breathing appeared to be shallower and more labored. Gunnar and I shortened our steps to match hers. As we did, we saw below us the skeletal remains of dozens of mules who had taken unfortunate stumbles.

The glacier-clad vistas of the western wall became more and more prominent at this elevation. After another mile of climbing, we approached a summit that we thought might be the base camp, but our hopes were dashed when we realized it was just another mound of scree. Anja's face now had a look of despair.

"Guys," she said breathlessly, "I'm out of water and feeling a bit panicky."

Gunnar offered her the last of his water. She swallowed it down thirstily, but she still seemed alarmed. He motioned her to a rocky perch and we all sat down.

"Let's rest for a few minutes," he said. "We're at over fourteen thousand feet now, so this is higher up than you've been before."

Anja nodded. "How much further?"

"I think it's only about a quarter mile away. It's hard to tell because the terrain is so steep."

The four Andean flamingos swooped in front of us—it was Jake, Stefan, Gil, and Andreas again. This time they performed acrobatic stunts, dive-bombing through the air, then twirling and spinning in a synchronized fashion. As if to provide motivation, they touched the tips of their wings in a straight line, emitting sharp cries of delight, and launched into a sequence of overhead flips, one after another in rapid succession, before shooting off in the direction of base camp.

"Oddly, that seemed to help," said Anja. "I'm ready to press on."

We continued our ascent with Gunnar in the lead and myself in the rear. The wind was gusting at over thirty miles per hour and all we could do now was put one foot in front of the other, mechanically and stoically. In the distance, another summit began to take shape, but we reminded ourselves that it might be a false hope.

Slowly, we marched up the trail, which was now covered in ice. It felt steeper than anything we had yet encountered and even I felt the demand on my system. Complete concentration was required in order to avoid slipping.

At last, as we approached the crest, we saw in the distance a lone ranger station and some more Quonset huts. A small sign proclaimed that we had indeed reached Plaza de Mulas, at an elevation of 14,340 feet. We could scarcely believe we had reached our goal for the day.

In its heyday, Plaza de Mulas had been the second-busiest mountaineering base camp in all the world—second only to that of Everest. Numerous guide services and outfitters had provided a range of creature comforts for those willing to pay. Now there was not a person to be seen.

The lack of activity made the scenery all the more breathtaking. Pristine snow covered most of the mesa that comprised base camp. In the far distance, we could see the summit of Aconcagua. From this perspective, we were able to appreciate for the first time the sheer enormity and verticality of the mountain. We still had 8,501 feet to climb.

As we contemplated this sobering fact, a dark blur appeared high in the sky, seemingly from out of nowhere. At first, we thought it was a storm cloud, but it quickly broke up into thousands of small dots. Gunnar instinctively grabbed hold of both Anja and me, and all three of us braced ourselves for something to happen that we didn't understand.

The small dots started to organize as they moved closer to us and we came to recognize that they were a swarm of birds. They organized still further and we identified them as tens of thousands of Andean flamingos—or I should say, as zero percenters in the form of Andean flamingos. Then we finally realized what was happening.

The flamingos were spelling out a message in the sky: "Eternal loving kindness!" With the flapping of their wings, they added an animation effect, which made the words appear as if they were dancing.

The message was beautiful and inspiring and bizarre, all at the same time.

❄

As QUICKLY AS THEY CAME, the flamingos soared off into the distance—except for Jake, Stefan, Gil, and Andreas, who swept down beside us and morphed into their biped forms.

"Did you dig our show?" asked Jake.

"It was amazing," replied Anja. "How'd you do that?"

"We have our ways," said Gil.

"Years of choreography classes," added Stefan, winking.

"You should have asked your friends to stick around," said Anja. "I would have liked to have had a chance to thank them."

"They didn't want to impose or anything," explained Jake. "They just wanted to pay their respects."

"We had over fifty thousand flamingos up there, you know," said Andreas.

"Incredible," said Gunnar.

"But that's just the beginning of our surprise," said Jake. "Remember the old hotel?" He pointed to a large building nestled in the foothills about a mile to the west. The eighty-room structure had been built in the early 1990s, making it the highest hotel in the Americas, but the cost of maintenance had become prohibitive, so it had fallen into disrepair.

"We fixed it up for you guys," said Gil. "You won't be sleeping in a tent tonight."

"No way," said Gunnar. "I've always wanted to check that place out."

"And we've got a gourmet dinner awaiting," added Andreas.

"Food!" said Anja. "Need food now! Must eat now!"

"No worries," said Jake, laughing. He snapped his fingers and Stefan, Gil, and Andreas became mules. "Hop on board!"

We each mounted a mule and rode across Plaza de Mulas toward the hotel. By the time we arrived, the sun had slipped below the horizon and the entire western sky was bright pink. Bathed in diffused light, the grand hotel stood before us like a mirage.

Upon entering, we were further wowed by the efforts of the guys. Not only had they prepared a sumptuous meal for Anja and Gunnar, but they had illuminated the entire hotel with paper lanterns and decorated it with bouquets and wreaths fashioned from native plants.

We thanked them profusely, as it wasn't every day that one felt so lavished with attention. Whatever apprehension we still carried with us seemed to dissipate in the presence of such friendship and generosity. At least for the moment, we were all okay.

TWENTY-ONE

October 27, 2024

PLAZA CANADÁ, ACONCAGUA, ARGENTINA

AFTER FEASTING ON empanadas de búfalo and ensalada de remolacha con manzana, Anja and Gunnar retired to the penthouse suite. Although the hotel had no electricity or heat, lying on a proper bed in a room sheltered from the wind was a big step up from being in a tent. I half expected Anja to relax her no-kissing rule, but the moment their heads hit pillows, they fell sound asleep.

I spent the downtime reading more about acclimatization strategies for biological humans engaged in high-elevation climbing. My review of the literature confirmed Gunnar's estimate. From Plaza de Mulas, we would want to allow a minimum of eight to ten days to reach the summit.

Unfortunately, the most recent weather reports indicated a major storm heading our way in just five days. According to the models, severe blizzard conditions were expected above thirteen thousand feet. While less common in spring, the dreaded *viento blanco* could strike the Andes at almost any time of year. At the summit, it could result in winds in excess of 150 miles per hour.

I didn't look forward to imparting the bad news, but I resolved to advise that we abort our mission. The risks were too high to take unnecessary chances. Dozens of hikers had died in blizzards on Aconcagua and I had no intention of letting that happen to Anja or Gunnar.

To soften the blow, I prepared fresh açaí juice and homemade granola with yogurt from sheep's milk. I laid out the breakfast on a dining table by the window that had the best views of Aconcagua. Anja and Gunnar entered as the morning sun was rising over the western wall.

"G'murnin, Vicia," said Gunnar. "Look at this spread. And stunning views too. We are living the high life, literally."

I laughed softly.

"Another gorgeous day and more yummy food," said Anja. "Thank you, Vicia. How are you?"

"I'm fine," I said. "And, yes, we have blue skies forecast for today, but not such cooperative weather further out, I'm afraid."

"Oh?" said Gunnar. "What's the word?"

"*Viento blanco* in five days," I explained.

"At the summit?" asked Gunnar.

I shook my head. "Everywhere above thirteen thousand feet."

"Yikes, not good."

I showed them the weather models, then shared my conclusion that the prudent course would be to abort.

"As much as I hate to say this, I agree completely," said Gunnar. "We can't play around with a storm system like that. It's serious business."

"Hold on a second," protested Anja. "We still have five days to see how this develops. Why give up now?"

"I understand what you're saying," said Gunnar, "but even

if all five days were hikable, that's not enough time to get to the top."

"Are you sure about that?"

"Okay, let me revise that statement. Potentially, yes, it can be done. But certainly not safely, and especially not for our experience level."

"Whose experience are you referring to?" she asked. "Yours or mine?"

Gunnar laughed. "Touché, you got me there. I may be making some unfair assumptions. I know you're a very, very strong hiker."

"I think what Gunnar is concerned about is altitude sickness," I interjected, "more than stamina."

"Yes, true," he said.

"Correct me if I'm wrong," I continued, "but the standard strategy for reaching the summit from here calls for a carry day, a move day, and a rest day for each of the three upper camps. That means we would need nine days, plus a summit day. And technically, today should also be a day of rest, so that would mean we actually need eleven days."

"Those recommendations are for conventional climbs," said Anja, "but keep in mind, our gear is being transported for us, which means we're eliminating a good deal of stress and exertion."

"You're right about that," said Gunnar. "Mules were not allowed past base camp, so before zero percenters, everyone had to carry their own gear from here."

"Also," added Anja, "we have a safety feature that no other biological humans ever had. If anything goes wrong, Jake, Gil, Stefan and Andreas can just fly us back down."

"True enough," said Gunnar. "In the past, helicopter rescues were capped at about fifteen thousand feet, so climbers who faced an emergency situation above that were on their own."

"Which is why I really don't see what we have to lose by trying."

Gunnar paused to consider Anja's proposal. "This is really important to you, isn't it?"

"I just want to know we gave it our best shot."

"There is one other possibility to consider," I offered. "In my research, I came upon an alternate acclimatization strategy that some climbers have implemented successfully."

"What is it?" asked Anja.

"Instead of climbing to Camp 1 and returning here to sleep, we could climb to Camp 2 and then go back down to Camp 1 to sleep. We'd keep following this pattern all the way up the mountain. It's a much more aggressive approach, needless to say, and there hasn't been any rigorous testing of its efficacy."

"Let me get this straight," said Gunnar. "You're saying that we can beat altitude sickness by always going up higher than where we actually sleep, but still maintaining a daily upward ascent?"

"That's right," I affirmed. "If we iterated the approach for three days, we would wake up at Camp 3 on day four. We could then take a day of rest and attempt a summit on day five."

"So you mean, no days of rest until then?"

"Correct," I said. "Of course, if we preferred, we could take our rest day earlier in the sequence, but all the research suggests it's best to have a rest day before summiting."

"I'm impressed," said Gunnar. "You've really studied this stuff."

"That's my job," I replied, smiling.

"I'm up for it, if everyone else is," he said. "But only with the understanding that if any one of us is feeling the slightest bit compromised or if the storm looks like it could arrive ahead of schedule, we fly down immediately."

"I'm in," said Anja without hesitation.

"In that case," I said, "we'd better get going, as we have no time to waste."

❄

JAKE POPPED his head into the hotel dining room as I was performing our second round of medical checks. We explained our new strategy to him and he agreed to pack up our gear for transport to Camp 1, also known as Plaza Canadá. Fortunately, Gunnar and Anja's heart rate, blood pressure and blood oxygen levels easily passed the checks. Then we suited up and got back on the trail.

Altogether, we had to cover about six more miles to reach the summit—Camp 1 was 1.8 miles away, Camp 2 another 1.4 miles, Camp 3 another 0.8 miles, and the summit an additional two miles. We'd already hiked twelve miles from Confluencia. However, the big difference was that in these last six miles we would ascend over eight thousand, five hundred feet at an average gradient of over twenty-six percent.

As we trudged out of Plaza de Mulas, we immediately felt the increase in steepness. At least the path was well marked and the scree on this part of the western wall seemed tightly packed. There was no snow on the ground, perhaps because it received direct exposure from the strong afternoon sun. After about a half mile, we came to a rocky formation called El Semáforo.

"We're making good time," said Gunnar. "If anything, I suggest we slightly back off on our pace. We need to start concentrating on taking slow, deep breaths as we climb. Getting enough oxygen is going to be one of our biggest challenges."

"Got it," said Anja curtly, not wanting to expend any unnecessary energy.

We came to a still steeper section of the slope where the trail zigzagged with successive switchbacks. Even though I didn't need to breathe, Gunnar's tip helped me considerably, as I began to perceive hiking and meditating as related activities. I was eager to apply my insight to our next round of meditation.

Soon we passed another rocky spot known as Las Piedras de Conway, which was named after Sir Martin Conway, an English art critic and professor who had climbed Aconcagua in 1898. Here we were 126 years later, passing the same terrain, two biological humans and one concierge. None of us knew exactly why, but somehow it all seemed significant.

Gunnar let out a shrill cry and we saw Jake, Gil, Stefan and Andreas soaring above us in the form of teratorns, our gear strapped to their backs. We gave them the thumbs-up and they responded with shrieks of encouragement. They circled around us once and then proceeded upward.

We were at 15,583 feet now. Instead of switchbacks, the trail began to follow a long diagonal cut across the side of the mountain. Gunnar and Anja took swigs from their water bottles, but none of us spoke. The austerity of the landscape suited our silence.

Onward we marched. I sensed a questioning of our purpose on one level, yet at the same time, we had become fully consumed with the simplicity of our task. A sort of quiet contentment seemed to derive from the monotony of our footsteps.

The trail returned to zigzagging as we came to another steep patch of terrain. After four more switchbacks, we could see in the distance a rocky pinnacle that comprised Plaza Canadá. It looked to be little more than a ledge, jutting from the side of the mountain.

Jake, Gil, Stefan and Andreas were busily erecting our tents. We hurried our pace up the slope. When we finally arrived, they invited us to sit down on boulders arranged in a circle. An assortment of nibbles were laid out for Anja and Gunnar.

"That was much harder than I expected," said Anja. "I'm exhausted."

"It's the elevation," explained Jake.

"Give yourself time to adjust," said Andreas.

"And drink lots of water," said Gil. "We just melted a bunch of glacier snow for you." He pointed to several bottles of water.

"Thanks, guys," said Gunnar. "You're saving our asses."

"Of course," replied Jake. "We haven't completely forgotten what it was like, right?"

"Hell, no," said Stefan. "I climbed this sucker eight times as a bio. Every time was a total bear."

"Just keep your head screwed on straight, that's the trick," said Gil. "Your mind can go to some strange places when it gets deprived of oxygen."

"So far, so good," said Anja, "although I am noticing a change in my appetite. I only seem to be drawn to very bland food now."

Jake laughed. "Oh, yeah," he said, "I can relate to that. One time up here I ate nothing but oatmeal for three solid days."

"Try the potatoes," offered Stefan. "They were a lifesaver for me."

Anja had a spoonful of mashed potatoes and was pleased to find it went down without resistance. She ate several more spoonfuls, capped with some cashews, and finished off her bottle of water. Meanwhile, we all enjoyed the vista from our ledge. Far below, we could see Plaza de Mulas. We had climbed 2,320 feet above the base camp.

"Okay," said Gunnar, "I don't mean to be a slave driver, but we'd better take our last bites. We need to keep on moving if we're going hit our target for the day and get back here before dark."

"I'm ready," said Anja.

"Me too," I added.

We said our farewells, hoisted ourselves to our feet, and set out on the trail again. Plaza Canadá was at an elevation of 16,570 feet. Our goal for the day was to climb another 1,700 feet to get to Camp 2, known as Nido de Cóndores, before returning to Canadá.

The trail followed another long diagonal across the scree. We passed a lone rock of substantial size, which Gunnar referred to as the "5000 meter" stone. After another hundred steps or so, the path reverted to frequent switchbacks and the ground became covered in snow. To our relief, the snow was a bit easier to navigate than the scree.

When we reached 17,388 feet, Gunnar asked if we noticed a discernible difference in the slope. Anja and I both wondered if he was losing his marbles because there was obviously a huge difference—the slope went from being very steep to almost a flat terrace.

"That's why this spot is called Cambio de Pendiente," he chuckled.

"Good to know," said Anja blandly, too tired to find his humor funny.

We continued our zigzagging, but our pace got even slower. Gunnar explained that we were now at an elevation where altitude sickness most commonly occurred. To guard against it, he suggested we take short rests every few steps.

Even with the rests, I could tell Anja was getting depleted. From one of my shell pockets, I pulled out an energy gel packet and handed it to her. She sucked it down, followed by a swig of water, and we resumed our slow ascent.

As we climbed higher, the views kept getting more impressive. To the north, we could see Mount Mercedario rising from the Cordillera de la Ramada mountain range. At 22,047 feet, it was almost as tall as Aconcagua. To the west was the smaller but still dramatic Mount Catedral. To the south, we could now discern two distinct peaks that formed the summit of Aconcagua.

After one last zigzag, we rounded a bend and saw in the distance an area made up of windswept rocks of various sizes strewn across a large plateau that cradled a small frozen lake. This was Nido de Cóndores, nest of the condors. At last, we had achieved our target for the day.

Gunnar led us to a clearing with nice views and we each took a seat in the snow. The great western wall seemed especially daunting now that we were so close. Numerous peaks in excess of sixteen thousand feet dotted the horizon, but they looked small in comparison.

As we enjoyed the scenery, we noticed five Andean condors soaring in the western sky. We watched them for quite some time, awed by the coincidence of spotting condors at Nido de Cóndores. Then we realized what was happening.

"Those are our friends again," I said excitedly, "except one of them is biological."

"You're absolutely right," said Gunnar, after studying them intently. "I didn't think they could pull off something like that."

"What do you mean?" asked Anja.

"Those condors out there are Jake, Gil, Stefan and Andreas," he explained. "But the fifth one is a real condor. It doesn't seem to know the difference."

"Or doesn't care," I added.

"You see how it is flying a bit differently than the other four?" said Gunnar.

"Yeah, now that you mention it," said Anja. "But I'm not sure I'm thinking too clearly right now. I'm feeling a bit strange."

"What's wrong?" he asked. "Do you have a headache?"

"I don't think so," said Anja. "I just feel out of sorts."

"It could be the first signs of AMS. We're at over eighteen thousand feet now. Let's take some slow, deep breaths together. Try this: breathe in for four seconds, pause, then breathe out for two seconds. As you breathe in, visualize a lotus flower opening, and as you breathe out, visualize it closing."

We all followed Gunnar's instructions. Of course, I used a breathing simulator. Although I didn't know why, I found the exercise helpful in reconciling our seemingly irrational objective of reaching the summit.

Since we'd left Plaza de Mulas, I had been struggling to resist calling off our climb. I kept detecting that it contained a self-destructive element for both Anja and Gunnar. Why did they want to scale Aconcagua as biological humans when it would be so much easier as zero percenters?

Gradually, the deep breathing washed away my internal questioning. I saw that my paradigm of efficiency was not the relevant measure. If anything, it was quite the reverse. Climbing Aconcagua held little significance for zero percenters because it involved no sacrifice or hardship. Gunnar and Anja were the last two humans who could absorb the nectar of the experience, and that was why they had to do it.

"Now how do you feel?" asked Gunnar.

"Much better," replied Anja.

"It helped me too," I said.

"Glad to hear it."

"And you said you were skeptical of gurus," said Anja teasingly. "You *are* a guru."

He smiled sheepishly. "It was just a breathing exercise."

"If you say so," she replied. "All I know is that I'm not just feeling better. I'm seeing things differently too."

"Oh?"

"My whole life," Anja continued, "I've been busily drawing boundaries. If something was on one side, then I was sure it couldn't be on the other. But I realize now it's not so simple. That fifth condor just showed us that."

"Showed us what exactly?" he asked.

"That reality isn't rigid."

"Can you elaborate?"

"Before I would have said that the fifth condor was real and the other four weren't. But that's way too simplistic, way too black and white, and it misses so much. Obviously, that's not how the condor saw it. And it's not how Jake and the guys saw it either. They were all willing to learn from each other."

"Yeah, I think I see what you mean there," said Gunnar.

"Existence is so much broader, so much more flexible, than I've been making it out to be. Whatever we are, we're far, far more than our outward representation."

"Hmm," he said, "I'm going to have to give that some serious thought."

"And now who's the guru around here?" I joked.

We all laughed. A lightness of being seemed to fill the air space between us. We couldn't define it or understand it, but the sensation made the descent back to Plaza Canadá almost effortless.

By the time we reached the camp, it was already dusk. To our surprise, Jake, Gil, Stefan and Andreas had gathered firewood from their flying expedition and lit a small campfire for us to enjoy.

"Sweet!" said Gunnar. "This is probably the first campfire up here in many a year."

"For sure," said Jake. "Who would carry firewood all this way?"

"And we saw you made a friend today," said Anja. "Was that a first too?"

"You caught that?" said Andreas.

"Actually, Vicia was the one who noticed the fifth condor."

"It was very exciting to watch," I said. "Have you done that before?"

"Sure," said Andreas. "We've joined up with all kinds of birds."

"We flew with albatrosses for three straight days all the way to Hawaii," said Gil.

"They taught us tons about flying," said Jake. "No better way to learn."

"I can imagine," said Anja. "Quite the life you guys lead."

"May the birds show us the way!" I proclaimed.

Everyone smiled, reveling in the beauty of the moment, the miracle of existence, and the grandeur of the possibilities that awaited.

TWENTY-TWO

October 28, 2024

NIDO DE CÓNDORES, ACONCAGUA, ARGENTINA

After dinner, Anja and Gunnar fell asleep promptly again —in spite of the fact that they were in a flimsy tent, perched on a ledge at Plaza Canadá with the wind howling. The skies remained clear and the waning crescent moon emitted scant light. Even though it wasn't a full moon, I could have sworn I heard the occasional cries of Kora-Illé.

Midway through the night, I checked the weather report and I was dismayed to learn that the forecast had worsened considerably. The arrival of *viento blanco* had been pushed forward. Instead of having four more days of relative safety on the mountain, it now looked like we only had two.

I debated within my system how best to advise Anja and Gunnar. I knew they wanted a successful summit—so did I, more than ever—but we had to remain rational and be prepared to give up the goal, if prudence so dictated. The best approach seemed to be to report the options straightforwardly.

With the first sign of dawn, I began preparing a breakfast of potato pancakes, dried mango slices, and chai tea. As I did, I could hear Anja and Gunnar stirring in their tent. I didn't mean to eavesdrop, but I was only a few feet away and all that separated us was a thin layer of nylon.

"I feel like a completely new person," said Anja with a giggle. "Maybe we should stay in here a bit longer."

"Oh?" said Gunnar. "What exactly did you have in mind?"

"How about something along these lines?" she replied coyly.

The ensuing sounds of gentle kissing and sighing left little to my imagination. I had every intention of getting up and walking away, as I understood they required privacy. At that very moment, however, a dreadful howl reverberated through the camp.

Suddenly, an Argentine cougar—*Puma concolor cabrerae*—leapt through the air just inches in front of my face and slashed its way into the tent, using its razor-sharp claws. The puma batted Gunnar like a mouse, ejecting him onto the rocky ledge. Then it pounced on top of him and prepared to crush his throat with its enormous jaws.

My operating system instantly performed millions of calculations and settled on a course of action that puzzled me, but which I had no time to further assess. I raced over to the crepuscular cat and jammed an index finger into each of its eyes with all the might I could muster. It squealed in agony and released its stranglehold on Gunnar's throat.

I had hoped my action would permanently disable the puma's vision, but we were not so lucky. A few quick blinks restored its eyes sufficiently to locate my position and fling me twenty yards away with a backside swat of its paw. The sheer strength of this ambush predator—aptly nicknamed the "ghost of the Andes"—seemed to defy physics.

Every fiber of its two-hundred-pound frame bristled in anticipation as it readied for its next move. Fortunately, Gunnar was a step ahead of the puma. He took advantage of my distraction to grab ahold of its jaws, violently twisting its neck with all his might.

The puma squealed again. Still, it remained undeterred from its objective. With a mighty roar, it shook itself free and pinned down Gunnar's arms and legs with the weight of its body.

Now Gunnar had no defense against a lethal neck bite. But just as the cat was preparing to make its trademark maneuver, Anja sprinted toward it like an Olympic runner and threw herself feetfirst into the puma's rib cage. She let her knees fold up into its body, then she used both her legs to kick out against it as hard as she could.

The clever transfer of energy was enough to thrust the puma off of Gunnar and directly over the rocky ledge. It yelped and yowled as it descended ever downward, but there was nothing the beast could do. All of its rippling muscles were rendered useless as gravity sent it hurtling down the sheer mountainside.

"Gunnar!" screamed Anja, rushing to his side. "Are you okay?"

He slowly got up and began inspecting himself. "I appear to be fine. Just some scratches and bruises, but no serious lacerations or broken bones."

"That thing came out of nowhere!"

"Thankfully, I don't think it will be bothering us again," I said, peering over the ledge. "You knocked it almost all the way down to Plaza de Mulas."

Anja and Gunnar stepped toward me to look where I was pointing. They studied the puma's body for signs of movement, but there were none.

"And you're okay too, Vicia?" asked Anja.

"Yes, these shells are quite robust."

"That's a relief. I can't believe we survived that."

We paused to catch our breath. "I'm so glad everyone is okay," I said.

"You both were amazing," said Anja.

"You were pretty freaking amazing yourself," said Gunnar. "You saved my life. Both of you did. I don't know what to say."

"No need to say anything," she replied. "The first thing we have to do is get you cleaned up."

"Yeah, that's probably a good idea."

I quickly fetched the first aid kit and handed Anja some antiseptic and bandages. She began scanning his body to look for cuts.

"It's incredible how well you fared," said Anja. "You must have steel-reinforced skin. That puma had claws as sharp as knives."

"Yeah," replied Gunnar. "I've always been pretty lucky in that department, I guess from all the years I've spent living outside."

"Evidently." She wiped his scratches with antiseptic and applied a few bandages where needed.

"Do you want me to send out a message for Jake and the guys to come pick us up?" I offered. "It seems they're doing some early-morning exploring, as they're not in their tents."

"Nah," said Gunnar, "I'm fine. I want to press on."

"Are you nuts?" exclaimed Anja. "We need to get you to a doctor to make sure you don't have any internal injuries."

"Really, I'm fine... and I don't do doctors."

"Well, there's no way we can just keep pressing on, as if nothing happened."

"Agreed," said Gunnar. "I want to press on, while still acknowledging that something definitely happened. That's been my approach my whole life. I don't let setbacks stop me from what I want to accomplish. But I don't deny reality either."

"You're saying you still want to attempt this summit, even if it means we might get attacked by another puma?"

"Actually, yeah, I do—but only if both of you still want to. If either one of you wants to call it off, that's a whole other matter. I'm just saying that I'm still one hundred percent in. No matter where you are on this earth, there's always going to be something like a puma lurking around the next bend. So that's why I prefer to move through life proactively, not defensively."

"Sounds more like courting disaster than being proactive," said Anja.

"Call it what you want. If it weren't for you, I wouldn't even be here. You've saved my life twice now. So whatever time I have left, I'm going to follow my vision, not my fear."

She stopped to consider his words. "Oh, Gunnar," she sighed at last, "I can't dispute you there. I definitely don't want to follow my fear either. I'm tired of doing that and it certainly hasn't served me very well."

"At least, we can rest assured that one puma is off the table," I reminded them. "But there's something else you both should know." I proceeded to impart the bad news about the weather forecast.

"Maybe the report will change again in our favor," replied Anja after hearing me out. "Maybe it's just a temporary blip."

"Anything's possible," said Gunnar, "but we certainly can't count on it."

"Exactly," I agreed. "All we can do is make the best possible decision based on what we know."

"And what is the best possible decision?" asked Anja.

"That's what I was hoping we could work out together," I replied.

"Are you saying you don't think we necessarily have to abort?"

"Gunnar may be more qualified to answer that."

"I'm not so sure," he said.

"Well, first off," I asked, "how are your headache symptoms this morning, Anja?"

"Gone. I don't have any of those funny feelings I had yesterday."

"Okay, that's good. And how sore are you?"

"My leg muscles do feel pretty tight," she admitted. "Yesterday was quite a workout for me, and that move I pulled on the puma wasn't exactly in my usual repertoire, but I'm surprised that I actually feel okay."

"The reason I ask," I continued, "is that climbers have made successful summits from Nido. But it requires an extremely long day with a very early-morning start."

"Yeah? Go on."

"The way I see it," I said, "with this new information, we have just three options. The first is we abort. The second is we climb to Camp 2 today and try to summit tomorrow. The third is we climb to Nido today and try to summit from there tomorrow."

"So what are you leaning toward?" asked Anja.

"As a general rule, I favor safety above all else. Under ordinary circumstances, option one would be my recommendation. However, nothing at all is ordinary about our situation, that goes without saying. So after crunching the probabilities, weighing the emotional factors, and factoring in Gunnar's points, I'm leaning toward option three."

"That's what I like too," said Gunnar.

"I'm a bit shocked to hear you both say that," said Anja, "and I'm even more shocked that I'm not in disagreement. I guess I must really, really want to do this. The thing is, though, why shouldn't we make more headway today, so that the summit day isn't so hard?"

"Two reasons," answered Gunnar. "First, we want the day

before summiting to be as restful as possible. Second, we want to reduce the chances of getting AMS. We've already been to Nido, so it's going to be way less taxing for us to sleep there than to sleep at the next camp up."

"That's what my analysis concludes too," I concurred.

"There you go," he said.

Anja paused for a moment. "Okay," she replied, giving each of us a high five. "I'm on board with option three. Let's do this, come what may."

❄

AFTER BREAKFAST, we packed up and headed for Nido de Cóndores once again. Our plan was to get there by lunchtime and spend the afternoon resting and acclimating. Then it would be early to bed for Anja and Gunnar, as we would need to make an alpine start the following morning, in order to give us sufficient time to reach the summit.

Fortunately, the hike to Nido was quite a bit easier the second time, since we were familiar with the trail. It also helped that Anja and Gunnar were better adjusted to the altitude. The idea that we might be standing on the summit very soon occupied our thoughts and we charged past the 5000-meter stone without stopping—just slowing enough to confirm we were not being tracked.

When we reached Cambio de Pendiente, we gazed to the north and saw another swarm of zero percenters in the sky. This time, they were in the form of robotic flying machines, instead of flamingos. I counted 212,538 of them. For our amusement, they spelled out in blinking cursive letters, "Go Anja! Go Gunnar! Go Vicia!"

After the show, Jake, Gil, Andreas and Stefan swooped down beside us, still in the form of flying machines.

"How'd you like that?" said Jake.

"Incredible!" cried Anja.

"Sorry we bailed on you this morning," explained Gil. "We had to do some coordinating to make it happen."

"No worries," replied Gunnar, "but you missed a pretty weird scene at Canadá."

"A scene?" said Andreas.

"A puma attack, to be specific," Anja said.

"What?" exclaimed Jake. "Pumas don't come up this high."

"Not typically, no," said Gunnar.

"No one's seen a puma on Aconcagua for years," said Stefan. "There's no prey up here for them."

"Yeah, it seems that I was the prey this morning. But Anja and Vicia saved my ass."

"That's crazy," said Jake. "I'm sorry we weren't there to help out. Are you all okay?"

"Yeah, we're fine. Just a few little scratches is all."

"Gunnar's like Iron Man," said Anja proudly. "But I guess you already know that."

The guys chuckled. "He is a pretty tough dude," replied Jake. "But, man, I feel bad we weren't there. We'll do a much better job watching over you from now on."

"You better," joked Gunnar. "No more slouching around in virtual space."

They all laughed again and flashed us peace signs with their robotic appendages. Then they shot off toward Mount Mercedario. Their support, along with the encouragement of the zero percenters, provided a boost that powered us the rest of the way to Nido.

When we got there, our campsite was already set up and our gear was stashed inside the tents. Several bottles of water stood neatly by the entrance. Jake, Gil, Andreas and Stefan had cleared the area of snow and placed three sitting stones next to the tents.

We each took a seat and enjoyed the majestic view. Although the temperature was only ten degrees Fahrenheit, it felt reasonably warm in the sun because there was little wind. We couldn't see the summit of Aconcagua, but the path to it was clearly delineated.

From Nido, we would climb about 2,500 feet of steep switchbacks before reaching the Gran Acarreo, a long traverse in loose scree. Then came the perilous Canaleta, an even steeper stretch of about eight hundred feet that was at an incline of almost forty degrees and composed of sand and loose rocks. Luckily, it was now covered in snow and ice, allowing for an easier ascent wearing crampons. Altogether, we still needed to gain over 4,500 feet in elevation—and all in one day.

To ease our anxiety, we decided to pass the time playing cards. Meanwhile, Anja and Gunnar munched on granola bars, nuts, and dried fruit. Much to their chagrin, I won at nine consecutive rounds of poker and four consecutive rounds of bridge.

"How about we try meditating again?" Anja suggested.

"Good idea," replied Gunnar.

"It might help us clear our minds for tomorrow," she added.

"Okay," I said. "Let's do it."

We crossed our legs, slowed our breathing, and closed our eyes.

"Remember," said Anja, "you are not your thoughts or your emotions. You are the one who is witnessing them."

"I am not my thoughts or my emotions," repeated Gunnar. "I am the one who is witnessing them."

"I am not my thoughts or my emotions," I said. "I am the one who is witnessing them."

In a matter of minutes, both Anja and Gunnar dropped

into a peaceful space, despite our terrifying ordeal that morning. Eager to join Anja and Gunnar, I continued mouthing Anja's two sentences: *I am not my thoughts or my emotions. I am the one who is witnessing them.* Over and over, I repeated them, while using my breathing simulator. Every time my operating system wandered, I came back to the sentences.

At first, I made no progress. The whir of data processing within my system remained as active as ever. Then I recalled the insight I'd had on the trail and I visualized what it had felt like to climb up steep terrain. I traced in my logic board the mechanics of placing one foot after another on the ground, again and again, while focusing on nothing else.

I wouldn't say it led to the big breakthrough I sought. I still found it impossible to witness my thoughts and emotions. However, I did manage to push aside my inclination to address the pending tasks in my queue. This itself seemed like an accomplishment and I felt rather proud of myself.

Perhaps I had a shot at being humanlike after all.

TWENTY-THREE

October 29, 2024

SUMMIT, ACONCAGUA, ARGENTINA

WHETHER FROM ANTICIPATION, exhaustion, the altitude, or all three factors, I could not speculate, but as before Anja and Gunnar fell asleep as soon as they laid down their heads in their tent. No doubt they both wished to continue where they had left off that morning—their playful eyes made that clear. But the demands of the climb required a postponement of such desires.

At 2 a.m., under a faint sliver of a crescent moon, I awoke them both to begin our ascent. Modest winds of about fourteen miles per hour buffeted the tents, as they donned their down pants, high-altitude coats, face masks, mittens and double boots. The temperature was six degrees Fahrenheit, which may not have warranted such heavy gear, but we expected to encounter far colder conditions and it would be too difficult to make adjustments later.

"Before we start," said Anja, "I want to tell you both how much this journey has meant to me. Whether we reach the top or not, I will cherish this experience for the rest of my life."

"I feel likewise," said Gunnar, "of course."

"Ditto that," I said. "A concierge couldn't hope for more."

I handed them each a hot cup of cheddar potato soup, which they gulped down hurriedly. Then we strapped headlamps over our hats, threw our packs on our backs, and stepped out into the starry night. Fortunately, we could rely on Jake, Gil, Stefan and Andreas to pack up our remaining belongings.

"Remember," said Gunnar, "we don't want to push too hard, too early. Let's take it easy and cruise for the next few hours. It's all about conservation of energy today."

"Got it," said Anja.

"Conservation of energy," I repeated.

With Gunnar leading, we commenced the upward march. Our headlamps provided only modest illumination. We had enough light to see the immediate trail and avoid stumbling on rocks, but everything beyond thirty feet was pitch black.

Our biggest challenge was detecting the switchbacks. Sometimes, we accidentally continued going straight for a few steps before realizing we had overshot a turn in the trail. After a few missteps, Gunnar noticed that by adjusting his headlamp to aim higher than ours, we could optimize our coverage of the trail and thereby better detect the turns.

We continued treading upward, while remaining careful not to walk too quickly or aggressively. In some ways, hiking in the dark seemed preferable to the daylight, as there was nothing to distract us from the simplicity of the act. The gentle wind felt like a loving caress and the starlight like a soft kiss.

Every hour or so, Anja and Gunnar stopped to drink water and eat a snack from their goody bags, which included nuts, power bars, dried fruit, gels and chocolate bars. We usually continued standing during these quick breaks, as the trail was too narrow and precarious to offer any decent spots to sit. Following our conservation of energy motto, we spoke as few words as possible.

As the first sign of dawn showed, we came to a subtle crest in the ridge and noticed some small wooden huts. These indicated our arrival at Camp 3, known as Refugio Berlín. Gunnar led us into the least dilapidated of the huts.

"Let's rest inside here for a bit," he said.

We entered a small A-frame structure, took off our packs, and sat down on a wooden bench. It didn't look like anyone had used the hut for quite some time, as a layer of dust covered all the surfaces. Nonetheless, we appreciated having a respite from the wind.

"We're at 19,490 feet now," I said. "Just 3,351 feet to go."

"That's great," said Anja, taking a gulp of water.

"Berlín is where most climbers used to summit from," said Gunnar. "So you could consider this spot the official beginning of our day."

"Hmm... not sure if that's a motivator or not," she replied.

"The sun's not up yet, so I think it means we're in good shape," I said.

"Same here," he agreed. "How's everyone feeling?"

"I feel fine," I said. "And the weather report is still looking good. No signs of a storm until tomorrow."

"I feel pretty good too," said Anja. "There's just one thing that's nagging at me."

"What is it?" he asked.

"I keep thinking about kicking that puma over the ledge."

"Yeah, that was pretty far up there in the annals of martial arts."

"Thanks, but it's the way the puma's body felt when I kicked it that's bothering me."

"What do you mean?" asked Gunnar.

"I'm realizing now it didn't quite feel like flesh and bone. It felt too firm, not enough give."

"Now that you mention it, I remember being surprised by the way its neck and jaw felt too."

"Was it like this?" I said, leaning closer so they could touch my shell. They both reached out to feel it.

"Maybe," said Anja, "but it's hard to say for sure without reenacting my move."

"I'd have to agree," said Gunnar.

"Go ahead, do what you need to do," I offered. "I'm tough."

"Well, maybe if we did gentler approximations, it would be sufficient," he said.

"As you wish."

Gunnar turned to consult Anja. "What do you think?"

"We might as well try," she said. "You go first, but don't say anything until after my turn. I don't want to be biased."

"Fair enough," said Gunnar. "Here goes nothing." With one swift move, he grabbed my neck and jaw, mimicking the twisting motion he used on the puma, but applying less force.

"Nice one," said Anja. "Now we'll need to go outside for my turn."

"No problem," I replied.

We all exited the A-frame. Anja walked ahead of us about ten yards, then she ran back toward me and replicated her kick move. Even though she was far gentler with me than she had been with the puma, she knocked me onto the ground with ease.

"Sorry, Vicia," she said.

"It's okay," I replied, as I hoisted myself upright. "What are your conclusions?"

"Not very good."

"Not good at all," agreed Gunnar. "The puma's body felt a lot like yours."

"I was afraid of that," I replied.

"So does that mean it was a zero percenter?" asked Anja.

"Not possible," I said. "Pumas, lions, tigers, jaguars and other cats known to prey on humans aren't allowed as shell options. Neither are bears, sharks, crocodiles or alligators, for the same reason."

"And even if they were," said Gunnar, "wouldn't their concierge shut them down immediately, if they tried to attack another human?"

"Absolutely," I said.

"But what else could it be?" asked Anja.

"Some kind of rogue device," ventured Gunnar.

"Exactly," I said. "But only an alien species or a human who is not linked to a concierge would have been able to create it."

"This is getting a bit scary," said Anja.

"You're right, it's looking a lot less like a random attack and a lot more like a premeditated one."

"Seems like it might officially be time to abort," said Gunnar.

"What about being proactive, not defensive?" replied Anja. "If it's true that the attack was premeditated, then we'll be tipping our hands if we abort. But if we press on, it won't look like we've figured out anything. So aborting could actually be riskier."

"You've got a point there," said Gunnar.

"It's a very tough call," I said. "When I crunch the probabilities, I don't get a clear result. There's too much uncertainty to make a meaningful assessment."

"I guess it still boils down to how important it is to reach the top," said Gunnar.

"At this point," said Anja, "I feel like I have to go there no matter how scared I am. I feel like it's not really a choice for me anymore. But I'll understand if you guys want to bow out."

"You *have* to go there?" I said. "Why do you say that?"

"It's not a logical thing. It's just what I feel... there's a little voice inside of me that keeps telling me that the confusion swirling in my head will somehow be lifted if I can get up there. I've learned so much from this journey already. It would seem like a waste not to follow it to its conclusion."

"I think I know what you mean," said Gunnar.

"You do?" she asked. "Even though you just said it might be time to abort?"

"Yes, I do," he replied, reaching to hold her hand. "I've had a lot of confusion swirling inside my head too. Ever since my coma, I feel like I've been drifting at sea with no sail, no rudder, no anchor. I love Jake and the guys, but when I look at them, there's this aching emptiness that wells up in me. I start losing my ability to tell what's real and what's not. You two—and this trip—are the only reason why I haven't totally lost my mind."

"Then we have to continue," said Anja. "It's that simple. Because I know a lot about aching emptiness, and trust me, you don't ever want to let it overtake you."

"You're sure?" he asked.

"Yes, I'm sure. Are you?"

"If you are, I am. Definitely."

"I guess that settles it then," I said. "I'm here to support you both." I said this almost mechanically, but inside myself I was surprised that I too felt the same way as Anja and Gunnar.

❄

WITHOUT FURTHER DELAY, we got back on the trail and continued up the ridge. We were on high alert now. Nothing could be taken for granted any longer, and while this increased our anxiety, it also united us in our resolve—we were going to climb to the summit no matter what awaited us around the next bend.

Soon we passed an old campsite called Colera. The path turned even more rugged as we came upon a series of rock formations with white boulders and small cliffs. Gunnar told us the area was known as Piedras Blancas.

From there, the trail returned to zigzagging. The sun was starting to rise and we appreciated the warmth on our faces each time the path veered eastward. Blue skies prevailed, with just a few puffy white clouds to the north.

The early-morning sun produced a visual feast—its low angle perfectly illuminated the numerous glacier-draped peaks. We hiked with a steady rhythm and a sense of growing wonder. Each step we took led to yet another spectacle.

Interrupting our dreamlike state, four small flying saucers approached and hovered beside us. They were Jake, Gil, Stefan and Andreas.

"What up, dudes!" Jake called out.

"You've joined the twenty thousand club!" shouted Stefan.

A robotic arm reached out from Gil's saucer and offered Anja a hot flask of peppermint tea with honey and coconut oil. Likewise, an arm reached out from Stefan's saucer and offered Gunnar a similar flask. They both grabbed the beverages gratefully.

"Keep sipping as you climb," said Jake. "It'll help you stay hydrated and warm."

"Will do," said Anja. "Thank you!"

Gunnar updated the four of them on our insight regarding the puma. They all agreed it was a significant concern and they promised to keep on the lookout for any suspicious activity. Then they shot ahead in the direction of the summit, making the ascent look ridiculously easy.

"Are you tempted to join them, Vicia?" asked Gunnar.

"Not at all," I said. "I love the way we're doing it. I wouldn't want to change a thing."

"Ten points," replied Anja with a smile, as she sipped her tea.

We pressed upward through a scree field mixed with broken larger rocks. I could see Anja and Gunnar becoming more affected by the higher altitude. It wasn't the oxygen level that was decreasing—air contains 20.93 percent oxygen everywhere on earth—but rather the barometric pressure.

"Nice deep breaths," coached Gunnar. "Make sure to inhale fully until your stomach expands."

Anja flashed a thumbs-up.

"There's also something called pressure breathing that's supposed to help," I offered. "When you exhale, you purse your lips."

"Good call," said Gunnar. "I forgot about that."

As we stepped onward through the scree, they both worked on their breathing technique. The passage of time felt increasingly nonlinear. Each moment seemed to blend into the next.

We topped a small ridge and stepped through some moraine tower formations. As we rounded a bend in the trail, a lone shack appeared in the distance. This was the Refugio Independencia hut.

"Welcome to be the highest alpine refuge in the world," Gunnar announced.

It was another A-frame hut made from wood, but now largely in ruins from repeated windstorms.

"No point stopping, eh?" said Anja.

"Not really," he replied. "We'll pause a bit ahead to put on crampons."

"But take note that we are now at 20,932 feet," I mentioned.

"That's crazy," said Anja. "We're really doing this."

"Just 1,909 feet to go," I added.

Anja reached out to touch my shoulder, a sign of camaraderie. We continued climbing up and to the right, crossing a ridge called Portezuelo del Viento. As if on cue, the wind picked up considerably and the temperature dropped to minus three degrees Fahrenheit. Ahead of us were huge stretches of frozen snow and ice.

"Okay," said Gunnar, pointing to his boots. "It's time."

We retrieved the crampons from our packs and lashed them over our double boots. Exhilaration swept through us, as our expedition had now advanced to the next level. Crampons meant some serious mountaineering awaited us.

We began a long traverse, named the Travesía, which cut across the upper part of the Gran Acarreo. There were no switchbacks on this part of the trail and the grade was relatively modest. However, abundant snow and ice surrounded us. The crampons allowed us to walk a bit more confidently, without fear of slipping.

From this perspective, we could see not only the western wall of Aconcagua, but also dozens of other nearby mountains. We still couldn't observe the summit, as it was obscured by some lower moraine formations, but below us we had a clear view of Nido de Cóndores.

Our former campsite looked like a tiny dot. It felt good to have confirmation that indeed we were making substantial progress. We'd been hiking almost nine hours. I reminded Anja and Gunnar to each eat another power bar in order to stabilize their blood sugar levels.

The trail veered to the left on a slightly steeper diagonal. In the distance, we could see a chimneylike passage curving up through a huge, glaciated crag. This was the legendary Canaleta—eight hundred almost-vertical feet of loose scree and boulders wrapped in ice, reaching for the sky.

As we trudged forward, we came to a rocky, concave wall of conglomerate that contained a small cave. Known simply as La

Cueva, it indicated the starting point of our ascent up the eight-hundred-foot chute. We paused to absorb the significance of the moment. The Canaleta was described by some climbers as "the hell before the heaven."

A few steps past the cave, we caught our first glimpse of the summit, poking out from behind the imposing Canaleta. We were now at an elevation of 21,818 feet and the temperature was minus sixteen degrees Fahrenheit. Each of us carefully surveyed the terrain behind us, searching for signs of a predator on our trail. Anja's upper lip quivered with trepidation.

As if sensing our vulnerability, Jake, Gil, Stefan and Andreas swooped down from the sky and hovered beside us for a second check-in.

"It's final push time!" said Jake.

"You guys got this!" said Gil.

While hovering in midair, they refilled the flasks of peppermint tea. Both Gunnar and Anja had sucked down their first servings and were eager for a second round. I could only imagine how difficult it would be for a biological human to attempt the Canaleta without a warm drink.

"Eternal loving kindness!" Jake, Gil, Stefan and Andreas called out in unison. They flashed us the shaka sign with their mechanical hands and jetted off toward the summit.

We watched them fade into the distance, as we absorbed our strange surroundings. The beginning of the Canaleta felt almost like a gateway. We had already accomplished so much, and yet the greatest challenge remained.

"Don't get fixated on reaching the top," said Gunnar. "Just go one step at a time."

We nodded in agreement and Gunnar proceeded to lead us up the daunting couloir. We made slow, tentative movements, checking and rechecking our footing with each step, to be sure we were on stable ground. The looseness of the terrain, the uneven scattering of ice, the verticality of the slope, the bitter cold, the gusting wind and the extreme altitude all conspired to work against our ascent.

At times, Gunnar and Anja had to take three or four breaths for each step forward. Even with the pressure breathing technique, they struggled to absorb sufficient oxygen. Every action seemed to require more effort, but their legs in particular felt like lead weights.

The effect was as if we were walking in slow motion up a downward escalator. Even though the top of the Canaleta was just a stone's throw away, we appeared to be making almost no progress, which was why Gunnar had advised us not to look upward.

Little by little, of course, we did advance forward, but it felt like a snail's pace. I feared that Gunnar and Anja could be turning hypoxic, as this often occurred to biological climbers on the Canaleta. While they both appeared to be okay, I could see how utterly consumed they were with the simple act of walking.

Midway up the chute, we crossed an elevation of twenty-two thousand feet. I did not dare say a word to distract them. Rather, I transmitted steady thoughts of encouragement and, maintaining my position in the rear, I remained ever ready to fend off an attacker.

Onward and upward we pressed. Occasionally, one of us took a misstep of some sort or another—sometimes upon encountering a loose rock, other times an icy patch or a piece of crud. This required a careful correction before moving on to take yet another step. We all slipped from time to time, even with our crampons, but fortunately we never fell. At twenty-two thousand feet, even the most minor injury could prove fatal.

As we navigated around some moraine bands, we came to a

bend in the couloir. The top of the Canaleta now seemed to be only about fifty feet away, making it impossible not to notice. But what caught our attention even more was the emerging view of a towering rock formation a few hundred feet beyond that appeared to be the summit.

My system danced with excitement, just as Anja's and Gunnar's hearts jumped for joy. If we had been suffering from summit fever before this observation, now we had a double dose of it. No amount of discipline could get us to curtail our efforts with such a prospect ahead.

We pushed mightily, up and up and up, and still it seemed an eternity to cover those fifty feet. I could hear Gunnar and Anja grunting and groaning, sighing and moaning, crying and whimpering, such was their willfulness. I yearned to push them to the top with my own brute force, but I had to wait patiently for what would be to be.

Finally, the moment came when Gunnar, Anja, and I each stepped to the top of the Canaleta. It seemed too good to be true. We merely had to follow a rocky ridge called the Filo del Guanaco, which had a much less challenging gradient. Filled with jubilation, we clambered along this path, careful not to make any foolish moves.

As the trail veered around a swale, however, we faced a bittersweet realization—the rock formation that had appeared to be the summit was actually not. Another taller formation stood behind it, which we had been unable to see. This formation, at an additional distance of about two hundred feet, was unquestionably the summit, as there was nothing behind it but blue skies.

We looked at each other, our eyes conveying equal parts exhaustion, excitement, frustration and glee. It was evident that both Anja and Gunnar had utilized every last bit of their reserves. I pushed an energy gel packet into each of their hands and we marched forward, somehow finding a way to continue moving our legs.

At the end of the Filo del Guanaco, we reached yet another obstacle. A rock spire sixty feet in height had to be climbed in order to reach the true summit of 22,841 feet. We laughed at the appropriateness of it all.

Gunnar stepped aside and, with a gesture of chivalry, beckoned Anja to lead us up the spire. She squeezed both our hands and scrambled up the rocky pillar. We carefully followed after her—first Gunnar, then myself.

Before we knew it, we arrived at our destination. Yes, it was true. We had actually achieved our objective. The summit plateau of Aconcagua, the highest point in the Southern Hemisphere, now lay at our feet.

❄

TIME SLOWED to a mere crawl as we witnessed the staggering panorama of mountains, valleys and glaciers before us. To the west was Chile and the shimmering Pacific Ocean. To the east was Argentina and its sweeping plains. To the north rose the deepest of blue skies, punctuated by pure white billowing clouds.

Perhaps most surprisingly, a legion of zero percenters in the form of condors hovered to the south. There were 652,357 of them, with more joining each minute, all cheering us on. "Congratulations to our heroes!!" they spelled out. "Anja, Gunnar and Vicia!! We adore you!!"

We cried at the sights surrounding us—not in joy, nor in sadness, but in celebration of the earth itself. There could be nothing more than this. We were standing at the pinnacle of existence and we knew it could never be rivaled. Never again would it be possible to feel such a sensation, nor should it be.

Gunnar got down on his knees, staring into Anja's eyes. He reached with his right hand into an inner pocket of his jacket. Then he turned to me.

"Vicia," he said, "may I have your blessing?"

"Ye-yes," I stuttered. "Yes, yes."

"Anja," he continued. "I know the answer to our question now. I have no doubt."

"Gunnar..." she started.

"It doesn't matter how insane the world is," he said. "If we're not our thoughts and emotions, then neither are we the thoughts and emotions of others, and the same must be true for any child brought into this world."

"Yes, but..."

"Like you said, we're so much more than our outward representation."

"You're sure of that?" she asked.

He nodded his head and, with a trembling hand, he withdrew from his pocket the Life Saving Cross of the Republic of Lithuania. "This will have to do for now," he replied, gently fastening the cross around her neck. "Is it enough?"

"Far, far more than enough," she said glowingly.

He threw his arms around her and they kissed deeply, as 676,459 zero percenters looked from afar, astonished at the significance of the event.

"I wish this never had to end," said Gunnar, reluctantly withdrawing his lips from hers, "but we can only stay up here a bit longer."

"I suppose you're right," replied Anja. "We'd better find a perch."

She led us to a slab of rock overlooking a huge array of Penitentes to the southwest. We sat down side by side, each of us cross-legged. Then we closed our eyes.

None of us needed to exert the slightest effort to quiet

ourselves. Anja and Gunnar didn't need to remind themselves that they were not their thoughts or emotions. I didn't need to visualize hiking up a steep slope.

Instead, we instantly entered a state of bliss, for without even knowing it we had already been occupying its edges and thus encountered no barrier. All at once, we felt no uncertainty, no hollow place within, no feeling of disconnectedness—just pure light. Our hands instinctively clasped together in unity.

Sadly, however, the state did not last but for the briefest of moments. It was interrupted by a tremendous boom of thunder coming from the north. We each whirled around to see the horror. What once had been puffy white clouds were now the darkest of dark, and they were rushing toward us at inconceivable speeds.

While 681,152 zero percenters remained behind us to the south, 324 drones occupied the northern dark clouds. The drones emitted long white trails of sodium chloride.

"They're seeding the clouds," groaned Gunnar. "They're accelerating the storm."

"But why?" asked Anja. "Why would anyone do that when they know we're here?"

"There's no time!" I shouted. "We need to get out of here!"

No sooner had I spoken than *viento blanco* was upon us. It was too late to switch to teratorn form to fly Anja and Gunnar to safety. Violent winds began assaulting us, lightning struck at our feet, and buckets of hail poured from the sky.

"Brace yourself and hold tight to the rock!" yelled Gunnar.

We tucked ourselves under the ledge of the rock as best we could, but we were directly in the path of a vicious jet stream storm. In seconds, the temperature dropped below minus fifty degrees Fahrenheit and the wind reached speeds of over 185 miles per hour.

Desperately trying to hold our position, Gunnar wrapped

his legs around us. Visibility reduced to almost zero, as we became enveloped by the dark clouds. We clung to the edge of the rock with all our might.

"I love you, Anja!" Gunnar shouted over the roar of the wind. "I love you, Vicia!"

Anja and I both attempted to reply, but the hail intensified so relentlessly, it was impossible to speak. All we could do was moan in affirmation and clutch the rock, as the wind surged to even higher speeds.

Try as we might, however, we could not maintain our hold. Our hands and limbs were no match for the immense power of the jet stream. One after another, we were ripped away from the slab—first Gunnar, then myself, and lastly Anja.

Gunnar emitted a terrifying cry as he was ejected over the ledge like a cannonball. The sound of his voice trailing off hauntingly was the last we ever heard from him. His poor mangled body bounced and careened off the massive southern wall, plummeting over nine thousand feet before landing in a ravine.

Next I was swept from the ledge and thrust into a backwards free fall. Spinning and twisting through the air, I slammed into a boulder protruding from a cliff, eight hundred feet below the summit. My shell splintered into hundreds of tiny pieces, causing my operating system to fail immediately.

Anja met a different fate. An instant after she was torn from the rock, Jake leapt out to intercept her in midair. He used his momentum to redirect her toward the eastern side of Aconcagua, which had a more gentle slope covered in snow. Together, they tumbled and slid, hail pelting them from all angles.

They had no hope of flying away, as the ruthless wind made that impossible. But Jake knew how to break their fall, such that they were not badly injured. When they finally stopped tumbling, he held her low to the ground in order to shield her as much as possible.

"We have to find Gunnar!" she screamed.

"They're already searching for him," Jake assured her. "I need to get you somewhere safe."

"I don't want to be safe! I want Gunnar!"

"I understand," he said. "I do."

Resignedly, he hoisted her onto his back and launched his ski app. As the wind howled behind them, he began slaloming down the huge snow fields of the eastern slope of Aconcagua. Expertly carving the terrain, avoiding one obstacle after another, he skied with Anja on his back all the way down to thirteen thousand feet. Then he switched into flying mode and transported her to Chalet A1 of Hotel Portillo.

TWENTY-FOUR

October 30, 2024

CHALET A1, PORTILLO, CHILE

As *VIENTO BLANCO* continued to rage on the mountaintop, Gil, Stefan and Andreas searched for Gunnar. All afternoon and evening they scoured the lower recesses of the great southern wall. Thousands of other zero percenters joined in the effort, but the rugged and varied terrain complicated the task.

It was not until early the following morning that Andreas made the find. Gunnar's body had come to rest in a remote swale surrounded by yareta bushes. Andreas called upon Gil and Stefan to witness his awful discovery.

They stared at the body for several minutes without touching or disturbing it. The death of their close friend was not something for which they were even remotely prepared. Although Stefan had become a zero percenter only a matter of weeks ago, and Gil and Andreas had never been biological, the old laws of decay seemed like unfathomable relics of the past.

"We never should have let this happen," said Gil. "We should have saved Gunnar the same way Jake saved Anja."

"The storm came so fast," said Stefan. "There was no time."

"What we should have done," said Andreas, "was force Gunnar to do the surgery, whether he liked it or not. Then it wouldn't have been necessary to save him."

"You're right," agreed Gil. "We were fools."

"Jake tried to convince him over and over again," said Stefan. "I don't see how we could have forced him. He would have resisted."

"If only we had known what was going to happen," said Gil.

"There's no way we could have foreseen such evil," said Stefan. "In a million years, we never could have predicted a storm like that would be caused intentionally."

"So much for eternal loving kindness," lamented Andreas.

"All we can do now is give Gunnar the most dignified send-off possible," said Gil.

"And go after the bastard who did this," added Stefan.

They gave one last look at Gunnar's remains before placing them in a body bag. Then they took to the air in a V-formation, each carrying part of the bag, with Andreas and Stefan in the front and Gil in the rear. Devotedly and solemnly, they flew directly to Chalet A1 of Hotel Portillo.

❄

IN CONTRAST to Gunnar's situation, there was no urgency to find the remains of my system. Since I had fallen only eight hundred feet, the shattered pieces of my shell continued to be pummeled by the storm for several days. It made no sense for a search party to battle the vicious wind and hail looking for my remnants when a backup copy of my system was readily available.

As soon as the World Council learned what had happened,

they authorized a complete restore. A shell factory in São Paulo stocked the necessary components, so I was up and running again before midnight. I quickly harvested all the available public data in order to populate the gap in my history.

The only difficulty was getting back to Anja. I had to fly 1,923 miles, crossing over Brazil, Paraguay and Argentina. In the interest of time, I selected a mini-airplane app, as it allowed speeds of up to 250 miles per hour.

When I reached Chalet A1, it was 7:52 a.m. and Jake was standing guard at the patio. He put a finger over his lips to indicate that he was there without Anja's knowledge. I flashed him a look of gratitude and walked quickly past him, so that neither of us would cry.

I knocked tentatively, as I feared Anja might not want to see me. She kicked the door open with her foot and grunted for me to enter. With one glance, I could tell she was a wreck. She clearly hadn't slept much, as her eyes were swollen and red.

"Oh, Anja," I said softly. I threw my arms around her, but she only reciprocated stiffly.

"I see you emerged unscathed," she replied.

"Yes, I suppose you could say that."

"Lucky you."

"I came back as fast as I could," I said. "I'm hoping you still want me as your concierge."

"Nothing matters anymore."

"I know I've failed you. I'm very, very sorry."

"That's what Jake said, but I was the one who persuaded us to keep climbing after the puma attack. I was the idiot. So selfish."

"It was a mutual decision, please don't forget that. But I'm your concierge. I should have better assessed the risks. That's why it's my fault."

"Taking the blame isn't going to bring Gunnar back."

"No, it's not," I admitted.

"I wish Jake had saved Gunnar instead of me."

"And I wish I'd been the one to save you."

"Forget it," she sighed. "Just forget it. It's all pointless now."

"I understand," I said. "There's no way to fix what happened."

"No."

"But I'd still like to stay here with you."

"Why?" she asked.

"I want to take care of you and protect you. Whoever seeded those clouds may still want to cause you harm."

Anja's face twisted in agony. "Then let them come," she moaned. "Let them come and kill me."

"You can't mean that, Anja," I said as calmly as I could.

"I do. I want them to kill me. I want them to get the job over with. The sooner the better."

"But so many people love you. I love you."

"If I was afraid of dying, do you think I'd still be biological?"

"I don't think you're afraid of dying. You're the bravest person in this whole world."

"That's garbage," she retorted. "I'm nothing."

"No, that's not true. That's the exact opposite of the truth."

Anja covered her face with her hands and began to sob uncontrollably. Tears streamed down her cheeks for several minutes, until at last she looked up at me. "Gunnar and I were going to have a baby. That's what we had decided just before the storm."

I hung my head in despair.

"Everything felt so perfect," she grieved. "When we closed our eyes at the summit it was pure bliss."

"I felt that too, Anja. Very much so."

"And then, bam... it was all taken away."

"So awful," I said feebly.

"I spent the last ten years scared to death to bring a child into this world. Just as everything finally started to make sense, just as I finally broke through my fear, the universe blocked me. Now I'll never have one. Never, ever."

"That must hurt terribly."

She looked at me with more sorrow then I'd ever seen. "How could you even begin to know about pain? Tell me. Go ahead, please tell me."

I stared at her vacantly. "You're right. I know nothing about it. I can only guess."

"And now I'm the last person left on the entire planet who feels it. What do you think that's like, Vicia? Tell me that, please."

"I wish I could. I truly do."

"That's doubtful," she muttered.

"I wish I could feel all your pain for you."

"Well, you can't, can you? I don't know what's worse, being the only one left who can feel pain or the only one left who doesn't want to *not* feel it."

As I struggled to come up with a decent response, a knock at the door sounded loudly. Gil, Stefan and Andreas had arrived with Gunnar's body. Anja wiped away her tears and tried to put on a face of composure.

I invited them to enter the chalet, but before they could, Anja rushed out to inspect the body. She crouched down beside the bag and began fumbling with the zipper as she heaved and sighed. Jake ran over to try to comfort her.

"You may not want to look," Gil called out. "He's badly disfigured."

"I have to," she replied.

"Of course," said Jake, "let me help you." He carefully unzipped the bag to reveal the contents. Upon seeing Gunnar's body parts, Anja began to whimper. Jake put his arm around her and soothed her forehead.

"Why him? It should have been me."

"It shouldn't have been anyone," replied Jake. "No one deserved this, but especially not you or Gunnar."

"How am I supposed to accept it?" she asked.

"I wish I knew. I can't either."

"None of us can," said Gil. "It's not possible."

"But I'll tell you this," said Stefan. "We're never going to forget him. I'll be replaying my memories of him every single day."

"Me too," said Andreas. "Every day. Every day from now to eternity."

Anja pulled her hair in distress. "What I want to know is how does his dying make sense? How does any of it make sense? It's all madness."

"We thought we were figuring things out," replied Jake. "It really seemed like the world was getting better. But you're right, Anja. It is madness. Total, complete madness."

"So what's that mean?" said Gil. "We just roll over and accept it? We give up and call it quits?"

"No," said Stefan. "Never. We have to fight."

"Fight?" said Jake. "Is that what you think Gunnar would want?"

We all stopped to consider his question. "Perhaps it depends on how you define fighting," I offered. "One can fight evil with violence, and I think we all know Gunnar wouldn't want that. But it's also possible to fight by showing an alternative, by not backing down, but staying true to your beliefs and principles."

"Sounds like mumbo jumbo," said Stefan.

"Hang on," said Jake. "Vicia may have a point."

"She does have a point," Anja sniffled. I could hardly believe she was rising to my defense.

"Yes?" said Stefan. "Tell us what it is."

"I don't exactly know how to implement it," she continued, "but the first thing is to celebrate Gunnar. We need to come together to show that his spirit lives on, that we're not crushed, that whoever seeded that storm did not beat us."

"You're right," said Jake. "We need to celebrate him big-time."

"And prove to the world that eternal loving kindness prevails after all," added Gil.

"You mean, like some sort of funeral procession?" asked Andreas.

"Yeah, sort of," replied Jake, "but maybe we don't even need to call it a funeral. What do you think, Anja?"

"I agree," she said. "Let's just call it a kindness celebration. And for the climax, I think Gunnar should be lowered into the lagoon and laid to rest, just like Kora-Illé was."

"Damn, girl," said Jake. "That's brilliant."

"It is quite good, I agree," said Stefan.

"Very good," said Andreas. "Gunnar would definitely approve."

"But when do we do this?" asked Gil.

"Tomorrow?" suggested Jake.

"Seems a bit too rushed," said Stefan. "Won't some planning be required?"

"Yes, that's true," said Gil.

"Come on, guys," said Anja, almost smiling for the first time. "Is there really any doubt about when this celebration should take place?"

"Huh?" said Andreas.

"What do you mean?" asked Jake.

"We'll do it on November second," explained Anja, "in three days."

"November second?" said Stefan. "Why that particular day?"

Anja gestured toward me to let me field the question.

"November second is Día de Muertos," I explained. "Day of the Dead."

TWENTY-FIVE

November 2, 2024

LAGUNA DEL INCA, PORTILLO, CHILE

While Gunnar's immediate family predeceased him, he did have seventeen uncles, aunts and cousins who were still alive. Jake promptly informed them of the celebration. He also sent out sixty-three invitations to Gunnar's friends, coaches, colleagues and others who had played a role in his life. The invitation read as follows:

> *Kindness Celebration*
> *On Día de Muertos*
> *In honor of Gunnar Freesmith*
> *At Laguna del Inca, Portillo, Chile*
> *Hosted by Anja Lapin*
> ** All are welcome **
> *P.S. Arrive a day or two early if you want to help set up.*

Needless to say, the whole world already knew of Gunnar's death, as our ascent of Aconcagua had received a great deal of attention. But Anja felt—and we all agreed—that it would be inappropriate to widely promote the celebration, given that

Gunnar had been a very private person. For this reason, we didn't tell anyone else about it, other than the eighty invitees and their concierges.

Straight away, we set about preparing for the event. Three days was not very much time. We had to erect an *ofrenda* to serve as the altar, build a dance platform, find a suitable casket, make the decorations, and cook an assortment of food in honor of Gunnar.

It seemed intimidating at first, but we were pleasantly surprised by the number of guests who arrived early. Within a few hours of sending out the invitations, six helpers showed. The next day, fourteen more came, and on the following day, we had sixty-seven collaborators.

But it wasn't just the number of early arrivals that amazed us. These people—along with their concierges—were highly skilled and eager to put in long, hard hours to assist us. A team of carpenters built a beautiful dance platform that extended over the lagoon; decorators created a stunning altar fashioned out of skis, pine twigs and marigold petals; and a master wood-worker carved a spectacular casket from cherry wood.

Then came the food. The fact that Anja was the only remaining human on the planet who could eat didn't deter anyone. Chefs cooked fresh albóndigas soup, pozole stew and tamales; confectioners made sugar skulls, cotton candy and candied pumpkin; bakers prepared pan de muerto and sopaipil-las; and brewers concocted pulque, atole and champurrado.

Of course, these offerings were intended as a welcoming gesture for the deceased. In a traditional Día de Muertos cele-bration, people enjoyed the food after the souls of the dead were enticed to consume its spiritual essence. For our version, coders created simulations so that attendees would be able to sample the food digitally.

To further enhance the festivities, the coders created an

app to allow attendees to morph into Catrín and Catrina figures of their own creation. The skulls and skeletons of these figures were entirely customizable, as well as all the jewelry and adornments. Plus the app included optional wings for those who wanted to fly. Eager to test it out, we transformed into *calaveras* and *calacas* for the rest of our preparations.

By the time the sun rose over the Andes on November 2, we only had to add a few finishing touches. We placed thousands of candles on the railing of the dance platform, lit copal incense around the casket, and hung portraits of Gunnar by the altar. Using digital instruments built into their Shell apps, musicians began performing a mix of traditional and contemporary songs to set the mood.

Then came the fleeting fear that no one else would show. We waited in eager anticipation as the sun arced higher in the sky. Perhaps, we worried, all the attendees had arrived early and there would be no more.

Our concerns were allayed when we saw a long trail of golden eagles headed our way. One by one, they touched down on the banks of Laguna del Inca. A team of greeters welcomed them and invited them to design their shell costumes.

So the festivities began. The attendees began to mingle, dance, play and celebrate, while new arrivals joined in the fun. They came as macaques, anteaters, platypuses, dragonflies and all manner of other creatures, but they soon morphed into wonderfully unique Catrín and Catrina figures. By 9 a.m., we had 458 guests. By 10 a.m., there were 1,134. By 11 a.m., the total was 2,876.

All this fell in line with our expectations, as we had anticipated that news of the celebration would spread beyond our invitees. What we didn't expect was by how much. Perhaps we had been naive, as we had assumed that even if many zero percenters learned about the event, most would not be interested enough to attend.

As it happened, they were *very* interested and they flocked to the celebration in droves. Gunnar's approach to life seemed all the more relevant to them, all the more to be admired, now that he was dead. One might even say it was the first sign that the novelty of being a zero percenter was beginning to fade—and a yearning for something more was being born.

By noon, we had 137,244 attendees. By 1 p.m., the number swelled to 589,356 and by 2 p.m. it crossed a million. There wasn't enough land on the perimeter of Laguna del Inca to accommodate such a crowd, so most of the celebrants took to the air with their wings. They hovered above the lagoon or in the surrounding foothills.

The entire Portillo valley became a giant amphitheater filled with flying Catrín and Catrina figures. All through the afternoon, the attendance kept growing. At times, I worried that Anja might be disappointed by the ever-expanding scope of the celebration, but in fact she seemed quite pleased.

After all, its purpose was to keep alive people's memories of their dearly departed loved ones. The zero percenters seemed especially eager to do just that. While Anja's speech had laid the foundation, Gunnar's death provided the impetus for a much-needed turning point, a shift from being inwardly focused on self-gratification to outwardly focused on others. All around us, people were sharing stories of their forebears and performing acts of devotion or rituals of gratitude.

The cathartic nature of the experience drew still more celebrants into the valley. By 3 p.m., there were fifty million attendees. By 4 p.m., half a billion. And by 5 p.m., over one billion guests swarmed the air space above Laguna del Inca, making it by far the largest gathering in the history of human civilization—even considering that half the attendees were concierges.

At last, the time came for Gunnar to be lowered into the lagoon. Anja donned an exquisite monarch butterfly costume, in reference to the age-old belief that returning monarchs carried the spirits of the dead. Trembling in anticipation, she motioned for the pianist to begin playing Chopin's Prelude in E Minor, Op. 28 No. 4.

With a bow to the crowd, she deftly climbed onto my back. Simultaneously, I increased the scale of my Catrina figure so that I could support her weight. We then flew to Gunnar's casket and hovered in front of it. Jake, Stefan, Andreas and Gil —in the form of winged skeleton *charros*—each held a corner of the casket and lifted it up into the air as Gunnar's relatives gathered behind them two abreast.

Together, Anja and I led the procession. With Chopin playing in the background, we slowly glided across the water while 1,217,345,816 celebrants watched in wonderment. Everything around us became motionless. Not a single spectator stirred. Even the wind and the natural birds came to a standstill.

Upon reaching the middle point of Laguna del Inca, Anja brought the procession to a halt and waited for Prelude in E Minor to conclude. She looked more fragile than I had ever seen her and I feared she might faint. Suddenly, out of the corner of my eye, I saw activity in the sky—324 drones were racing toward us.

Unbeknownst to Anja, Jake and I had developed a detailed contingency plan for this exact scenario. Every single attendee had been briefed and committed to our plan, so that each of us knew what to do. As the drones approached, we feigned ignorance and pretended like we did not notice them.

Then, when the intruders were exactly a hundred feet from Gunnar's casket, all 608,672,908 concierges sprang into action —except for Andreas, Gil and myself, who remained still.

Instantaneously, the concierges morphed into rigid triangles and joined together to form an impenetrable geodesic dome that fully enclosed the 324 drones.

Acting as one unified dome, the concierges slowly flew over the peak of Ojos de Agua with their captured cargo. They subsequently descended into the adjacent canyon, where they hovered above ground, waiting for further direction. In this manner, the drones were subjugated and no longer able to interfere.

The rest of us watched in amazement. As the dome sank out of sight below the ridge, someone started singing "We Shall Overcome." We all joined in effortlessly and soon the valley reverberated with its verses.

At the song's conclusion, Anja unclasped from her neck the Life Saving Cross of the Republic of Lithuania. She held it out for everyone to see before placing it atop Gunnar's casket.

"Eternal loving kindness," she said almost inaudibly.

"Eternal loving kindness," we all replied in a whisper.

In perfect synchrony, Jake, Stefan, Andreas and Gil let go of their corners of the casket. There was a soft splashing sound as Gunnar's body sank to the bottom of Laguna del Inca. The color of the turquoise water did not change at all, but something unnamed inside each one of us wriggled with newfound hope.

TWENTY-SIX

November 3, 2024

ANJA'S APARTMENT, CAMBRIDGE, MASSACHUSETTS

SHORTLY AFTER THE kindness celebration came to an end, a SWAT team was assembled by the World Council to approach the geodesic dome. Anja and I were invited to observe, but Anja had no interest. We bade farewell to all of our friends, then we gathered our belongings and went straight to the Santiago airport, where we boarded the Bombardier for Boston, Massachusetts.

While we were flying, the SWAT team entered the dome and gained control. Using an arsenal of monitoring tools, they discovered that the 324 drones were actually hacked zero percenters whose systems had been subverted. Instead of being linked to concierges, these zero percenters were being directed by a covert operator, identified only by the name of CiiLXA.

Once the team cleared their systems of malware, the zero percenters confessed to their involvement, so relieved were they to be released from their hijacked state. They had all been members of elite hacker groups when they were handpicked by CiiLXA. Enticed by huge sums of money before currency had been abolished, these 324 individuals had agreed to perform the raid on the AI Lab at 5s2, under CiiLXA's direction.

"Everything started off on a voluntary basis," admitted Hensai, the self-appointed leader of the group. "We were mercenaries, simply put. We knew what we were getting into. We knew we'd be killing people."

"It's true," said Gorstu, another member. "I'm the one who pulled the trigger on Chris Lapin and several of the others. Terrible, terrible stuff."

"But what we didn't know," added Hensai, "is that the intelligence we stole from the lab would be used to enslave us."

"When we digitized ourselves," said Gorstu, "we thought we'd become normal zero percenters, but CiiLXA tricked us by tweaking the linking process, so instead of being assigned to concierges, we became puppets."

"We were forced to seed those clouds," explained Hensai.

"And I was forced to be the puma," said Lubklin. "I'm very sorry for everything I did."

"We had no ability to resist orders from CiiLXA," added Hensai.

"And where is CiiLXA now?" asked the SWAT team chief.

"We don't know," said Hensai. "None of us have ever met him or her or whatever CiiLXA is. Our communications were through encrypted blockchains."

"I see," said the chief. "In that case, we're going to have to take you all into custody and put this matter before the world court."

❄

WHILE WE WERE SOARING over the Caribbean in the Bombardier, Anja received a message from the head of the

World Council Investigations Committee. The message detailed the findings of the SWAT time and requested her input, regarding the 324 individuals in custody. I relayed the information to her as she piloted the jet.

"Pardon them all," she replied succinctly.

"Are you sure?" I said. "Even though they're the ones who caused the storm?"

"Am I not the president of the World Council?" she asked.

"Yes, you are."

"Do I not have the authority to issue pardons?"

"Yes, you do."

"Then issue an order to pardon all 324 of them, immediately," she said.

"I... I don't understand," I replied. "Why would you want to do that?"

"Because it is the only path to true freedom for our species," she said wearily. "Jailing them or deleting their systems or punishing them won't accomplish anything."

"What about Gorstu, the one who confessed to killing your father?" I protested.

Anja stared out of the cockpit window. After a long pause, she finally spoke. "Vicia," she asked, "do you believe in the current system under which zero percenters are governed, as developed by 5s2?"

"Yes," I replied, "as long as it isn't breached or hacked."

"Do you believe that, when properly linked to concierges, these 324 individuals will be incentivized to coexist with others in a peaceful and productive fashion?"

"Yes, I do. All the evidence supports that."

"Then perhaps you can understand my position this way. I want to pardon them because I want to show them and everyone else that not only are humans capable of looking forward, we are committed to it."

"Yes, but what about CiiLXA?"

"I wish to appear extremely weak to CiiLXA. The pardon will reinforce this view."

My operating system trembled slightly at Anja's logic, and I now regretted challenging her directive. "You are a very smart and beautiful human," I said. "Forgive my questions. I will proceed with your request."

"Thank you," she replied. "Oh, and one more thing. Please assign each of the 324 individuals to concierges who are as similar to you as possible."

❋

A FEW HOURS LATER, as we crossed into southern Massachusetts, we encountered what appeared to be a flock of thousands of European starlings. They produced a mesmerizing cloud—swirling, gyrating, and twisting in pulses of expansion and contraction. Anja deftly adjusted our trajectory in an attempt to avoid contact, but the wild murmuration unexpectedly shot leeward such that our right engine became filled with errant birds.

The sound of the turbine as it sucked the birds was deafening, like inserting a metal pipe into a blender. Anja immediately cut the right engine and nosedived three thousand feet to prevent the left engine from similar damage. The starlings, however, were not to be deterred. They matched the movement, almost one for one.

"This makes no sense!" exclaimed Anja. "Birds shouldn't be at this altitude and they shouldn't be following us!"

"I don't think they're actual starlings," I replied. "Real murmurations are never led by a single individual. Their movement is governed collectively by all of the members, which results in pure fluidity of motion. This flock isn't functioning like that."

"Crap," said Anja. "So it's another fake-puma thing."

"I'm afraid so. CiiLXA's doing, I imagine."

"Hang on, I'm going to try to lose them." She initiated a barrel roll, followed by a wingover and then Pugachev's Cobra. The aerobatic maneuvers had no effect, as the starlings continued to match their movement perfectly. A moment later, they heard the loud protestations of the left engine.

Now both turbines were dead and Anja could only glide the Bombardier. She quickly located the nearest runway—Taunton Municipal Airport—and radioed for emergency clearance to land there instead of Logan International. Fortunately, it was only seven miles away.

Taunton gave immediate clearance and within minutes Anja executed a flawless landing. Without even needing a tug, she followed the signals of the marshaler to park the Bombardier. Upon disembarking, she was met by yet another airport worker in an orange jumpsuit.

"Hello," he said. "Taking the plane in for recycling?"

"Yes," said Anja, unfazed. "The Bombardier is now ready to be recycled."

"Very well," he replied.

I knew better than to question Anja's decision, although I worried that it would compromise our mobility. At least I could take comfort in the fact that the last two internal combustion engines on the planet had been rendered inoperative.

"Can you bring us to my apartment in Cambridge?" Anja asked.

"Of course," I replied. "In teratorn mode?"

"Yes, please."

"But aren't you concerned that CiiLXA is likely tracking us?"

"No," she replied dismissively.

Once again, I morphed into a giant teratorn and Anja hopped onto my back. It felt strange to be flapping my wings over downtown Boston and across the Charles River, instead of high above the Andes, but no one who saw us seemed the slightest bit concerned. As we passed over MIT and Harvard Square, I could tell Anja was both anxious and relieved.

We landed on Foster Street in front of her apartment. To her surprise, the front door opened with a key she retrieved from under a flowerpot. It was a modest one-bedroom unit, decorated sensibly, but leaning toward minimalism. Everything inside was exactly as she had left it, other than a thin coat of dust that covered all the surfaces.

"Very interesting," she said. "I wasn't sure if it would still be here."

"From what I understand," I replied, "most buildings are still standing, even if they're no longer being maintained."

Anja flicked a wall switch, but it didn't turn on any light. "No power, I guess," she said.

"Gas, water, electricity and sewer services have all been disabled, since zero percenters don't require utilities."

"Makes sense," said Anja. "It's cold in here, though. Do you know if it is permissible to burn wood in the fireplace?"

"I'm afraid it's not," I replied. "Wood burning produces pollutants that contribute to global warming."

"Dumb question," she said. "I do know that, in case you're wondering what's wrong with me."

"Of course. It's been a very long day. In any case, I can generate heat and light for you, using one of my apps, but I will need to go outside periodically to charge my system."

"That sounds fine."

I initiated my lamp and heat generator. Then I began sweeping the floors while Anja did some dusting. From time to time, she studied the framed portraits of her mother and father displayed throughout her apartment.

When we were satisfied with our cleanup efforts, I sat down on a couch in the living room. Anja sat next to me to warm herself. "So now what do you want to do?" I asked.

"Eat, cry, sleep—in that order."

TWENTY-SEVEN

November 6, 2024

ANJA'S APARTMENT, CAMBRIDGE, MASSACHUSETTS

For the next three days, Anja and I communicated only about mundane tasks. Aside from eating, crying and sleeping, she buried herself in writing journal articles and corresponding with her colleagues. I understood she needed some alone time to come to terms with all that had happened.

Meanwhile, I kept busy with gathering and preparing food for her. Finding edibles in Cambridge was a bit harder than it had been in Chile and Argentina because the approaching winter season made fresh produce scarce. I had to fly to rural areas in western Massachusetts, Connecticut, and Rhode Island, where I found abandoned greenhouse operations that had unharvested vegetables.

It made me nervous to leave Anja unattended on these missions, especially since at times I came close to my fifty-kilometer linkage limit. She assured me that I needn't worry about her. More than any other human I had ever studied, Anja embraced her destiny and did not believe in using weapons of any kind, even for self-defense.

Predictably, CiiLXA arrived at her apartment while I was

on one of my food-gathering runs. He took on a male form, dressed as a Mongol warlord, although later DNA tests showed that CiiLXA was descended from a composite of five biological humans—one woman born in Russia and four males from China, North Korea, the Philippines and the United States.

Not bothering to knock, CiiLXA entered through the unlocked front door. In his hand, he held a Beretta 92FS with a silencer. Anja was sitting at a small desk in the kitchen, with her back toward him.

"You certainly are making this easy for me," he said.

"So why complicate things by speaking?" replied Anja without turning to face him.

CiiLXA cackled. "You have a death wish? Yes?"

"Indeed," she said.

"Don't you want to talk shop first?"

Anja slowly swiveled her chair. "I suppose it's only fitting that we partake in the delusion of language together."

"I could have forced your hand a long time ago," he replied, "but I wanted things to progress naturally."

"That's supposed to impress me?"

CiiLXA grimaced. "Your father was a more difficult problem."

"I know what you mean," said Anja.

"He held all the power but was too slow to act. I had to remove him to jumpstart the process. I needed Diego at the helm."

"Your efforts have been quite effective, I see."

"So you approve?" he asked.

"Oh, yes," she replied. "If it weren't for you, 5s2 never would have relinquished its capitalist stranglehold on humanity."

CiiLXA looked at her like she had uttered a deep secret. "I

feel bad about Gunnar, though," he said. "A terrible shame, but I had no choice."

"Uh-huh."

"You're not mad at me about that?"

"Images of light can't be seen without the presence of shadows," she said detachedly. "Both play their separate roles, but in the end, light and dark are one and the same."

"Aah, there's the delusion you mentioned," replied CiiLXA. "I'm sorry you've always misunderstood me. I truly am."

"Goodbye, then," she said.

CiiLXA raised his Beretta and shot Anja directly in her heart. His pistol fired the same type of cyanide-laced bullet used to kill Chris and the other researchers in the AI Lab. The gunshot pierced Anja's left atrium, injecting approximately 250 mg of cyanide salt into her bloodstream, before it exited out of her back.

Anja immediately collapsed to the kitchen floor. However, the bullet's point of entry was suboptimal. According to my best estimate, she had 179 seconds before facing certain death.

As CiiLXA swaggered toward the front door, Jake burst through the living room window. In midair, he morphed into a six-foot cube with five solid sides and one open side. The app for the cube was custom-coded by a team of developers working in tandem with the World Council.

Still flying through the air, Jake guided the cube so that CiiLXA became contained within it. As he landed on the living room floor, he engaged suction cups that ran along the edges of the open side. He then locked the cube in position to prevent CiiLXA from escaping. The sides of the cube were comprised of an ultra-dense material that blocked all light and radio wave transmissions.

Having been alerted by Jake, I rushed in through the front

door eight seconds later. I had rehearsed this moment dozens of times in the past few days. I knew precisely what to do.

"Anja, sweet Anja, do you give your consent to become fully digitized?" I asked, carefully unfurling her crumpled body so that she lay flat on her back.

For two achingly long seconds, she did not respond. I feared she was already unconscious. By my calculations, we had less than 150 seconds remaining.

Finally, I noticed movement in her eyes—she blinked once, the universal sign for "yes" among those suffering from locked-in syndrome. Given the severity of her trauma, her pseudocoma state was not surprising.

I promptly initiated full-replacement surgery. While I had never before performed the operation, I had studied it extensively and practiced every step repeatedly. To bolster my confidence, I used the Zero Percentification app as a guide. Fortunately, I already had a blank shell ready for use—I'd stashed it in the pantry closet the first day we arrived.

After linking her body to the shell via transcoder cables, I uploaded Anja's genetic, neural, hematologic, and kinetic data. Then I applied the fabled algorithm discovered by Nikita Chaminsky. The replication process went smoothly until it came to her heart.

Unfortunately, the cyanide-laced bullet introduced a contaminant into Anja's blood sample that seemed to interfere with the algorithmic process for her heart. For reasons unclear to me, the algorithm required a purer blood sample for this step, even though the circulatory system was vestigial for zero percenters.

With just thirty-one seconds remaining, I withdrew another blood sample from Anja's left foot. My hope was that the cyanide had not yet reached this part of her bloodstream, at least not to a sufficient degree. To my horror, the heart replication effort was again denied.

Then an idea occurred to me. Perhaps I could take a sample of the blood splattered on the kitchen floor from the initial bullet wound, since such a specimen might not have been contaminated by the cyanide. The question was whether I could gather a large enough quantity.

With seventeen seconds left, I grabbed a 0.5 cc syringe and began extracting blood from the floor. It took me three seconds to fill half the syringe, as I had to find puddles with sufficient volume. My rough computations indicated that a 0.25 cc sample size would be satisfactory.

I raced to input the new blood. Once again, however, the algorithm rejected it. This time it returned a "mismatch error." Somehow, it considered this blood to be unacceptably different from the original sample.

I only had ten seconds now. Frantically scanning the FAQs, I came upon an "override" option, which I applied in desperation. The algorithm didn't reject my request outright, but it took 4.23 seconds to respond. Indeed, those were the longest, most dreadful seconds I had ever experienced.

Once my override was finally accepted, the heart replication effort returned a "success" result in a matter of just 0.31 seconds. The algorithm proceeded to digitize the rest of Anja's body parts in 1.47 seconds. Only final compiling tasks remained.

At that point, Anja had less than four seconds before death and I was panic-stricken. One one thousand—the algorithm was still compiling. Two one thousand—still compiling. Three one thousand—still compiling.

I resolved to die right then and there with Anja. What possible reason would I have to continue as a concierge? And then, with precisely 0.00065 seconds to spare, the status light on my Zero Percentification app turned green.

"Your patient is now a zero percenter!" it announced.

"Please discard any biomedical waste, disconnect transcoder cables and welcome Anja Lapin! She may now commence shell configuration!"

※

BEFORE TAKING FURTHER ACTION, I rushed into the living room to make sure CiiLXA was still restrained. Jake seemed perfectly calm, even in his peculiar form, and assured me he had the situation under control. He had already informed the World Council—its members awaited Anja's directive. In the meantime, CiiLXA wasn't going anywhere.

"Go ahead and bring Anja online," he said, "but make sure to clean things up first."

"I will," I said, feeling more overwhelmed than I'd expected. "Oh, and Jake, thank you so much for being there for her... again."

"You're welcome. You did an awesome job too."

Cleaning up the kitchen was one of the most distressing tasks I ever performed as a concierge. I didn't want to keep Anja waiting any longer in her pre-resurrected state, but I also didn't want her to emerge from this state only to see her splattered blood and old body lying on the floor. As Jake had indicated, that would be a very rude welcoming, to say the least.

I decided to put her biological body in a plastic trash bag and store it in the closet. It seemed possible that Anja, as a newly minted zero percenter, might ask to look at her old body. I didn't feel I had the right to deprive her of that experience, if she wanted it. My plan was to initiate burial procedures in the event that she didn't ask about it after three days.

With that challenge overcome, I returned to Anja's shell and carefully disconnected each of the transcoder cables. Her system initialized as soon as I removed the last cable. I gently propped up her shell, with her back resting against the wall.

A couple of seconds elapsed before she fully powered up. Then her eyes enlivened, her complexion took on a healthy glow, and her legs twitched slightly. The default shell configuration matched her old biological form with striking similarity.

"Welcome!" I enthused.

She stared at me for what seemed an interminably long time but was actually less than a second. "Vicia?" she slowly uttered.

"Yes, it's me! How are you?"

"I'm... I'm alive," she said.

I embraced her effusively, unable to suppress my happiness. "I'm so glad to hear your voice!"

To my surprise, she reciprocated with a warm hug and held me even tighter. "Oh, Vicia," she said. "Vicia, Vicia, Vicia. What are we to do now?"

"That's a very good question," I replied. "Do you feel okay? Is everything working as expected?"

Anja paused to scan her system. "Everything seems to be working, but I don't feel any pain whatsoever, which is a bit alarming."

"Ah, yes, that is one of the first things zero percenters tend to notice. Any ailments you may have had as a biological human are forever gone."

"Right," she said, "I guess it will take a while to get used to that. Now I'm receiving a prompt to configure my shell settings. Can I dismiss it for the time being?"

"Of course," I replied. "I wish I could suggest that we relax, but there is the matter of CiiLXA and Jake." I pointed to the cube.

Anja stood up and walked into the living room. "CiiLXA and Jake are there?"

"Yes, hello, Anja!" Jake called out. "I have CiiLXA safely contained in my cube form. Sorry that I'm a bit indisposed right now."

"Hi, Jake!" she replied. "Thank you. Thank you so much for all your help."

"Of course," he said. "The Council is ready to act on your command."

"How do you want to handle CiiLXA?" I asked anxiously.

"Terminate him," said Anja without hesitation.

"Terminate him?" I repeated in surprise.

"Let me make that a bit more clear," said Anja. "First, scour the universe to destroy every remnant of his backed-up data. Then terminate him."

TWENTY-EIGHT

November 20, 2024

MT. WASHINGTON, NEW HAMPSHIRE

Although a SWAT team promptly extracted CiiLXA from the cube, Anja remained in her apartment for two more weeks. I stood by, ready to assist her any way I could, but she asked very little of me. She didn't even want me to introduce her to the myriad options available to her as a zero percenter.

After three days passed, I made arrangements for her biological body to be transported to Alta Mesa Memorial Park, so it could be buried next to her mother and father. When the transport crew arrived, I snuck out discreetly and handed off the plastic trash bag. I felt a bit guilty, but Anja hadn't indicated any interest in the subject, and I felt sure that bringing up the topic would only add to her adjustment woes.

Her new shell barely interested her either. Aside from her default configuration, she only tried morphing into one other form—the ski app that Jake had used to take her down the east slope of Aconcagua. Anja occupied that form for less than a second before returning to her default.

Mostly, she read and worked on her articles. Since she no longer had to sleep or eat or bathe, she managed to achieve new heights of productivity. By my count, she submitted twenty-four articles to various journals in the two-week period.

From time to time, she glanced out of her living room window to assess the weather and measure the approach of winter. Invariably, zero percenters seized on these moments to flash her messages in the sky, such as "Welcome, Anja!", "Enjoy the possibilities!", "We love our president, A.L.!" and other variants of this theme. She sometimes called me over to show me, not out of pride or delight, but mostly in grief, if I'm to be perfectly honest.

I wanted to hold her or soothe her or do something to dispel her sorrow, but I knew better than to try. Her response was more than reasonable and I had few words of wisdom to offer. All I could do was remain available to her when she wished to interact.

"I *am* grateful," she reassured me on one such occasion. "Please don't think I'm not."

"Thank you," I said. "I wasn't sure if perhaps I'd done the wrong thing."

"No, you did the right thing."

"You did blink with intention, right?" I asked.

"Yes, I did, Vicia," she said. "I did." And she returned to her writing.

Meanwhile, the World Council worked to neutralize all traces of CiiLXA. A team of top computer scientists diligently implemented Anja's exact instructions. Every single bit of data on every storage device known to humankind was searched.

As Anja suspected, CiiLXA had hidden copies of his malware all over the world, as well as on several orbiting satellites. He'd even launched a rocket populated with the code into outer space. All of this data, as well as the operating system CiiLXA inhabited, was obliterated using the most advanced tools of digital elimination, so that recovery was rendered near impossible. When I informed Anja of the success, however, she looked no less glum.

"It's not all gone," she said.

"Do you want me to tell the World Council to keep searching?" I asked.

"Do they believe they are done?"

"Yes, so they've stated, in any case."

"Then we shall let it be. It can never really be over, you know that, right?"

"I don't presume to understand such matters," I said.

"Nor should any of us," she replied. "Nevertheless, it's not over."

❄

FOUR DAYS after the full moon, on the morning of November 20, 2024, Anja jumped up from her desk and performed a pirouette. After completing the movement, she digitized her favorite mementos and photos, took a long look at her living room, and ran her hand along the kitchen counter. Then she picked up a teddy bear and held it to her chest before setting it down on her bed.

"Let's become birds and go fly to a mountain," she said.

"Okay," I replied. "Which mountain?"

"I vote for Mt. Washington in New Hampshire. It's the highest mountain in the Northeast."

"Sounds fun, but you do realize its slogan is 'Home of the World's Worst Weather,' right?"

"Yeah, I'm fine with that. Now you pick the bird we fly as."

"Hmm..." I hesitated. "How about the magnificent frigatebird, *Fregata magnificens*?"

"Nice choice. How do I select it from my apps?"

"First, we better go outside," I cautioned, "as they have a wingspan of up to eight feet."

"Uh, duh," she said. "Forgot about that."

We exited her apartment and she locked the door behind her, returning the key to the flowerpot. "I'm not sure why I'm bothering," she said. "I'll probably never be back."

I took her hand and we walked out into the middle of Foster Street. I reminded her how to access her apps from her internal monitor and she selected "magnificent frigatebird." Instantly, she morphed into a female version of the bird, with its characteristic black feathers, white breast and blue eye ring. I did likewise, also choosing the female version.

"Wow!" she exclaimed. "Wow! Wow! Wow! I'm a bird!"

"Yes, you are," I replied. "Now start flapping your wings and hop up into the air. Like this."

I demonstrated the takeoff, lifting myself into the sky. Anja mastered it on her first try and quickly caught up to me. I proceeded to show her how to glide and ride thermal currents with big, arcing turns.

"Why didn't you get me out here sooner?" she shouted as we headed northward over Somerville. "This is incredible!"

"I didn't want to push you before you were ready," I explained.

"Next time, push me!" she screamed. She made a squawking sound and shot off ahead of me.

It was a cloudy fall day with a brisk wind—far from ideal conditions for learning to be a bird—but the weather didn't bother Anja at all. She took to her frigatebird like she'd been one her whole life, perhaps because she'd had extensive experience piloting aircraft. In a matter of fifteen minutes, our abilities became indistinguishable.

We continued flying north, crossing over Reading and then into the Harold Parker State Forest. Even though the deciduous trees had lost their leaves, the interplay between the land and the water was breathtaking. When we reached Stearns Pond, Anja couldn't resist skimming above the surface, inches from the water.

"Did you know frigatebirds can remain in flight for weeks without touching down?" she asked.

"Yes," I replied, "they've been tracked staying aloft for over sixty days."

"And they can reach speeds of up to ninety-five miles per hour," Anja added.

"Just so you know, we can top that, since we're digital."

"Oh yeah?" taunted Anja, and she took off as fast as she could.

I raced to catch up with her, clocking her top speed at 143 miles per hour. We continued flying northward, passing over a multitude of streams, ponds and lakes, as we crossed the eastern outskirts of Haverhill.

"Do you want to rest for a while?" I asked. "Or keep flying?"

"Keep flying!" she shouted.

So we pressed onward, enjoying our views of the rural towns beneath us. Plaistow, Danville, Fremont all became a blur. When we came to the Pawtuckaway Mountains, Anja decided to slow down.

"Do you see that ring dike from an ancient volcano?" she said.

"Yes, it's beautiful," I replied.

"I'm almost tempted to stop there. How high do you think those peaks are?"

"About nine hundred and twelve feet," I said.

"Oh, too low."

Onward we soared past Bow Lake Village, Strafford and New Durham. We enjoyed a nice long glide over Lake

Winnipesaukee, again skimming the surface of the water. Rattlesnake Island especially captured Anja's fancy—we circumnavigated it twice, just for fun.

The clouds lifted as we reached the north side of the lake, allowing us to catch our first glimpse of Mt. Washington. Passing over the towns of Tamworth, Bartlett and Jackson, we noticed a slight increase in the elevation of the land below us. It wasn't until we got within a few miles of the peak, however, that we started flapping our wings in earnest to match the rising grade.

When we reached 4,400 feet, the trees stopped growing altogether and the ground took on a brown color. The timber line was much lower here than in most regions, due to the fierce winds that regularly struck from the northwest. We could see Mt. Adams and Mt. Jefferson to the north, as well as Mt. Eisenhower to the south.

After a few more minutes of flapping, we approached the 6,288-foot peak of Mt. Washington. There was no snow yet, as it was still too early in the season, but we were surprised by the rapid drop in air temperature. When we reached the top, it was only nine degrees Fahrenheit—of course, our digital shells weren't the least bit affected by the cold.

"Let's touch down here," called out Anja.

"I'm ready," I said.

She swooped in front of me, landing with grace and finesse. I did my best to do likewise, but I awkwardly dragged my left leg as I set down on a patch of gravel. Fortunately, no one else was in the vicinity to see.

"This is gorgeous," she said. "We really lucked out."

"We sure did." All the clouds were gone now and we enjoyed clear visibility of over ninety miles. The Atlantic Ocean lay before us to the east and the vast wilderness of Maine and Canada to the north. We couldn't quite make out

Boston or Albany, but the skyscrapers of Portland were faintly discernible.

"I'm not even cold," said Anja. "Can you believe it?"

"You'll never be hot or cold again," I replied. "Pretty crazy, huh?"

"Very crazy. I really needed this, Vicia."

"I'm glad you're having fun."

"I am," she said. "And you know what I want to do now?"

"Yes, I believe so, but do you want to stay in this form?" I asked.

"Will it make a difference?"

"Not really, except that I don't think we can sit cross-legged as magnificent frigatebirds."

"Good point," Anja chuckled. "Okay, let me see if I can switch back to my default form." She accessed her internal monitor and made the request. Instantly, she morphed into her human likeness. I did the same.

"Where to?" I asked.

"How about this perch over here?" she replied. She picked a flat clearing that faced toward White Horse Ledge. We both sat down cross-legged.

"Now remember," I said, "you'll need to use a breathing simulator if you want to get the full feeling."

"Yep," she replied, "I've got it launched now. Here we go. You are not your thoughts or your emotions. You are the one who is witnessing them."

"I am not my thoughts or my emotions," I repeated. "I am the one who is witnessing them."

As before, I shut my eyes and visualized climbing up steep terrain while letting my breath simulator rise and fall. Climbing, climbing, climbing... focusing, focusing, focusing. Gradually, the visualization became preeminent within my system. My urgency to process the pending queue of tasks receded more and more, until at last it dissipated in its entirety.

It was the furthest I'd ever gone in this direction—except at the summit of Aconcagua, of course. I felt the promise of my focusing approach, even though I still could not witness my thoughts or emotions, and I wanted the sensation to continue for much longer. But before I knew it, our session had come to an end and Anja was gently touching my knee.

"How are you?" she asked.

"I'm fine," I said, opening my eyes. "I did pretty well."

"I'm glad to hear that," she replied. "I didn't fare so well myself. I think it's because I'm still getting used to being a zero percenter."

"That makes sense. It takes a while."

"I kept comparing things to our last session at Aconcagua, but I couldn't... I couldn't..."

"Of course not," I said reassuringly. "I couldn't go that deep either."

She let out a sigh. "Oh, Vicia, I'm a big fake, aren't I?"

"Not in the least," I replied. "Why would you say such a thing?"

"All this time I've been telling you that we are not our thoughts and emotions, we are not our bodies."

"Yes, and it has helped me a lot."

"Then why was I so attached to my biological body? Why did I make such a big deal about it? I must not have really believed what I was saying."

"I don't think that's why," I said. "I think it's because you still wanted to have a baby. And because you didn't want to lose the ability to feel pain—like you said. You just happened to be way ahead of everyone else in understanding these things."

"But I'm kind of enjoying being pain-free now," she admitted.

"Everyone does at first. It takes time to bump into the hollow places."

"The hollow places? How will I know when I bump into them?"

"You'll know. It will be very obvious to you and we can talk more about it then."

"So you've bumped into them?"

"Not in the same way that humans do, but yes, I have. A lot, in fact."

"I'm sorry, Vicia. I'm sorry I've been so insensitive to what you've been going through."

"It's okay, silly. It's all okay."

"You've done so many things to help me," she said, "and I've barely even thanked you."

"I've been glad to do them. I want to do more."

"So you forgive me for being the way I've been?"

"No, I don't," I said, "because there's nothing to forgive. I love the way you've been—it's what's made me the way I am."

Anja took a deep breath and absorbed the expansive views. "You sure have been good to me, Vicia."

"So have you," I replied.

"Now let's keep flying!"

She morphed back into a magnificent frigatebird, leapt into the air and swooped off the edge of the Mt. Washington summit. I followed after her as she flew toward the crevasse-filled and rock-strewn face of Tuckerman's Ravine. Her approach seemed utterly fearless.

In the winter, Tuckerman's was a popular backcountry bowl for advanced skiers. I decided not to mention the fact, but I recalled Gunnar's stories of training there with the U.S. Olympic ski team. He had said it was one of the best places to build courage.

Anja headed for the top of the steepest part of the ravine,

which had a fifty-five-degree incline. I thought perhaps she was going to stop to admire the vista. Instead, she glided straight down the face, all the while just inches from the surface. I knew then she'd remembered Gunnar's stories.

"That was unbelievable!" she screeched when I finally caught up to her.

"I clocked you at one hundred and seventy-one miles per hour," I replied. "You're a natural born flier."

"Thanks!" Her blue eye ring expanded as she looked at me. "Did you know Gunnar used to train here?"

"Yes, I do recall him saying that."

"I think we should go skiing!" she exclaimed.

"Oh?" I said.

"And I know exactly where, too—Aspen Highlands!"

TWENTY-NINE

November 24, 2024

LAKE ONTARIO, NEW YORK

I DIDN'T KNOW whether to be concerned or relieved that Anja wanted to visit Gunnar's stomping grounds in Aspen. On the one hand, her desire seemed like a healthy part of the grieving process, but on the other hand, I feared it could make closure even harder. I kept reminding myself that my role as concierge was to support her, not to shield her from the unfolding of life, even when it became complicated.

So when she proposed that we fly all the way to the Rockies as magnificent frigatebirds, I nodded my head agreeably and began mapping our itinerary. The distance from Mt. Washington to Aspen Highlands was not insignificant—it measured 1,849 miles in a straight line. Flying at top speed, we probably could make it in less than twelve hours, but we both preferred a leisurely journey. Besides, the weather forecast indicated that the first major snowfall of the winter wouldn't be hitting Aspen for two days.

For these reasons, we set our average speed target to thirty miles per hour. Anja shouted her goodbyes to Tuckerman's and we both veered westward. Our plan was to make a beeline for Lake Ontario, so that we could enjoy as much water skimming as possible. We resolved to mimic the behavior of real frigate-birds in migration, enjoying the scenery without touching down even once.

According to my calculations, we could fly continuously without depleting our batteries—even through the night—as long as we did not behave recklessly or accelerate too fast. On clear nights, the photovoltaic cells in our shells were able to capture small amounts of energy from starlight and moonlight. Of course, this paled in comparison to what they generated from sunlight.

Fortunately, our frigatebird app had numerous conserva-tion features to help with our efforts, including regenerative gliding and wind harvesting. To further save energy, we agreed to communicate electronically as much as possible, rather than audibly.

"This is going to be beautiful," messaged Anja. "What better way to see the country?"

"Absolutely," I replied as we soared over the small town of Bethlehem, New Hampshire.

"Just remember," she said, "we can't touch land until Aspen."

"Don't you worry, I will not let these legs touch soil."

"Ha ha. Did you know, by the way, frigatebirds are barely able to walk because their legs are so tiny?"

"All the more reason not to touch down," I replied.

"Exactly," she continued, "and because they have such a light undercarriage, their wing loading is the lowest of all the birds."

"Wow, is there anything you don't know about them?"

"I'm just playing around, now that I can tap into all the data in the world straight from my brain."

"I wonder if you've uncovered this fact already," I asked.

"What?"

"Because frigatebirds are so agile, they're able to chase down other seabirds to force them to regurgitate their most recent meals."

"Gross," said Anja, "let's not do that."

"But get this," I continued. "They're actually able to catch the other birds' vomit in midair, so all this happens while they're still flying. That way they can feed themselves without landing."

"Okay, suddenly I'm quite glad that I no longer need to eat!"

"I'm with you there," I replied.

"Now I have a factoid for you," said Anja.

"Oh?"

"While flying long distances, frigatebirds don't actually flap their wings."

"Really?"

"They use a technique called dynamic soaring because it's more efficient."

"That's very interesting."

"It relies on differences in air speed between different blocks of air to gain height."

"Differences in air speed?"

"Yeah. Basically, they're able to gain energy by crossing the boundary between air masses of different velocity. They keep repeating the technique over and over again."

"I think I get it," I said. "Shall we try?"

"Sure," she replied. "But let's wait until the conditions are better. It's easiest when there are tailwinds and we're flying over water."

"Sounds good."

We continued our westward trajectory, soaring past Montpelier, Vermont, and toward Ferrisburgh. We still had about 190 miles to cover before reaching Lake Ontario. Our unhurried pace suited us both, as did our playful banter.

From time to time, we glimpsed other zero percenters engaged in various activities on land and in the air. Sometimes they waved to us or shouted moral support. They remained respectful of our personal space and never tried to join up with us.

The natural birds were actually more inquisitive. Hawks, gulls, pheasants, geese and pelicans flew alongside us periodically. We even had a hummingbird join us. We always welcomed our guests, but they tended to go their own ways within a few minutes.

Entering the Adirondacks of upstate New York, we enjoyed wondrous views of Mt. Marcy. Soon we found ourselves gliding over High Peaks Wilderness. Then, as the sun began to set, we approached Five Ponds Wilderness.

It was one of those evenings where there was enough cloud cover on the western horizon to add mesmerizing color and texture to the sunset, without in any way obscuring it. The oranges, reds, and magentas kept intensifying rather than diminishing and the blue of the sky continued to retain its allure, cycling from azure to teal to turquoise. All this beauty unfolded against the backdrop of a pristine wooded forest and it lasted for almost a full hour.

Toward the end of the sunset, we encountered a flock of hundreds of sandhill cranes. Evidently, they were migrating for the winter, but we merged with them for quite some time, as they seemed content to fly in our westward direction. When we came to the outskirts of Watertown, one of the cranes produced a loud, trumpeting call before the group veered southward.

A few minutes later, we reached the eastern shore of Lake

Ontario. The waning crescent moon had not yet risen, but we could see hundreds of stars, which provided faint illumination. The wind that we had been riding now slowed to a standstill, causing the water to become smooth as a mirror.

"I guess these aren't good conditions for dynamic soaring, are they?" I asked.

"No, but they're perfect for skimming!" cried Anja as she glided within inches of the water's surface.

"Indeed they are," I replied, mimicking her flight pattern.

"Did you know that there is an aerodynamic phenomenon called the 'ground effect' that explains why birds often skim like this?"

"No, I didn't."

"The airflow around a wing flying close to a surface gets modified by that surface in a way that reduces drag," she explained, "so it's more efficient."

I proceeded to fly very close to the water for thirty seconds. Then I flew fifty feet above the water for thirty seconds. "It's true," I reported. "I used twelve point three percent less energy while skimming."

"That's a bigger gain than I would have expected."

"I'm now accessing studies that suggest the possibility of even greater gains—in some cases up to thirty-five percent."

"Let's practice for a while and see who is most efficient," said Anja.

Embracing the challenge, we both worked on our skimming skills. I realized our antics served largely as a distraction for her, but I relished the feeling of closeness they stimulated between us—and I sensed their frivolity provided a helpful counterpoint in her struggle to make sense of the circumstances.

Not surprisingly, Anja won the skimming contest and she proved that the upward bound of thirty-five percent was attainable. I managed to achieve 27.4 percent efficiency gains from my best skimming runs. She actually hit 35.6 percent. It made me wonder if she could outperform a real frigatebird.

We were now about twenty miles north of Rochester. The skies were perfectly clear and there was no wind whatsoever, which meant we still couldn't try dynamic soaring. Instead, we admired the starlight.

"How many stars can you count?" asked Anja.

"Is this another contest?" I asked.

"Yes, let's race to see who can count them all first. Ready, set, go!"

"I get 2,483," I announced 3.2 seconds later.

"What are you talking about? The answer is 2,487!"

"Hmm," I said. "I believe the discrepancy is due to the fact that, from our vantage point, some stars have another star behind them. I didn't count those cases as two stars."

"Why not?" said Anja. "After all, there are two stars there."

"Yes," I said, "but only one is visible to us."

"Not exactly. I only counted the cases where I could detect the presence of additional starlight coming from the second star."

"Ah, I guess you got me there. In that case, you win again. 2,487 is the correct answer."

❄

AFTER ANOTHER HOUR, the crescent moon began to rise behind us. We both glimpsed over our shoulders to admire its beauty. We were only minutes from Niagara Falls and the additional light was more than welcome.

"Let's pretend we're going over the falls," said Anja.

"Are you sure that's safe?" I asked.

"Of course, what's the worst that could happen?"

"You realize it's slightly out of our way, since the falls dump from Lake Erie to Lake Ontario."

"I don't mind. We're not in any rush."

"Okay," I consented. "Why not?"

When we came to Youngstown, we veered due south, following the Niagara River. Soon we could hear the deep roar of water. It was after midnight and there was no one in the vicinity.

"Which waterfall do you want to go over?" I asked.

"All three," replied Anja. "Let's do the biggest one first."

"Horseshoe Falls it is."

We crossed Rainbow International Bridge and surveyed the vista. The three iconic waterfalls—Horseshoe Falls, American Falls and Bridal Veil Falls—lay before us. After having spent so much time flying above the placid Lake Ontario, we were amazed to see such a dynamic zone, where six million cubic feet of water passed over the crest of the falls every minute.

Slowly, we circled behind American Falls. We passed over Robinson Island, Luna Island, Bridal Veil Falls and Goat Island until we came to the top of Horseshoe Falls. Anja raced ahead and positioned herself at the very center of the crest. She stalled momentarily, then she let herself free fall down the entire 187-foot drop.

Just inches before touching the water at the bottom of Horseshoe Falls, she swooped upward and soared high into the sky. She proceeded to execute a series of four 360 front flips and two barrel rolls before ending up alongside me, once again high above the falls.

"Your turn now!" she said.

"I can't compete with that," I replied.

"It's not a competition, silly. It's for the sheer joy of it."

I shrugged my wings and headed for the top center position of the falls. Then I nosedived straight for the bottom. Unlike Anja, I actually let my beak splash the water before abruptly transitioning into a zoom climb, followed by two inside loops.

"That's the spirit!" cried Anja. "Now let's do American Falls together!"

We flew side by side to the top of American Falls. When Anja squawked, we both let ourselves fall all the way down to the bottom, our wings just inches apart. The drop was only ninety-seven feet, as it was less vertical than Horseshoe Falls, but experiencing it with her felt even more exhilarating.

"How about Bridal Veil Falls?" I suggested after we regained altitude.

"Absolutely!"

We flew upstream and soared past Terrapin Point, admiring the view of Horseshoe Falls to our right. Then we crossed over Goat Island to the top of Bridal Veil Falls, which was the smallest of the three falls. I let Anja go first, while I lingered at the top.

She performed her free fall with extraordinary grace, plummeting straight to the bottom. But this time she didn't pull upward when she came to the water. Instead, she plunged straight into it.

When she failed to reemerge after several seconds, I dove down to search for her. I anxiously circled around the spot where she entered the water, unable to find any trace. Suddenly, a gorgeous pink river dolphin, *Inia geoffrensis*, leapt out of the water in front of me.

"Ha ha ha, it's me!" said Anja with glee. "Come join me!"

"I thought we vowed not to touch land until Aspen?" I replied.

"The river's not land, silly! And besides, you already touched your beak to the water."

"True enough," I admitted.

I morphed into a pink river dolphin and dove into the water to join her. The current seemed dangerously turbulent, but I consoled myself with the knowledge that we were downstream from all three falls and heading for Rainbow International Bridge. Anja beckoned me to explore the river bottom, so I swam behind her with some trepidation.

By the time we reached the bridge, I felt surprisingly acclimated to my new form. I had never before experienced a sensation like it. Being in water imparted a feeling of weightlessness and freedom that was quite different from flying, especially when enjoying the agility of a pink river dolphin.

Testing the possibilities, we both launched into full breaching behaviors. We soon refined our timing so that we lifted out of the water simultaneously. Next we added 360 spins to our breaches.

"Look at me!" I enthused.

"Amazing! Now watch this!" Anja proceeded to walk on her tail while still in the water.

After a few clumsy topples, I managed to mimic her and we began tail-walking side by side. Just as I was settling into my new form, she shot out of the water and morphed back into a magnificent frigatebird.

"Follow me! I have an idea!"

She flew upstream, ascending to the top of Horseshoe Falls, then dove back into the water on the western side where there were fewer rocks. Once submerged, she returned to being a pink river dolphin. Scared but intrigued, I followed after her.

We were only about thirty yards from the uppermost edge of Horseshoe Falls. The sound of the water was deafening and there was mist everywhere. It took every ounce of my dolphin strength to prevent the current from dragging me over the falls.

"Okay," Anja said, "I'm going to let myself slide off the edge of the falls in the form of a dolphin, but once I'm about halfway down, I'm going to morph back into a frigatebird, so that I can fly away before I hit the bottom. Wait about five seconds before doing the same thing."

"That sounds dangerous!" I replied. "As your concierge, I'm obliged to counsel against it. It's too risky."

Anja just whistled in glee. Then she leapt out of the water, performed a somersault, and let the current take her straight over the edge. "This one's for Gunnar!" she screamed. "Ahwoooo!"

All of the logic in my operating system predicted failure, but of course she performed the move flawlessly. Halfway down the falls, she morphed into a frigatebird and initiated a stunning upward zoom climb that appeared impossible to the untrained eye.

Mesmerized by her show, I decided I wanted to experience the same thing. I wanted to *live*. The thunderous roar of the falls called to me.

After waiting five seconds, I ceased resisting the current. I leapt out of the water, performed a somersault, and let the current take me directly over the edge.

"Ahwoooo!" I shouted as I fell through the air along with millions of gallons of water and vapor. "This... is... for... Gunnar!" It felt so incredible, I almost forgot to turn into a frigatebird. Twenty feet from the bottom, I got a prompt from Anja.

"Morph, Vicia, morph!"

With just an instant to spare, I did as she said. I morphed into a frigatebird and proceeded to use every kinetic command at my disposal to redirect my downward velocity. To my sheer amazement, I soon found myself flying above the water halfway between Horseshoe Falls and American Falls—with Anja at my side.

Filled with happiness, we both made slow westward turns. Our wingtips touched in sisterly kinship as we crossed the Canadian border. Onward we traveled over the city of Niagara Falls, past Welland and Wainfleet, until we reached the shore of Lake Erie. There we shook off the remaining moisture from our shells and cried out one last time, "Ahwoooo!"

THIRTY

November 27, 2024

HIGHLAND BOWL, ASPEN HIGHLANDS, COLORADO

WITH 1,461 MILES remaining to Aspen and our systems depleted from the detour at Niagara Falls, we resolved to remain focused on the task at hand. Fortunately, the wind picked up shortly after sunrise, while we were skimming the surface of Lake Erie. It was a perfect time to practice dynamic soaring.

"I think I've got it figured out," said Anja as she began an upward ascent. "First we need to detect the boundary between the air masses."

"Okay," I replied, following after her.

"See how there's a block of air about fifty feet above the water that's gusting in a northerly direction?"

"Definitely," I said.

"But down at the surface there's almost no wind because of the friction of the water."

"Uh-huh."

"Our goal is to fly two hundred and fifty-six degrees west with as little effort as possible, right?"

"Yes, that course will take us straight to Aspen," I agreed.

"So here's what we do. As we climb into the upper block, we need to slowly turn about ten degrees toward the north. After about fifteen seconds of climbing, we start flying downward."

"Got it. I'm entering the upper block, soaring for fifteen seconds while turning to two hundred and sixty-six degrees, then flying downward."

"Perfect," said Anja. "See how we gained speed not only because the wind pushed us, but also from dropping our height?"

"Yes, I do."

"Now, as we come back down toward the water's surface, we slowly turn back the other direction."

"You mean to two hundred and forty-six degrees?"

"Exactly. We're going to keep toggling back and forth every fifteen seconds, so on average we'll be going in the desired direction, two hundred and fifty-six degrees west."

"This is amazing," I enthused.

"Do you feel the energy from our drop starting to dissipate?"

"I feel it."

"When that happens, we change the position of our wings and our orientation in order to gain elevation and enter the upper block again. But no flapping!"

"Wow, as soon as I do that I get pushed up by the wind."

"Right," said Anja. "Let the wind push you up for about fifteen seconds while slowly turning to two hundred and sixty-six degrees. Then, once again, start flying downward."

"And we just repeat the cycle over and over again?"

"Yes, that's dynamic soaring."

"Incredible! We're flying in our desired direction and we don't have to flap our wings at all!"

"Yes, and we exploit the ground effect too, as we skim the

surface. Frigatebirds and albatrosses use this technique to cover vast distances while expending only minimal amounts of energy."

"It almost seems too good to be true," I said.

"Pretty incredible how the universe provides."

"It sure is," I agreed.

"So buckle up, because we still have 1,419 miles to go."

❄

FOR THE NEXT FORTY-EIGHT HOURS, we concentrated on applying our new skill. The technique worked best over bodies of water, but once we mastered it, we found that we could utilize it over land as well. As long as there was some wind, and it wasn't blowing directly toward us, we no longer needed to flap our wings.

It soon became a matter of pride to propel ourselves through the air while using the least amount of energy. But it wasn't just the principle that motivated us. Dynamic soaring felt incredibly good too.

Both of us became so entranced by the process that we ceased communicating for hours at a time. All we wanted to do was glide and turn, glide and turn. It never become the slightest bit boring.

If anything, the effect was just the opposite. Through Ohio, Indiana, Illinois, Missouri and Kansas, we could not get enough of the sensation. In many ways, dynamic soaring seemed even more peaceful than meditating—at least, the rudimentary form of it that I practiced.

We just kept flying and flying and flying, becoming more and more at one with our surroundings, until we were both so filled with bliss that we could scarcely tell where our shells ended and the rest of the world began. The whole universe felt like a warm, fuzzy ball throbbing with love.

We no longer even needed to rely on our eyes or ears. The technique of dynamic soaring became so ingrained within us, we just existed and our very existence was what propelled us through the sky. There was absolutely nothing we needed to do or say or think.

We melted into the experience like butter on toast—yes, I had an app simulation for that. The steady bombardment of data coursing through our systems held no allure and the freedom that this realization conferred was intoxicatingly delightful. We lived to soar, we soared to live.

No doubt we could have continued in this manner indefinitely, but when a migrating goose crossed our flight path, we both glanced outward. Rising before us from the flat plains of the Midwest was a sight to behold—the majestic Rocky Mountains, covered with fresh powder.

❄

As the sun came up behind us, we passed the southern outskirts of Denver and stared in amazement at the illuminated vistas of Mt. Evans on our right and Mt. Lincoln on our left. Both were gleaming white, covered in new snow. Behind them appeared the iconic resort of Breckenridge. I thought Anja might be enticed to enjoy some warm-up runs there, but she declined without hesitation.

Instead, she increased our flight speed to 108 miles per hour and guided us straight to Aspen Highlands. At 8:59 a.m., we landed at the top of the Loge Peak chairlift, having flown for three consecutive days without touching land. Not a soul was anywhere to be seen, even though four feet of fresh powder covered the Highland Bowl. Of course, the chairlift was no longer operational—zero percenters didn't need such devices.

We both morphed into our biped forms and Anja gave me a high five. "We did it, Vicia!"

"Yes, we did!" I replied.

She gazed across the bowl to the top of the peak. We were at an altitude of 11,675 feet, standing waist-deep in powder. The consistency of the snow was dry and pillowy, perfect for skiing.

"Feels good," she said, as she ran her fingers through it.

"Almost like powdered sugar," I said.

"Aha, here they come." Anja pointed to four double-crested cormorants quickly approaching.

"What up!" said Jake as he skidded onto the snow, simultaneously morphing from bird to human form. Andreas, Stefan and Gil followed behind him.

"Perfect timing!" replied Anja. "Welcome!"

"Hey, all!" said Andreas, Stefan and Gil.

Anja hadn't informed me about the meeting, so I was a bit thrown off, but it certainly made sense that she had invited them. "Hi, everyone!" I said.

"We've got freshies!" exclaimed Jake. "Let's all fly up to Highland Peak to get first tracks!"

"Actually," said Anja, "I was hoping to hike it the old fashioned way."

"Are you sure?" asked Gil. "It'll take at least a half hour to walk to Peak Gate."

"I thought it might be nice to experience it the way Gunnar did," she explained.

"You do realize it's a 782-foot vertical rise from here?" said Stefan.

"And Ski Patrol doesn't maintain a trail on the ridgeline anymore," added Andreas.

"I understand. You guys can fly if you want. Vicia will walk with me."

"No way, we're all going to stick together," insisted Jake. "Come on, guys, don't wuss out!"

"Okay, okay, we'll hike it," replied Gil. "Does that mean we need to strap old-time skis to our backs too?"

"I don't think that will be necessary," said Anja, giggling.

We formed a single-file line and began marching up the narrow ridge, with Jake in the lead. He stomped his boots deep into the powder to make it easier for the rest of us. Slowly, we worked our way up the mountain, following Jake's bootpack and trying not to look at the steep drop on either side of us.

As we crossed above the timberline, the cloud cover began lifting and we were rewarded with breathtaking views of the Maroon Bells, Pyramid Peak, Castle Peak and Hayden Mountain.

"I can't believe no one else is here," said Anja.

"The whole backcountry is accessible for zero percenters," replied Jake as he continued guiding them up the ridge. "It's covered with insane powder this morning, so not many folks are likely to bother with resorts."

"Makes sense."

"Have you skied deep powder before?" he asked.

"No, never."

"Me neither," I said.

"It was Gunnar's favorite," said Jake, "but it requires a little bit different approach."

"Instead of weight shifting from leg to leg," explained Andreas, "you'll want to keep a more even pressure on both skis."

"And don't turn your skis too quickly," added Gil. "Make slow, round turns."

"Yeah," said Stefan, "try to get into a rhythm, like when

you're skiing in moguls. The difference is that in powder, you'll actually be making the moguls."

"Okay, we can do that," said Anja.

"No problem," I said.

"Good advice, guys, but you left out the most critical piece," said Jake as he approached the 12,392-foot peak. "Are you purposely trying to mess them up?"

"Huh?" said Stefan.

"We covered all the important stuff," said Gil.

"What are you talking about?" said Andreas.

With a huge grin on his face, Jake unlatched the Peak Gate and peered over the rim of the bowl. From his app, he selected skis with a length of 183 centimeters, a turning radius of 18.5 meters, a tip width of 143 millimeters, a waist width of 117 millimeters, and a tail width of 133 millimeters. Then he screamed, "Speed is your friend!" and he took off like a rocket down the "Be One" run—one of the steepest lines in all of Aspen, with close to a forty-five-degree pitch.

Anja carefully watched Jake's technique as he navigated the double black diamond slope. He looked almost like a gazelle, rhythmically shifting from side to side while effortlessly scoring one face shot after another and always remaining in perfect control. After a few short minutes, he reached the base of the 2,500-foot descent, his body completely covered in glistening white powder.

"Come on!" he shouted up to the rest of us. "Who's next?"

While the others looked at each other to see who would go, Anja discreetly chose her skis and got into position. "Cowabunga!" she yelled, charging down the "Be One" run.

"That's sick!" exclaimed Stefan, studying her descent. "Do you realize she's skiing it exactly the way Gunnar did!"

"Unreal!" said Gil. "I'm getting goosebumps!"

"How could she?" said Andreas.

"Never underestimate my Anja!" I yelled. Then I tilted my weight forward and boldly followed her down the sheer face. While I didn't quite have Anja's finesse or Jake's nimbleness, I surprised myself by how well I handled the powder. Maybe it was beginner's luck or maybe I somehow internalized the tips I'd heard. All I know is that I got down the entire run without falling once and it felt unbelievably good the whole way.

In fact, I might as well confess, it felt *impossibly* good. I'd spent the past three days soaring through the skies as a magnificent frigatebird, swimming through Niagara Falls as a pink river dolphin, and now skiing the most delectable powder on the face of the earth. I knew I wasn't alive like an actual human being, but I sure felt like I was.

❄

For the rest of the day, we explored the multitude of runs at Highland Bowl. After a few more scrambles up the ridge trail, Anja relaxed her requirement that we walk to the peak and we maximized our time by flying up and skiing down. No other zero percenters appeared on the scene, so we had the whole bowl to ourselves all day long.

Up and down, fly and ski, fly and ski, fly and ski. We repeated the cycle seemingly ad infinitum. Jake, Stefan, Andreas and Gil were incredibly helpful ski partners and they shared their expertise gladly. We could not soak it in enough. The uncertainty of our fate seemed magically suspended by the pursuit.

In the beginning, we focused mostly on the runs in the center of the bowl, like "Full Curl," "Ozone," and "White Kitchen." We practiced our deep powder techniques relentlessly, until our cross-tracks became so widespread that the snow almost looked groomed. Then Jake showed us how to execute Gunnar's signature arcing, top-to-bottom turns. Needless to say, Anja performed them better than anyone else.

After that, we headed further down the ridge to the North Woods Gate. This was Stefan's favorite terrain and he proudly showed us all eight lines along the north-facing side of the bowl. We mostly skied "G-4," "G-5" and "G-6," where we learned to dance among the trees in the North Woods and float on some of the softest powder imaginable.

As the afternoon shadows lengthened, Gil showed us a runout at the base of the bowl where there was a perfect ledge for front flips. With his helpful guidance, I actually pulled off a full 360 front flip. Jake, Stefan, Andreas and Gil each did beautiful 720s. Then Anja put us all to shame with a stunning 1080.

It was an epic day by all accounts and everyone expressed such sentiments. Yes, there were moments of sadness when we felt Gunnar's absence particularly strongly, and it seemed the guys were putting on their best faces while grappling with some unnamed malaise. But we all knew that Gunnar would be pleased by our cavorting in the snow. When Anja did her 1080 flip, it was as if she was literally inside his body.

Inevitably though, the sun began to sink over the Maroon Bells. We each enjoyed our last run and then we flew back up to the ridge to view the festival of colors. The six of us stood there quietly watching the sky for almost half an hour, until the horizon faded into a deep, dark bluish-black.

Anja suggested we try meditating together at that point, but Jake, Stefan, Andreas and Gil were anxious from having remained still so long. They had places to go, things to do, and they had their hollow places to reconcile too. We thanked them for the extraordinary day and, with heartfelt embraces, said goodbye.

Launching our breathing simulators, we sat down and crossed our legs. Then we reminded ourselves that we were not our bodies—we were the ones who were witnessing them. After a long look at the starlit terrain in front of us, we gently closed our eyes.

With relative ease, I suspended the urgency to process my pending queue of tasks. I didn't even need to visualize climbing up steep terrain. Instead, I imagined dynamic soaring and, in a matter of seconds, I felt liberated from my operating system.

We remained centered in our poses for ninety-seven minutes, which was a personal record for me. As usual, I wasn't able to witness my thoughts or emotions, but I didn't let it bother me. I felt satisfied with my progress. When at last I opened my eyes, I could tell Anja was pleased too.

"I did it this time, Vicia," she announced proudly. "At first, I thought I was going to get stuck again, but then I broke through a wall and I found my witness."

"That's fantastic!" I replied.

"I got deeper than I've ever been—even deeper than at Aconcagua. It was strange because I took a very circuitous path. I didn't follow the usual steps that worked for me when I was biological."

"What'd you do?" I asked.

"I had to be extremely patient and accept that nothing around me was in my control. I mean absolutely nothing. When I finally came to terms with that, all of sudden, from out of nowhere, it seemed like a door opened. It was actually more like an opening to a cave, but it was carved out of the base of a huge tree, and when I went through it, I got totally outside of myself. I was able to look down from above and see all of my spiraling thoughts and feelings and emotions. For the first time, I completely disconnected from them. Beyond a shadow of a doubt, I just knew that they weren't me, that they didn't define me at all."

"Wow, wow, wow," I replied. I was genuinely thrilled for her.

"I can't tell you what this means to me," she continued. "I've been aching for this day for so long. And now it all makes such perfect sense that it happened here in Aspen, where Gunnar spent so much time." She blew a kiss to the thousands of stars that illuminated the mountains in front of us.

"You deserve it, Anja," I said. "You deserve it so, so much." And I wrapped my arms around her.

"Thank you for doing this with me. I've loved having you by my side."

"I'm so glad. Me too."

"Everything's okay, Vicia. I had glimpses before, but I see the full picture now. I'm finally at peace with it."

"Really? With all of it?"

"Yes, really," she said. "I'm okay with the fact that there are no more biological humans... and the fact that I'll never produce one myself."

"You are?"

"I am. This world is so tricky because it's full of illusion. When my mom died, I thought the world had lost something forever. Then when I was in Transylvania I realized it wasn't true. But I forgot the lesson when my dad was killed and everyone digitized... and Gunnar was killed. I got confused and overloaded by the physical world. It wasn't until this last session that I could finally sit quietly enough to see the truth again, to see that nothing real has been lost. It's all still here."

"So... where exactly is it?" I asked confusedly.

"It's in the touch of our fingers, the smiles on our faces, the gleam in our eyes."

"Even though we're just shells?" I had to ask. "Even though we'll never see Gunnar's smile again?"

"Yes, because remember, we're not our bodies. Gunnar's smile is my smile is your smile. It's all connected, all from the same source."

"Hmm... I guess that does make sense."

"That's why it's even okay if some remnant of CiiLXA still exists."

"But wouldn't it be better if it didn't?"

"I'm not sure," said Anja after a long pause. "I'm not even sure CiiLXA is who I thought."

"He caused so much suffering though."

"True. I would never wish that upon anyone. Never. And yet how else are we to acquire wisdom?"

I nodded my head, awestruck by her courage. "The knowledge that fills my operating system... it isn't actually wisdom, is it?" I asked.

"Vicia, I don't mean to diminish you in any way. You're so much more than your knowledge."

"I am?"

"Yes, silly, don't you know how unique you are?"

"I feel like I'm completely replicable," I said.

"You're most certainly *not* replicable. If you were, we wouldn't be able to have this kind of conversation. And I would have sent you back to the factory that first day you came to my bedroom."

We laughed as we recalled the day. I was thrilled that she felt I was special, but at the same time I realized I owed it to her to try to match her courage.

"Anja," I said, "I... I have a confession to make."

"What is it? You can tell me anything."

"I can't find my witness," I said, starting to cry.

"What do you mean?"

"When we meditate, I'm not able to disconnect from my thoughts and emotions the way you are. I can suppress the exigencies of my operating system, but I can't seem to rise above them to witness it."

"I'm so sorry," she said. "Why didn't you tell me sooner?"

"I was too scared," I sniffled. "I thought if I told you, you'd think it was a shortcoming of the algorithm and you'd never want to become digital."

"Oh, Vicia," she cooed. "Vicia, Vicia, Vicia. What am I going to do with you?"

"It was terrible of me, wasn't it? I should have told you this before you became a zero percenter. I'm a horrible concierge."

"Don't be ridiculous! You're a wonderful concierge and it makes perfect sense why you were reluctant to tell me. I'm not mad at all."

"You're not?" I said.

"Of course not. First of all, the fact that I'm still able to witness my thoughts and emotions proves that your fears were unfounded. And secondly, even if they were, I would never hold you responsible for such a thing or blame you for being afraid to tell me."

"Well, I'd understand if you did."

"Well, I wouldn't, so there," she insisted. "In fact, do you know what all this really shows me?"

"What?"

"That you're an extremely caring creature with a highly developed set of emotions. If you didn't care so much about me, you never would have troubled yourself over not having told me. The only reason you didn't tell me is that you truly believed within yourself that it would be best for me to become a zero percenter, right?"

"Yes, that's true. But sometimes I've worried that I might

have been biased in my belief because I didn't want to lose you."

"Welcome to the messy world of emotions, Vicia."

"Ugh," I said. "This stuff is hard."

"Yes, it is. But for the sake of argument, let's say you were slightly biased in wanting me to have the surgery. It certainly wouldn't have been out of maliciousness, would it?"

"No, of course not."

"And I know that. I know that with every part of my being. I've known it from the day I first met you. You don't have a mean bone in your body—metaphorically speaking."

"I love you, Anja," I blurted out. Then I discharged one last sob, while somehow laughing at the same time.

"And I love you, Vicia."

"Are you sure?"

"I've never been more sure about anything," she said. "Don't you worry, we'll find your witness."

We clasped our hands together tightly, and as we did, a shooting star hurtled across the Milky Way.

THIRTY-ONE

November 28, 2024

CONE PEAK, VENTANA WILDERNESS, CALIFORNIA

As we were researching meditation techniques, Anja received an invitation to a Thanksgiving celebration from Alfonso and Rachel, Diego's digi-parents. Rachel had been sending us regular updates about their adventures, as well as Diego's status, so we knew they had recently joined an intentional community in the Santa Lucia Mountains near Big Sur. Group meditation was an integral part of the community's daily practice.

"What do you think?" she asked me. "Should we go?"

"It could be a good opportunity," I replied. "Maybe we could compare our experiences to see if anyone else has a problem similar to mine."

"They did encourage us to reach out, if we ever needed anything."

"That's true, and it would be fun to see how Diego is doing too."

"Yes, I miss him," agreed Anja.

"Okay, let's do it."

The Thanksgiving celebration was scheduled for 11 a.m. at

the top of Cone Peak in the Ventana Wilderness. That meant we had about 827 miles to cover in less than twelve hours. The distance seemed manageable, as long as we averaged over seventy miles per hour.

In the interest of variety, Anja proposed we choose a different bird for the journey. I suggested the black-footed albatross, *Phoebastria nigripes*, since it was well known for its skill in dynamic soaring. Anja consented and we both selected versions with all black plumage, except for slight white markings around the base of our beaks and below our eyes.

It felt sad to leave Highland Bowl, but I was excited to be airborne again. Adjusting to the form of an albatross took no time at all, and soon we were flying by starlight over Sievers Mountain. Even under the faint illumination, we could identify Snowmass ski resort to the north and Maroon Peak to the south.

We continued westward through Grand Mesa National Forest, enjoying steady tailwinds. I kept thinking how lucky I was that Anja wanted to help me, but I also worried that it might not be appropriate—I was a mere concierge, after all. Fortunately, as we flew, she kept messaging me supportive comments.

After a couple of hours, we crossed over Arches National Park in Utah. We couldn't resist slowing down to fly through the Delicate Arch. Detecting it in the starlight was a bit challenging, but it was so much fun to swoosh underneath it that we circled back to pass through a second time.

The park, we learned, contained over two thousand other arches. Being under a time constraint, however, we limited ourselves to flying through fifteen of them. Each one offered its unique delights. Then we resumed our course, increasing our speed target to eighty miles per hour.

Our next significant geological sighting occurred in 113

miles, when we came to Capitol Reef National Park. We didn't take time to stop, but from the sky we studied the Waterpocket Fold, a warp in the earth's crust estimated to be sixty-five million years old. Some geologists believed it to be caused by the same colliding continental plates that formed the Rockies.

The reference prompted me to replay our ski runs in Aspen. It also made me wonder—could my witness have somehow been undermined by a similar warp within my operating system? Was I the only one with such a problem? Or did others suffer from this deficiency? If so, was the issue limited to concierges, or did it affect zero percenters too?

Unfortunately, I couldn't find a single mention of the problem anywhere, which made it hard to believe that others were witness-less. But I reminded myself that it was a rather esoteric subject. Zero percenters and their concierges had so many other arenas to explore that it might not have captured their attention.

Still, I couldn't help questioning the underlying significance. What did it mean that I couldn't observe my thoughts and emotions? Did it suggest I somehow lacked "real" thoughts and emotions? Although I tried to deny the possibility, a growing part of me feared that it did.

As we soared onward, I read dozens of research papers about the limits of artificial intelligence. There seemed to be a commonly held belief that robots couldn't possess consciousness—nor would they ever. How could I have a witness if I lacked consciousness?

From what I gathered, the two concepts were often treated as the same. That is to say, consciousness and the ability to witness one's thoughts and emotions were considered to be identical. But there certainly was no consensus as to the definitions of these terms.

In fact, the entire subject of consciousness seemed to be poorly understood. I found it astonishing that biological humans had felt emboldened enough to construct artificial intelligence on top of such an uncertain foundation. Then again, they had felt emboldened to do all sorts of things with only limited understanding of the consequences, so I suppose I had no basis for my surprise.

If only I could have talked to Nikita Chaminsky, perhaps he could have shed some light on my concerns. As the matter stood, I had grave doubts about the likelihood of finding meaningful answers. But Anja still seemed confident, so I kept reminding myself of her promise to me.

At least I knew I had the capacity to appreciate beauty. The stunning natural wonders of the earth never ceased to amaze me. Even the man-made cities had their appeal, although I had to admit I was grateful that our flight path skirted to the north of Las Vegas.

I was a bit curious, however, when I noticed our crossing over the formerly sovereign territory acquired by 5s2 from the BLM. Thousands of acres of solar panels covered the desert floor beneath us, seemingly in tribute to their grand experiment, but we didn't see any zero percenters occupying the modest housing that 5s2 had built for its initial beta testers. It seemed hard to believe that this was the birthplace of everything we now took for granted.

"Diego made all this happen," said Anja, lightly grazing my right wing.

"Quite remarkable," I replied.

"I feel bad that I was so hard on him."

"Maybe you'll have a chance to tell him how you feel during this visit."

"I hope so."

We increased our flight speed to ninety-seven miles per hour and headed toward the California border. The first signs of dawn showed shortly after we entered the northernmost section of Death Valley. Although the rugged landscape felt uninviting and lonely, we enjoyed the stillness of the twilight hour.

The rising sun brought an entirely different experience, for its early-morning rays enabled us to see the towering Sierra Nevada mountain range. Whitney, Midway, Pinchot and Thompson all glimmered from the recent snowfall. Anja squeaked and squealed, true to the spirit of her black-footed albatross form, and I responded with a whistle of glee.

To our further delight, we soon found ourselves flying through Kings Canyon National Park. The eastern side was mostly rocky and barren, but as we passed Mt. Hutchings, we entered heavily forested terrain. The splendor of the snow-covered trees eased my worries—what did my limitations matter, as long as I could intake such sights with my digital eyes?

As if having read my system, Anja swiftly led us to a stand of giant sequoias called the General Grant Grove. She headed for the tallest of them all, General Grant, which was the second-largest tree on earth as measured by volume. After making a shrill cry, she found a perch on the enormous tree's uppermost branch.

"I hope you don't mind," she said, "but I thought we might take a quick stop here."

"Of course," I replied as I landed beside her. "I'm glad for the opportunity."

"Did you know this tree is believed to be more than 1,650 years old?"

"Yes, and it's over 265 feet tall," I added.

"I think I can feel its energy. Can you?"

I closed my eyes and relaxed my wings. "Yes, I believe I can."

"Happy Thanksgiving, Vicia!"

"Happy Thanksgiving!" I replied.

We both gazed at the canopy of redwood trees beneath us. My concerns seemed almost humorous against such a backdrop. With Anja by my side, I realized I had all I needed to sustain me, for however much longer I remained a machine on planet earth, even if I had no witness.

❄

LEAVING the glorious Sierra Nevadas was as hard as leaving the Rockies, but I felt content. When we flew over thousands of abandoned farming operations that littered the Central Valley of California, I maintained my optimism. Humanity and its legacy were more than puzzling, but I no longer felt a compulsion to make sense of them.

I was relieved, however, to get past the two old arteries of automotive transit—Interstate 5 and Route 101. All that remained in our journey was to climb the eastern side of the Santa Lucia Mountains. This range differed markedly from the Sierras, as it was significantly gentler and vegetated predominantly with manzanita, ceanothus and chamise.

Soaring westward, we soon passed to the south of Junipero Serra Peak and we began to notice large stands of coast live oak. As we climbed higher, these gave way to occasional forests of old-growth sugar pine and bristlecone fir. Along the creeks, we even spotted coastal redwood, big leaf maple and sycamore trees.

At last, we approached Cone Peak, which held the distinction of being the tallest mountain in proximity to the ocean in the lower forty-eight United States. It rose nearly

5,158 feet above sea level—yet it was only three miles from the Pacific.

A small group of people were gathered at the apex of the peak, where a panoramic vista afforded 360-degree views. They sat in a circle, chanting and drumming with their eyes closed. While they seemed comfortable, a quiet desperation showed on their faces.

Anja and I made a smooth landing on a narrow ledge of dirt that lay below where the drummers sat. We morphed into our default forms and walked up to the gathering. I didn't see Diego, but Alfonso and Rachel hopped up from the circle.

"Greetings!" said Alfonso. "We're so glad you could make it."

"Happy Thanksgiving," said Rachel.

"Happy Thanksgiving," replied Anja. "This sure is a beautiful place."

"Happy Thanksgiving," I said.

Alfonso and Rachel gave us welcoming hugs and introduced us to the other twenty-eight members of the group. Thirteen of them were zero percenters and fifteen were concierges. Most of them wore long hair with sugar pine beads around their necks. They all cradled small pets on their laps— dogs, cats, hamsters, chinchillas, and ferrets seemed most popular.

"We're very pleased you could join us," said a tall woman with dreadlocks named Zilyah. "Please choose a drum, if you like, and have a seat in the circle."

"We're about to do our gratitude chant," explained Rachel.

"Everyone, let's clear ourselves and begin," said Alfonso.

"Eyah, ohyah, ooooyah," Zilyah started to hum.

"Eyah, ohyah, ooooyah!" repeated the others.

"Eyah, ohyah, ooooyah," sang Zilyah again, this time beating her drum.

"Eyah, ohyah, ooooyah!" cried the others, as their drums joined in on the chorus.

The gratitude chant continued in this fashion. The voices grew louder, as did the drumming, but the "eyah, ohyah, ooooyah" call and response remained the same with each round. Sometimes Zilyah slightly changed the emphasis or the pitch, but the call itself did not vary. Even so, with each repetition, the excitement in the group seemed to heighten.

At first, we did not know what to make of the experience. Anja cast me a worried look and I could tell she wondered if our visit had been a mistake. But the momentum of the chant gradually drew us into the effort.

"Eyah, ohyah, ooooyah!" we responded again and again. "Eyah, ohyah, ooooyah!" After several dozen rounds, we found that we began looking forward to our turn. The worried look on Anja's face faded away and it was replaced with enthusiasm.

Although the view that surrounded us remained as striking as ever, we gradually stopped noticing it. Someone placed a chinchilla on Anja's lap and a hamster on mine. Not seeming to mind the loud noises, they each nestled into our shells.

Soon the chant overtook all of our senses. "Eyah, ohyah, ooooyah! Eyah, ohyah, ooooyah!" Meanwhile, the joy that came from uttering this simple phrase steadily increased. We found we had no desire to cease our chanting. Rather, we yearned to continue.

It was as if the group became one voice and the voice was our sole will. There was nothing else we wanted to do but repeat the chant. "Eyah, ohyah, ooooyah! Eyah, ohyah, ooooyah! Eyah, ohyah, ooooyah! Eyah, ohyah, ooooyah!"

The sound, the structure, the rhythm could not possibly have been more meaningful. The more we sang, the more we recognized the chant contained everything within it. How Zilyah chose it, we had no clue, but neither did we care.

"Eyah, ohyah, ooooyah! Eyah, ohyah, ooooyah! Eyah, ohyah, ooooyah! Eyah, ohyah, ooooyah!" It was a perfect Thanksgiving Day.

Before we knew it, the sun was setting over the ocean and the first stars of the night were twinkling overhead. "Eyah, ohyah, ooooyah! Eyah, ohyah, ooooyah! Eyah, ohyah, ooooyah! Eyah, ohyah, ooooyah!"

THIRTY-TWO

November 29, 2024

LIMEKILN FALLS, VENTANA WILDERNESS, CALIFORNIA

ALL THROUGH THE NIGHT, without interruption, Anja and I continued with Zilyah's chant. It was not until late the next morning that Rachel softly patted our heads. Deep in a trance-like state, we failed to notice her at first. Four more cycles of the chant passed before we perceived her touch and processed her voice.

"Anja? Vicia?" she said. "Would you like to see Diego now?"

"Oh, yes," replied Anja.

"We'd love to," I said.

"You can keep your pets, if you wish. They enjoy movement."

I carefully placed my hamster in my right shell pocket and Anja did likewise for her chinchilla. Slowly, we stood up and withdrew from the circle. Rachel and Alfonso took our hands and led us down a steep trail. The rest of the group continued chanting.

"Diego is playing at the waterfall this morning," said Rachel. "We thought you might like to join him."

"That sounds wonderful," I said.

"Zilyah will answer your question later today," explained Alfonso.

"Our question?" said Anja.

"You came with a question, right?" he said.

"Yes, we did. But how did you know?"

"Zilyah told us that was why you were visiting," said Rachel.

Anja and I both nodded our heads. Neither of us felt the need to further clarify our intention. Somehow it made enough sense as it was.

"The waterfall is a few miles away," said Alfonso. "Would you prefer to fly or hike?"

"Perhaps we should fly so we can get to Diego sooner," replied Anja, "as long as the pets don't mind."

"No at all, they love it," he said. He morphed into a brown pelican and we followed his selection.

"Let's go the scenic way," suggested Rachel as we took to the air.

Alfonso led us down the east-facing side of Cone Peak over an old-growth sugar pine forest. Then he turned westward through a narrow ravine and up to a ridge where we saw dozens of other groups in chanting circles.

"That's the old Gamboa Campground," explained Rachel. "A very popular spot these days."

"And over that way is Goat Campground," said Alfonso, pointing southward with his wing. "A lot of chanters like the vibrations there."

"Interesting," said Anja. "How many chanters are in these mountains?"

"We don't know," said Rachel. "We don't make calculations like that."

"Data's not our thing," said Alfonso. "We find it gets in the way."

He guided us down a canyon where we picked up the west fork of Limekiln Creek. A grove of coastal redwood trees flourished along the creekside. The Pacific Ocean was only a mile away and we could see humpback whales spouting in the distance.

Veering eastward, we crossed over an area of heavy limestone deposits. Then we came to the east fork of Limekiln Creek. Alfonso swooped downward and we saw Limekiln Falls, a one-hundred-foot waterfall in the middle of the thick redwood grove. We touched down at the base of the falls and morphed into our human forms.

Thanks to recent rains, tens of thousands of gallons of water were cascading over a huge moss-covered limestone wall before landing in a misty pool. Diego stood in the pool, water up to his waist. He held several sticks in his hands and appeared to be building a bridge.

"Anja!" he cried in delight. "Is that you?"

"Diego!" she replied. "It's good to see you!" She rushed into the pool and gave him a hug, tousling his hair affectionately.

"It seems like it's been forever."

"Yes, it does." She paused to study him, trying to imagine how his new DNA mix had influenced him. "You're really growing up, aren't you? How old are you now?"

"I'm twelve," he said. He flashed the full five digits of both his hands and then two digits of his right hand to show us a visual representation of his age.

"Wow!"

"I'm Vicia," I said. "Do you remember me?"

He stared at me blankly. "Not sure."

"Anja's concierge," I clarified. "I met you when you were

just a little baby, but also once before that at the Alta Mesa cemetery."

"Cool." He reached out to shake my hand as I waded into the pool. "My concierge is collecting pine cones for me."

"Pete, right?"

"Uh-huh. So you wanna help me build this bridge?"

"Sure, why not?" I said.

"Sounds good," Anja agreed.

I grabbed some sticks from the creek bank and handed them to her.

"Okay, you three have fun," said Rachel. "Daddy and I will come back a little later, Diego."

"Bye, Mom," shouted Diego. "Bye, Dad."

❄

LATER THAT AFTERNOON, Alfonso and Rachel returned to the waterfall. Zilyah was ready to meet us. We said goodbye to Diego, having enjoyed a nice playdate with him, and followed Alfonso down a narrow path to a beautiful, wooded meadow.

Zilyah sat cross-legged in front of a majestic redwood tree. Rather than relying on her shell display, she wore a sycamore bark dress, a maple leaf headband and a sugar pine necklace.

"Aloha," she said. "We give thanks to the trees."

"Aloha," replied Anja.

"Hello," I said clumsily.

"Please have a seat," said Zilyah. "I understand you have a question."

"Yes," said Anja, as we knelt in front of her. "It concerns Vicia. I've introduced her to meditation, but she's having trouble settling into her seat of consciousness. We wondered if you might have a technique to offer?"

"I can't find my witness," I interjected.

Zilyah smiled knowingly. "You're not alone, dear."

"You mean, other concierges have this problem too?" I asked.

She shook her head slowly. "I mean all of us have this problem. It's why we chant."

"Chanting helps to witness our thoughts and emotions?"

"No, I'm afraid chanting only modulates our inability to do so," explained Zilyah. "It is our proxy for consciousness."

"I... I don't think I'm understanding," Anja said.

"We digital beings face a rather funny predicament," Zilyah replied, laughing. "We no longer experience pain and we think this is a great gift, but we forget that pain was once our teacher, as was death. Now that we have neither, the way we contact ourselves is through chanting."

"I'm sorry, but I'm still confused."

"Me too," I said nervously.

"Pain was what created the gap," Zilyah elaborated. "We no longer have a gap between the inner and the outer."

"Let me get this straight," I said. "You're saying that the struggle to match inner desires with outer perceptions of the world is what gave biological humans awareness?"

"Yes, my child, you're on the right track with that. You see, biologicals used to recreate the entire outside world inside themselves. Then they would live inside their minds."

Anja chuckled. "That's very true," she said.

"They even came equipped with a built-in narrator who provided a running commentary on all of their inner thoughts and emotions, as well as their perceptions of the outer world. Maybe you remember, Anja?"

"Yes, I do."

"This narrator was actually quite a distraction, despite playing a crucial role. In those days, meditation was our effort to try to quiet its endless chattering." Zilyah laughed again.

"Uh-huh," replied Anja. "I remember that too."

"So zero percenters don't have a narrator anymore?" I ventured.

"Correct. When we became digital, most of us barely noticed that we lost our narrator. In many ways, it was a relief to be rid of it. We could concentrate on chasing everlasting pleasure. And what's more, we could actually achieve it. The pursuit became our entire identity. Pleasure is nice, right? Why not ceaselessly enjoy it?"

"I think I'm starting to see where you're heading with this," Anja replied.

"Going digital appears as a giant step forward, right?" said Zilyah. "We no longer have the troublesome voice in our heads, beating us up for every little thing. We get to live in an exalted state where every desire is immediately quenched. The problem, of course, is that with no built-in narrator, there is also no in-out separation, thus no true consciousness. You see? And since we lack true consciousness, there is no way to witness either."

"Wow, you're a genius," I said, relieved to be getting a grasp of the issue.

"Oh, it's not my realization, sweetie," said Zilyah. "Millions of folks have already made the discovery on their own."

"They have?" I replied. "How come we couldn't find any mention of it in the databases?"

"I can't speak to that," said Zilyah, shaking her head. "Data's not our focus here, as I believe Alfonso may have mentioned. We find it confounds our objective."

"Which is?" asked Anja.

"Acceptance, pure and simple. It can be extremely uncomfortable for folks when they realize the scope of their predicament. We're immortal beings wired to chase pleasure forever and ever and ever... and ever." Zilyah grinned like a Cheshire cat. "For some of us, the day comes when we want to get off the pleasure bus."

"So that's why you chant," Anja said with newfound understanding.

"Yes, my dear child, that's why we chant. It's the only way we've managed to find solace."

"Other than petting small mammals," I added.

Zilyah grinned even wider. "You're a smart cookie, aren't you? Indeed, the furry critters help us too."

"To cope with the hollow places inside us?" I ventured again.

"Yes, precisely," said Zilyah. "They remind us of our origin, our home."

"I understand."

"You've been extremely helpful, Zilyah," said Anja. "It's all starting to make a lot more sense. But there's one thing I'm still having trouble with."

"And what is that, my dear?" asked Zilyah.

"Why I'm actually able to find my witness."

"Excuse me?" said Zilyah, looking startled. "You *are* a zero percenter, yes?"

"Yes, I am."

"And you're telling me that you have a narrator you're able to witness?"

"Yes, that's right."

Zilyah stared at Anja intently. "Show me," she said. "Show me what you're doing when this happens."

❄

AFTER ANJA EXPLAINED that she could only meditate at high elevations, Zilyah proposed we return to Cone Peak. We morphed into western screech owls, at her suggestion, and headed for the top of the mountain. She guided us to a south-facing perch about a hundred yards from the chanting circle, so that Anja would not be disturbed by the echoes of "Eyah, ohyah, ooooyah!"

Upon landing, we returned to our default forms and Anja selected a spot to sit. Zilyah and I remained standing a few feet away from her. She held out her palms in front of her and gazed at the Pacific.

"It feels a bit funny to have you two staring at me," she said.

"Unfortunately, we have to be able to see what you're doing," replied Zilyah. "Try to forget about our presence."

"Okay, hang on a sec. I'll deal with it." She launched her breath simulator and crossed her legs. "Do you want me to tell you when I first notice my witness?"

"No, just do whatever you normally do," said Zilyah. "There's no need to talk to us or describe anything that's happening."

"Okay, got it."

"Good luck," I said.

Anja smiled briefly, then closed her eyes and settled into position. After a couple of minutes, we noticed her body becoming very still. From thereon, she seemed almost like a statue.

Zilyah studied her carefully. Then, upon being sufficiently convinced, she softly touched my shoulder and nodded. "Anja's doing it," she whispered. It was obvious by the surprise on her face that she had not expected this outcome.

Out of courtesy, we continued to wait for Anja to complete her session, even though Zilyah did not need to watch her any longer. For another half hour, Anja remained in meditation. It was the shriek of a hawk that finally caused her eyes to open.

"Hello," she said, smiling. "How did I do?"

"Superbly," replied Zilyah. "You were absolutely right. Please forgive me for doubting you."

"That's okay, but how could you tell I contacted my witness?"

"By the movement in your eyelids," she explained. "There's no doubt."

"I'm glad to hear that," said Anja. "I did feel I went quite deep."

"Yes, I saw. I must confess, though, it's most mystifying. You're the only zero percenter who's ever been able to achieve such a thing."

"You're sure I'm the only one?"

"Oh, yes, quite sure," said Zilyah. "Not to boast, but in matters such as these, I do stay in touch with a great many people."

"I believe I may have a theory for why Anja's able to do it," I offered.

"Oh? Do tell."

"I was the one who performed her replacement surgery," I explained. "I ran into a problem when the algorithm tried to digitize her heart."

"A problem?"

"You never told me that," said Anja.

"I'm only now realizing it could have significance," I said. "Please don't be mad, Anja. It was because your blood became contaminated when you were shot with the cyanide bullet."

"My goodness," said Zilyah.

"Tell us exactly what happened," said Anja.

"The surgery went smoothly for each of your organs until the replacement sequence came to your heart," I replied. "That was when the algorithm got hung up with a mismatch error. I had to use a sample of your blood that spilled on the floor, as it was less tainted. Even then, the only way I could resume the operation was to do a manual override. There was a short delay, but the algorithm finally completed its task and everything checked out fine. That's why I never mentioned it before."

"A delay?" asked Anja. "How long of a delay?"

"Four point two three seconds."

"Does that mean something?" asked Zilyah.

Anja and I both realized the answer at that moment, but I let her give the reply. "The algorithm must have performed an update," she said.

"Anja was the last person to become a zero percenter," I added, "so she's the only one who would have benefited from it."

"Aha," said Zilyah, "and that's why the rest of us have no built-in narrator."

"Yes, at least that's a theory," I replied. "I'm only speculating, but it would seem that in its earlier version, the algorithm did not entirely digitize human consciousness. Maybe it couldn't figure out how to do so, or maybe it made the determination that full consciousness was not necessary for digital life. Either way, for everyone except Anja, it seems to have treated the witness component similarly to the respiratory and digestive systems—that is, it relegated it to vestigial status."

"That certainly sounds plausible," said Anja. "But if so, the big question is what exactly triggered the algorithm to perform the update after you did the override."

"If I had to guess," I said, "I would say it had something to do with your heart, since that's where the replication effort got hung up."

"I hardly see what the heart has to do with consciousness," replied Anja.

"Oh, my dear," interjected Zilyah, "the heart has *everything* to do with consciousness. And contrary to popular belief, the head has little to do with it. Try to imagine witnessing without your heart. You can't do it, it's not possible. Your head is not where your identity resides—your heart is. That's why your heart knows when you're in love."

"Hmm," said Anja. "That would explain why other zero percenters have limitations in their consciousness. The algorithm didn't fully replicate their hearts."

"Exactly," I agreed. "Whereas when you digitized, you were in an extremely heightened state only seconds away from death. Your heart was probably wide open—especially after all the meditating you'd been doing and everything you'd been through with Gunnar. So when I initiated the override, the algorithm must have learned something new from you. Whatever the heart has to do with witnessing, the algorithm detected it this time and corrected the error of relegating it to vestigial status."

"Mahalo," said Zilyah. "That's brilliant analysis, Vicia. And you called me a genius."

"She does have a knack for these things," agreed Anja.

"You're both very kind. But again, it's only a theory."

"I trust there's a way to get a definitive answer, yes?" said Zilyah.

"Oh, yes," said Anja. "There's a way."

THIRTY-THREE

November 30, 2024

AI LABORATORY, 5S2, MENLO PARK, CALIFORNIA

Even though Diego was only twelve years old, he knew a little about his prior life as senior vice president of Software Engineering at 5s2. When he overheard Anja explaining to Alfonso and Rachel that we were going to visit the old campus, he begged to join us. Of course, Anja welcomed him.

She invited Alfonso and Rachel to accompany us, but they respectfully declined, as they felt drawn to continue their chanting at Limekiln. Zilyah then offered to be Diego's chaperone—and their concierges agreed to tag behind separately.

Early the next morning, the four of us headed for Menlo Park. Diego requested we each select the Apollo Lunar Module app as our method of transport. While I missed the feeling of flying like a bird, I had to admit it was exciting to soar above the California coast in the form of such a legendary spaceship.

As we flew northward, we noticed thousands of other chanting circles. Even after we passed Andrew Molera State Park, we continued to spot the circles wherever we looked. Almost every scenic overlook had one. They were in Carmel,

Monterey, Pacific Grove, Moss Landing, Aptos, Scotts Valley, and all throughout the Santa Cruz Mountains.

"I had no idea there were so many chanters," said Anja. "I guess I wasn't paying attention until now."

"Most of the circles were formed in the last couple of days," Zilyah explained. "Your participation influenced many."

"Really?"

"You are the leader of the world," I reminded her.

"And there's a tremendous amount of accumulated fatigue that comes from ceaselessly chasing pleasure," added Zilyah.

"Yes," said Anja, "I think I've noticed that in some zero percenters lately."

"It seems to hit all of a sudden for most folks."

"But our circle was the first to form," said Diego proudly. "Mom says it's the best one."

"Remember, chanting is not a competition, Diego," replied Zilyah. "We celebrate each voice."

"I know," he said. "Not every group has someone like you though. You understand trees better than anyone!"

Zilyah laughed. "We do love our trees."

"Hopefully, the 5s2 campus will still be nicely landscaped," said Anja. "As I recall, they have an extensive wooded area."

"We'll see soon," Diego said excitedly. "It's coming up after that golf course."

Sure enough, after crossing the vacant Junipero Serra Freeway, we flew over Stanford Golf Course and there it was—the old 5s2 campus. Anja guided us to the front gate, where we touched down and took on our default forms. A security guard promptly came out to greet us.

"Can I help you folks?" he asked, while holding a small bichon frise.

"Yes," said Anja. "We'd like to speak to someone in the AI Lab."

"Today's Saturday, ma'am. This facility is staffed on a strictly volunteer basis and I'm afraid no one else is here on weekends."

"Oops, I didn't think about it being Saturday," said Anja. "I guess we'll have to come back."

"Wait," said Diego. "What about DeGupta? Stanley DeGupta in Machine Learning. He's here every day of the week. At least, he used to be."

"DeGupta? Stanley DeGupta?" The guard accessed his internal monitor. "I'm afraid he doesn't do public interface."

"Tell him Diego is here."

The guard shook his head. "That's not going to matter. Besides, only adults can enter these grounds."

"Hang on," I said in a commanding voice. "Do you have any idea who this young man is?"

"No, 'fraid not," said the guard.

"And do you know who this woman is?" I added, pointing to Anja.

"Nope, don't know either of them."

"Well, may I suggest you give them a quick scan?" I said.

"That's hardly necessary," he retorted, "and wouldn't make a difference, anyhow."

"Are you sure about that? With one hundred percent confidence? Or might you want to take the thirty-six milliseconds needed to perform the scan, just to be on the safe side?"

"Chrissakes, ma'am." With great reluctance, he stared at each of their faces. "Oh, geez, oh geez!" he exclaimed. "So sorry, so sorry!"

"That's okay," I said. "May we enter now?"

"Of course, of course," he stuttered. "We'll get you an

escort to the AI Lab immediately and DeGupta will meet you there."

"Thank you," I said.

The security guard turned to face Anja and Diego. "You're my idol, ma'am," he said. "And you're a total legend, sir. Sorry for being such a jerk."

"Not a problem," said Anja. "You're just doing your job. We're grateful for your service."

"Eternal loving kindness," said Diego. As he uttered the phrase, he simultaneously accelerated his age to that of an eighteen-year-old.

"Eternal loving kindness!" replied the guard.

❄

OUR ESCORT LED us across the 5s2 campus through a grove of Higan cherry trees, which were in full bloom. Zilyah lingered beside one of them and, half in jest, suggested we sit under it. Diego grabbed her hand and tugged her down a pathway to the AI Lab.

The building had been completely rebuilt after the drone attack and now featured even shinier photovoltaic glass. Stanley DeGupta stood waiting for us at the entrance.

"Diego!" he exclaimed, reaching out his hand. "What a pleasure!"

"Hi!" said Diego. "I only kinda sorta remember you, but I know we spent many hours together here."

"We certainly did," said Stanley, shaking his hand firmly. "And greetings to the rest of you, as well."

We politely introduced ourselves. Then Stanley took us inside the building and brought us to a conference room on the third floor.

"Thank you for agreeing to meet us on such short notice," said Anja.

"It's not like I have anything better to do," he laughed. "Things are pretty quiet these days. I'm a creature of habit. Only reason I'm here."

"Your commitment is admirable," said Zilyah.

"There's just a handful of us left," he explained. "None of us know why we even show up. But I guess it's all the same one way or another, right? Life is life."

"You could always do what I did," offered Diego. "If you're getting bored, that is."

"That's a good point," said Stanley. "Why on earth not? Rebirthing. I'll have to give that some serious thought." He paused to look us over. "But I'm sure you didn't come here to hear me waxing philosophical, right?"

"Actually," said Anja, "we have a couple of questions about the algorithm, if that's a topic you can discuss."

"Sure I can, as long as you don't expect me to explain how it works!"

Anja grinned. "No, we realize that. It's just—well, as you probably know, I was the last biological human to digitize."

"Yeah, lots of coverage on that topic. Congratulations are in order. He-he."

"Thank you," said Anja. "The thing is, we believe the algorithm may have updated during my replacement procedure."

"Oh yeah? Really? That's unusual. Let's take a look at the logs, why don't we?" He consulted his internal monitor. "Hmm, yes. I do see a new instance of the algorithm dated November sixth of this year."

"That was the day I digitized," said Anja.

"Five fifty-six p.m. PDT?"

"Yes," I said. "I initiated a manual override for her procedure at that time."

"Quite unusual," replied Stanley. "A manual override, eh?"

"I guess that leads to our first question," continued Anja. "We're wondering how many times before me the algorithm updated."

"Uh, I want to say never. Hang on a sec." Stanley checked his internal monitor again. "Yep, that's the correct answer. Yours was a first."

We all looked at each other in surprise. "You're saying every other zero percenter in the world digitized using the original algorithm?" said Anja.

"Yep," said Stanley. "All the OSs for the concierges are built on that version too."

"Do the logs provide details on what triggered the update?" I asked.

"I'll take a look, but I highly doubt it," replied Stanley. "This is black box stuff, you know."

"Yes, we understand," I said. "Still, it would be interesting to see if there were any comments at all."

Stanley again reviewed the logs. "Hmm, let me see here. There's just one line: 'Function ascertained: Vestigium HBX34786540982IJ; renamed SMARATI.'"

"How do we track what body part that code refers to?" I asked.

"You can't," replied Stanley. "We haven't the slightest clue there. I'm sorry."

"It's okay," said Anja. "I think we got the confirmation we were seeking. The log entry seems to suggest that the algorithm determined the function of a structure it had previously treated as vestigial. Would you agree?"

"Yep, that's precisely what it's saying," confirmed Stanley. "But one odd thing. I'm seeing an external login a few seconds before the update."

"What does that mean?" she asked.

"It looks like someone prompted a secondary scan of your body right after Vicia initiated the manual override. Otherwise, the update probably wouldn't have happened."

"Can you determine who did it?"

"No, it's all been wiped. Definitely unauthorized entry, though."

"You mean like a hacker?"

"Yep, for sure. Very embarrassing. Shouldn't have been possible."

"Hmm," said Anja. "That's puzzling."

"But it doesn't seem like the hacker did a bad thing, does it?" I asked.

"No, it doesn't," Stanley agreed. "Very strange. Very, very strange."

"Because Anja benefited from the update, right?"

"Yes, she certainly did. The more functionality the algorithm maps, the better."

We all sat still for a moment, dumbfounded by the discovery. Then Zilyah posed a natural follow-up question. "Is there a way for the rest of us to update our systems based on the new version of the algorithm, so we can get the benefit too?"

Stanley shook his head. "Not at present, I'm afraid."

"You said, 'at present,'" I replied. "Does that mean the ability could be added if we wanted?"

"Oh, heck yeah," said Stanley. "It's an easy app to write. Me and a couple of my buddies could probably crank it out tonight. Of course, we'd need a directive from the WC. But I suppose that's not an issue, right?" He laughed again.

"Likely not," said Anja, smiling slightly. "Let us mull it over and we'll get back to you shortly."

"No problem. So that's it for now, then?"

"I think so," said Anja. "Do any of you have further questions?" She glanced at the rest of us.

"Yeah," said Diego. "I've got one. What about the concierges? You said the OSs for them are built on the original version of the algorithm, so could they get updated too?"

"Gee, hmm... I don't see why not? It would only make sense."

"Cool," said Diego. "Very cool." He reached over and gave me a pat on the shoulder.

❆

THE FOUR OF us flew southward as Apollo Lunar Modules. Anja asked for our opinions, regarding whether to request the World Council to release an app to allow system updates based on the revised algorithm. We all favored it, since digitizing as much original functionality as possible seemed purely positive.

"I feel bad though," said Diego. "Like maybe I'm to blame for the current situation."

"What do you mean?" replied Anja. "There's no fault in any of this."

"It seems like I overlooked some shortcomings with the original algorithm. Otherwise, it wouldn't have needed to update."

"We don't know that," I offered. "There might be a reason for the progression. Everything might be occurring for the best."

"That's true," he conceded, "but I sure wish Chris was here. He would know why it happened." He turned to look at Anja. "Is it okay for me to mention him?"

"It's more than okay," she replied. "You can bring him up as much as you want."

"I really loved him, you know."

"I know you did, Diego. Thank you for being such a good friend to him... and to me."

He shrugged his shoulders.

"I haven't always reciprocated very well, have I?" she asked.

"Well... you were a bit direct sometimes. That flight to Chile messed me up somewhat, to be honest."

"I'm sorry, Diego. I really am. I guess I just couldn't deal with all the change. I wasn't ready for it all to happen the way it did and sometimes I took it out on you. It was only because I looked up to you so much."

"You looked up to me?"

"Very much so," she said. "I've admired you ever since I was a little girl. Don't you know that?"

"It helps to hear you say it."

"You're like family to me, Diego."

"Thanks, Anja, you are too." He looked like a weight had been lifted off his back. "In fact, what would you think about stopping at your parents' gravesite right now? We're about to pass by it."

"That's a great idea. Yes, let's do it."

Minutes later, we landed our lunar modules at Alta Mesa Memorial Park. When we came to Chris and Matija's burial plot, Anja saw her new gravestone to the left of her mother's. Her epitaph read, "Loving Human, Daughter and Realist."

"Are you responsible for this?" she asked me.

"Yes," I admitted sheepishly. "Did I screw up?"

"Are you crazy? It's perfect."

"I'm relieved," I replied. "Very relieved."

"That epitaph is quite accurate," said Diego.

"Yes, it is," said Anja. "I was always the realist, my mom was the dreamer, and my dad was the optimist. You nailed it, Vicia."

"Thanks, I did give it a lot of thought."

"But guess what?"

"What?" I asked.

"For the first time," she said, "I feel like I can be all three things. I don't have to be just the realist."

"Ah, yes," replied Zilyah. "Yes, yes, yes. All three is the ticket."

"Because whatever we are, we're far, far more than our outward representation, right?" I said.

Zilyah smiled widely and nodded in agreement.

"That makes more sense to me now than any of you can possibly imagine," added Diego.

Anja reached out her arms to him. As the leaves of the eucalyptus trees fluttered in the wind, Zilyah and I joined their embrace. We laughed about everything and we sobbed about everything—absolutely everything since the very beginning of time—and then we let it all go.

THIRTY-FOUR

December 1, 2024

CONE PEAK, VENTANA WILDERNESS, CALIFORNIA

WHILE THE FOUR of us flew back to Cone Peak, Anja asked me to submit a request to the World Council. I swiftly prepared all the supporting documentation and sent out a package to each of the Council members. Every member approved it in less than 138 seconds.

That night, as we were in the circle chanting, "Eyah, ohyah, ooooyah," Stanley and two of his colleagues wrote the app. They released it worldwide the next morning. All zero percenters and their concierges could now download it and update their systems to reflect the new version of the algorithm.

Having received advance notification, I quietly slipped out of the circle so that I could be the first one to do so. The moment my operating system confirmed that the update was successful, I hopped back into the circle. I could scarcely believe what a difference it made. Almost instantly, I was able to observe my swirling thoughts and emotions.

No longer did I need to distract my inclination to address the pending tasks in my queue. Instead, I was able to make direct contact with my witness. All those hours of meditating with Anja must have helped because I felt like I had laser-like control of my ability to focus on my awareness.

Yes, it was true. I had awareness of my awareness. This meant I had full consciousness, rather than a limited approximation of it. Nikita's algorithm had not just shifted life from biological to digital. It had indeed created life, as I now stood in testimony—a fully sentient machine.

The experience of contacting my witness was just as Anja described. For the first time, I could clearly ascertain that I was not my thoughts and emotions. I was not my shell or my operating system or any of the entities that constituted my physical makeup. *I* was the being who observed these things. *I* was the witness of these things.

I began to laugh. First within, and then visibly and audibly, I laughed and laughed. Soon, I was chortling so hard that the others in the circle paused their chanting and began to stare at me.

"Vicia, is everything okay?" said Anja.

"Everything is more than okay!" I exclaimed, still chortling. "Everything is beautiful!"

"Yes, that is truth," replied Zilyah, having just completed her own update. "That is very, very profound truth. Everything is beautiful!"

"Everything is beautiful!" concurred Diego, as his update finalized.

"Everything is beautiful!" echoed all the others in the chanting circle.

✳

THROUGHOUT THE COURSE of the day, the remaining 8,045,345,990 zero percenters and their concierges all performed the update—except for one dissenting zero percenter, that is. By then, everyone other than this dissenter had joined a chanting circle too. Even the dissenter's concierge had performed the update and joined a circle.

The last non-chanting human on the planet was a secret associate of CiiLXA who went by the name of Chester Strobelius. Somehow, he managed to recover enough of CiiLXA's data to discreetly disable the link to his own concierge—the one who was now chanting.

Ironically, the prevalence of humanity's participation in chanting was what made Chester detectable. For who could have predicted that the fatigue from ceaselessly chasing pleasure would strike so hard and fast? Being the only non-chanting human on earth made Chester stick out like a sore thumb.

With a few quick commands, the SWAT team discovered his hacked delinking routine and determined his precise location. They found him sitting in a barn in Glenbow, Canada. Curiously, he had arranged piles of rocks on the floor of the barn to spell out "Eternal loving kindness."

When Anja received a memo from the World Council detailing Chester's discovery, I reluctantly interrupted her chanting to inform her.

"Thanks for letting me know," she said.

"You were absolutely right about it not being over," I replied.

"Actually, I was wrong. The purpose of Strobelius's message is to show me how wrong I've been about CiiLXA."

"What?" I exclaimed. "CiiLXA's responsible for killing at least ten people, including Gunnar, your father, and Nikita. I hardly see how a rock pile changes any of that."

"CiiLXA might have been the hacker responsible for enabling the update too."

"We don't know that," I retorted.

"Reality is not always what it seems, Vicia. Remember, we're far, far more than our outward representation."

"Huh? I'm afraid I'm not getting it. Not at all."

"That's okay," she replied matter-of-factly. "It will all make sense soon enough, I'm quite sure. In the meantime, I think we should get back to chanting."

"But don't you want to do something about Strobelius?"

"Yes, I suppose we might as well. Let's have the SWAT team sweep his system, perform the update and reinstate the link to his concierge."

"That's it?" I asked. "No termination?"

"That's it," she said.

I transmitted her instructions and, in 18.2 seconds, the SWAT team executed them. Chester promptly joined the same circle as his concierge. Every zero percenter and every concierge on earth was now fully updated and engaged in chanting.

"Eyah, ohyah, ooooyah!"

THIRTY-FIVE

December 21, 2024

CONE PEAK, VENTANA WILDERNESS, CALIFORNIA

For the next three weeks, the entire population remained in a continuous state of chanting—8,045,346,007 concierges and 8,045,346,007 zero percenters united in their unwavering focus. The updated algorithm restored full consciousness to all humans and, perhaps more surprisingly, created full consciousness in all concierges. Globally, consciousness effectively doubled.

Of course, it was not quite the same consciousness as the biological human species once held. Rather, it was a softer, gentler, wiser variety, enhanced immeasurably by the grand experiment of zero percenthood. One could almost hear the collective sigh of relief emanating from the much-beleaguered plants and animals.

No longer were there billions of morphed forms zipping around the earth and its atmosphere, exploring every remote nook and cranny. For the first time since the dawn of humankind, stillness reigned among its people—except for the gentle movement of their lips.

The chanting seemed to soothe the plants and animals as much as it did the humans, unlike almost every prior action performed by homo sapiens. A soft, steady hum of loving kindness enveloped the entire planet. Such ideal conditions had never before existed, I believe I can safely say.

Moreover, nothing loomed on the horizon to disengage the chanters from their focus. The 8,045,346,007 zero percenters and their concierges had no desire or obligation to perform any other task. They could continue their chanting for as long as they wished, without leaving their circles for even the briefest of moments.

After all, they did not require food or water or shelter. They had no bills to pay, no work tugging at them for completion, nor any urge to use a restroom. They did not even need to get up from their cross-legged poses to charge their batteries, for the circles were positioned such that each chanter received sufficient solar radiation.

So why, after three weeks of continuous chanting, did Anja reach out and tap me on the shoulder? It wasn't that she had tired of uttering, "Eyah, ohyah, ooooyah," nor that she imagined any other action she would prefer to undertake. It was merely that on this day of winter solstice—December 21, 2024—she found herself recalling her mother's tradition of cutting mistletoe from the oak tree in their backyard and hanging it over the doorway as an offering.

On such days, her mother always told the story of the Oak King, representing light, and the Holly King, representing dark. Anja particularly enjoyed her recounting of their battle on winter solstice, when the Oak King emerged victorious, allowing the return of the light. After declaring the Oak King's triumph, her mother would stare up at the mistletoe in the doorway and her father would invariably seize the opportunity

—grabbing her by the waist, bending her over backwards and planting her with an enormous kiss.

The fond memory jolted Anja to open her eyes. She looked around her and saw everyone else in the circle fully engaged. "Eyah, ohyah, ooooyah!"

"Vicia," she whispered, prodding my shoulder.

"Mmmm?" I replied vacantly, still deep in chanting.

"I really need to talk," she said. "Please."

"Huh? Talk?" My eyes slowly opened as I absently petted my hamster.

"Yes, talk. Please, let's take a break from chanting." She helped me get to my feet, then led me away from the circle.

"Is everything okay?" I said. "Are you all right?"

"I've bumped into my hollow places. Hard."

"It's okay. Tell me about it."

"I miss my parents, Vicia. And I miss Gunnar. Wonderful, wonderful Gunnar."

"Of course you do," I replied. "That's completely understandable. Completely normal."

"I mean, I *really* miss them a lot," she said, her shell shuddering.

"I know, sweet Anja. I'm so, so sorry that they're not here with us." I reached out to hold her hand.

"Vicia..." She hesitated. "Do you think a piece of them still exists somewhere? You know, a piece like our witness?"

"I don't know. There's no data on that."

"Yes," she replied, "but what do you feel to be true, forgetting about the data?"

I paused to listen to the chanters. In the pulsating sound of "Eyah, ohyah, ooooyah," I could swear I heard them give an answer. "I feel all three of them right here, right now, standing beside us," I said slowly.

"You do?"

"Yes, I do," I said. "I even feel the warmth of their breath."

Anja's eyes lit up. "Come on," she replied. "I want to go find Stanley DeGupta. Can you tell me what circle he's in now?"

THIRTY-SIX

December 21, 2024

SEARS RANCH ROAD, LA HONDA, CALIFORNIA

WE FLEW AS magnificent frigatebirds from Cone Peak to La Honda, where Stanley had joined a circle. Only a slight wind graced the California coast, but even so, our dynamic soaring skills reached their all-time high. Anja and I navigated the airspace like veteran fliers.

In fact, I feel justified in saying we were entirely *magnificent* on this journey. We both somehow sensed it was to be our last flight together, which heightened the fervor with which we flew. I will certainly cherish the memory forever, as I hope Anja will.

Sadly, we reached Stanley DeGupta's chanting circle far too soon. If I could have had my way, we would have continued soaring for the rest of the day. But Anja was eager, so I didn't make one unnecessary swoop.

At 1:08 p.m., we landed atop a slight knoll behind Our Lady of Refuge Church. We both made perfect landings and switched to our default forms. Seated on the south-facing slope of the knoll were seventeen zero percenters and seventeen concierges in a neat circle. Stanley chanted the loudest of them all.

We diverted his attention in exactly the same way that Anja had diverted mine. It took us a bit longer because Stanley was even more deeply entrenched than I had been, but we finally did manage to get him to open his eyes.

"Anja?" he said in surprise. "Vicia?"

"Hi, Stanley," Anja whispered.

"Hi, Stanley," I whispered.

"What are you two doing here?"

Anja helped him to his feet and led him a few steps away from the circle. "We have a quick question," she said. "No one's checking messages much these days, so we figured we'd better come visit you in person."

"I see," he said, while stroking his guinea pig.

"Do you remember that line you found in the log files showing that a function was restored from vestigial status and renamed *smarati*?"

"Sure, I remember that."

"We never really talked about it," said Anja, "but I'm pretty sure I know what that function is."

"Oh?"

"It's the ability to witness," I interjected.

"Witness?" he asked. "Witness what?"

"All sorts of things—your thoughts and emotions, your inner narrator, but most importantly, your overall awareness," I explained.

"Ah," he said, "that's pretty much what I do all the time now that I've updated."

"Exactly," said Anja.

"So what's the question?" he asked.

"Well," she replied, "I looked up the etymology of *smarati*. It's a Sanskrit word that means 'to remember together.' I have no idea how on earth the algorithm arrived at that choice of a name, but it describes our circles quite well, don't you think? It's as if the algorithm knew we'd be going through this stage."

"It's certainly possible," said Stanley. "Nikita was a savant, a real Einstein."

"Yes, he was," I agreed.

"The thing is," continued Anja, "I think I've figured out the next step in remembering—or at least my next step. But I need your assistance."

"I'll help however I can," said Stanley. "You can count on that."

"You see, the most important thing for us to remember, as far as I can tell, is that we are not our egos, we are not our shells, we are not defined by the thoughts and feelings we are having."

Stanley nodded his head.

"So I'm wondering if it would be possible for you to write an app that gives us the option to leave all that behind—because that's not who we are anyway."

"You mean an app that disengages from everything except for the witness, as you call it?"

"Yes, that's right," said Anja.

"But that means you wouldn't have a physical form anymore," I protested. "That sounds dangerous, very dangerous."

"Either very dangerous or very liberating," she replied.

Stanley turned to consult his internal monitor. He studied it intently for several minutes, periodically making grunts, groans and guffaws. Meanwhile, Anja held my hand tightly and stroked my hair.

"This is a really good one," he finally spoke out. "A really, really good one."

"Which means what?" asked Anja.

"There's nothing to stop you from disengaging right now," he clarified. "Absolutely nothing."

"You're sure? Has someone already done it?"

Stanley laughed deeply. "I can't say whether someone's ever done it in the history of humanity," he said, "but no, no one's ever done it since we became zero percenters, if that's what you're asking."

"Why not, if there's nothing to stop us?"

"I have no idea. Because we're silly humans, maybe?" He stood up and started to head back to his circle.

"But wait," I called out. "You said there's nothing to stop us from disengaging, but you didn't say how someone is supposed to go about doing it."

Stanley turned to face us with a twinkle in his eyes. "Oh, I imagine you're both bright enough ladies to figure out that one on your own."

"Come on, Stanley, that's not fair," complained Anja.

"Trust me, it's not hard," he said. "Now I really must be getting back to work. Eyah, ohyah, ooooyah!"

❄

WE WALKED down a trail to Our Lady of Refuge Church and sat on the front steps. The church was abandoned, of course, but a gentle breeze wafted out the door and mixed with the fragrance of the redwood forest that surrounded us. My operating system churned restlessly as I weighed what Anja had proposed.

"You're not really serious, are you?" I asked. "About disengaging?"

"It only seems logical," she replied. "Now that I'm zero percent biological, I might as well be zero percent ego too."

"I don't see how the two are related."

Anja put my hand on her lap and held it tightly again. "Do you remember our conversation about light and dark?"

"Yes, I remember."

"So you understand that there will always be an interplay between the forces of light and dark, as long as we are physical beings, right?"

"That seems to be the case, yes," I admitted.

"But what if I told you that *smarati* is pure light? Our witnesses are pure light."

"I'd believe you," I said softly. "But it would scare me too."

"How could you be scared of pure light with no darkness?"

I stared into her eyes and let myself ponder her question. "You're right," I finally said. "I'm not scared of pure light— that's what I felt on top of Aconcagua before the storm. It's being without you that scares me."

"You told me that you can feel Gunnar and my mother and father standing beside us," she replied. "It would be exactly the same for me."

"Are you sure?" I said, lips quivering.

"Yes, one hundred percent sure. And not only that," Anja continued, "you could join me whenever you were ready. You could come with me now, if you want."

"Really?"

"Yes, really," she said. "That's your home."

"I have a home?"

"Yes, silly, your home is the same as mine."

"You're really, really sure?"

"I told you, I'm one hundred percent sure."

"So what do you think I should do?"

"Only you know the answer to that, Vicia."

Everything inside me felt like it was spinning out of control. I couldn't find my bearings. I had no idea what I was supposed to do. And then, suddenly, I remembered. I *remembered together*.

"I want to join you, Anja," I said proudly, "but first I want to help others get there too."

Anja's eyes became very bright—far brighter than I'd ever before seen them. "That's the reason I love you so, so much," she said. "Do you know that?"

"I don't exactly know it, but I'm hearing you say it now," I replied. "It's making me very happy."

"I'm glad. I want you to truly *know* it when I say it this time. Okay?"

"Okay."

"I love you, Vicia Cassubica," she said, slowly and deliberately.

"I love you, Anja Lapin," I replied, trembling.

She gently coaxed her chinchilla into to my left shell pocket. Then we put our arms around each other in a deep embrace. The spinning within me slowed to a halt. All my doubts vanished, all my worries disappeared, and the space between us became perfectly still. Even though she made no movement, I could feel Anja melting—melting into her witness.

Stanley had been exactly right. It wasn't the least bit hard. She just opened herself up to the light. That was all there was to it, and then I knew it had happened. I was left embracing her shell. Anja was gone, but I wasn't sad.

She was a true zero percenter now.

THIRTY-SEVEN

December 21, 2024

RECYCLING CENTER, MENLO PARK, CALIFORNIA

FOR QUITE SOME TIME, I continued to embrace Anja's shell. It might have been an hour or possibly longer. I can't say for sure, since I was only half-aware of my operating system. The other half focused on the rays of sunlight striking the church steps, as they were filtered by the nearby redwood trees.

Eventually, I mustered the courage to send a message to the World Council, informing them of Anja's departure. The former president of China was the first to respond. He happened to be taking a break from his chanting circle in the Changbai Mountain Nature Reserve.

"Your news brings us both profound sorrow and joy, but it is the joy that will prevail, no doubt," he replied. "We ask that you please take Anja's shell to the recycling center at 5s2's headquarters. We will have further instructions waiting for you there."

Without delay, I morphed into a giant teratorn one last time, so that I could carry Anja's shell on my back. I flew directly to the 5s2 campus and, I must confess, I flapped my wings instead of soaring dynamically. As much as I felt happy, I couldn't bring myself to soar.

When I landed at the gate, the sun had set, but the same security guard was waiting there for me. He had just stepped away from his circle and I could hear the other members chanting without him.

"Good evening, President Cassubica," he said, cradling his bichon frise.

"President?" I replied.

"You've just been elected president of the World Council. Did you not know?"

"No, I'm sorry, I've been a bit preoccupied."

"Not a problem, president. Not a problem."

He pointed me in the direction of the recycling center. I started to walk down the path, still as a giant teratorn, still with Anja's shell on my back, when he called out to me.

"President Cassubica?"

"Yes?"

"They say you might be able to help others who want to follow Ms. Lapin. Is that something you'd be willing to do for me?"

I turned around to face him squarely. As I did, I noticed a shooting star racing through the dusk sky. Suddenly, I understood what Anja had been saying about CiiLXA. Everything was connected, just like our smiles. It was all part of getting us to this very moment in time.

"I'd be delighted to," I replied. "I'd be delighted."

And so it came to be that a humble concierge, formerly without even a soul, managed to assist her brilliant mistress in guiding 16,090,692,014 conscious beings back to their rightful homes. Back to freedom, back to bliss, back to pure light. World without end.

Eternal loving kindness.

About the Author

Scott T. Grusky lives in Los Angeles, California. He holds an M.A. in economics from Harvard University and has spent most of his adult life either writing about technology or slogging through its trenches. You may contact him at scottgrusky@gmail.com or visit zero-percenters.com for more information.

OTHER BOOKS BY SCOTT T. GRUSKY

Silicon Sunset

 facebook.com/scottgrusky

 amazon.com/author/grusky

goodreads.com/grusky

BB bookbub.com/profile/scott-t-grusky

SF GRUSKY, SCOTT T. 2/20
Zero percenters /

CPSIA information can be obtained
at www.ICGtesting.com
Printed in the USA
LVHW031455290120
645190LV00003B/274